DEATH AND THE DRAGON

DAVID HANKINS

Lost Bard Enterprises

Death and the Dragon

by David Hankins

EBook ISBN: 978-1-962740-05-0
Trade Paperback ISBN: 978-1-962740-03-6
Dust Jacket Hardcover ISBN: 978-1-962740-04-3

First Printing – December 2024

Published by
Lost Bard Enterprises LLC
PO Box 32
Bettendorf, IA 52722
david@davidhankins.com

To Beatrix, may dragons always be real.

To Michelle, my love. Thank you for following me
through Hell and back.

To all bureaucrats everywhere, know this:
I will fight your red tape to my dying breath.
You have been warned.

REAPER

Also by David Hankins

Grimsworld

Death and the Taxman
Death and the Dragon
Death and the Immortal
(Coming 2026)

Grimsworld Tales
(Companion Collection)

These books and more available at
www.davidhankins.com

CONTENTS

Chapter 1

PURGATORY

I, THE GRIM REAPER, terror of men's souls, shall forevermore despise bureaucrats. For bureaucrats are of the Devil, and bureaucracies are but poorly furnished reflections of Hell.

Lovetta, the Guardian spirit behind Purgatory's expansive Soul Processing Desk, was the epitome of bureaucratic indifference. She resembled a gray werewolf with thick fur under her white robes. Cheap floral perfume wafted from her in waves. She sported purple claw polish, matching eyeliner, and the put-upon expression of bureaucrats everywhere when you ask them to do any actual work.

"I'm here to see Minos the Judge," I said.

Beside me, Frank the Taxman leaned on the chest-high Processing Desk and threw Lovetta what he probably thought was a dashing grin behind his salt-and-pepper beard. She didn't even glance at him.

"Wait like everyone else," Lovetta growled at me, still smiling that toothy smile. A clawed finger pointed imperiously toward Purgatory's milling souls behind me. A hint of angry satisfaction smoldered in the back of her eyes.

I returned her stare, but Frank followed her gesture, flipping his reaper's cloak behind him and leaning back with both elbows on the desk. Frank was a large man, practically the opposite of my skeletal form. He'd been my apprentice for a full six months now, and I still wasn't used to having him around. Sure, the company was nice, but the former IRS auditor's incessant cheerfulness was wearing on me. Death is a serious business.

He gawked like a tourist at the throng of souls packed into the roped-off aisles. Purgatory was a vast waiting room with cloud-dappled blue skies for a roof, overshadowed by a mountain that pierced the clouds. That view was Purgatory's one redeeming feature. The heavens above stretched for eternity in every direction. A vision of hope for those souls headed upward.

For everyone else, Purgatory's bureaucratic morass was all the warning they needed of their torments to come.

I tapped a bone finger on the Guardian's desk and matched her growl. "Death. Does. Not. Wait. Either announce me to Minos the Judge or stand aside."

Lovetta didn't budge. She merely cocked an eyebrow, prepared to wait me out.

Bloody bureaucrats. I hadn't visited Purgatory in centuries—Death's business keeps me busy—but surely, I retained *some* influence.

I needed to have words with Lucifer. To find out why he'd allowed Hell's rumored reorganization—dubbed Nigel's New Order after the demigod behind the change—to steal souls from Purgatory before they were Judged. Souls like my friend Abigail's. I'd promised her that I would personally investigate her case after she helped me evade the Auditor six months ago. And I would. But I wanted to talk to Minos first. Get the inside scoop before wading into Lucifer's realm.

To do that, I had to get past Lovetta.

I drummed my fingers on my scythe *Grace*. Time to use the only language bureaucrats understand: direct threats.

"You do not want to make an enemy of Death. Remember what happened to Charon the Ferryman?"

Lovetta's expression turned contemplative. She eyed me for a long moment before leaning forward to whisper, "The Year of the Dragon will end."

I leaned forward as well. "I. Don't. Care. I am not here to discuss the Chinese calendar. I'm here to see Minos about grave errors in soul management." I cracked my palm onto the desk. "Now let me pass!"

Lovetta straightened, her expression hardening as though I'd failed some test. But she swung open a section of the Soul Processing Desk and waved toward the arched door behind her. "Right this way."

I nodded tightly. That was better.

I should have paid attention to that bureaucrat's toothy smile. It was the smile of malicious compliance.

I swept past Lovetta in a swirl of black cloak. I leaned into the heavy door which opened with an ominous *creak.* Like any physical manifestation in the spiritual realms, it looked, felt, and smelled real. Rough oak with a distinctively aged scent. While spirits like me could pass through objects in the mortal realm—switching between corporeal and incorporeal was as easy as a thought—doing so here was ... problematic. Especially for me. Death has more power among the mortals than among the spirits. But my position always granted me special access to those in charge. I stepped into the chambers of Minos the Judge.

"Minos!" I intoned. "We need to talk."

The expansive chamber was more of a throne room than an office, the furniture sized for a giant, and unlike Purgatory's waiting room, it was fully enclosed. Hanging censers filled the air with a heady mix of cherry blossoms and sulfur; Heaven and Hell perfectly balanced on opposite sides of the wood-paneled room. Minos's massive hardwood desk dominated the room with an equally massive high-backed chair.

An empty high-backed chair.

I stopped before the Judge's desk, my footsteps fading into silence. Torches spluttered in ornate sconces along the walls. I glanced around. Where was Minos?

It was only then that I realized I stood on the cold marble Petitioner's Block where souls were Judged.

I took an involuntary step back. Judgment. I'd avoided Judgment for millennia. It had taken some fast talking to convince the Archangel Gabriel to turn me into the Grim Reaper after my original sin, but he'd bought my argument, and I'd sidestepped Judgment.

I shook my head. I was being ridiculous. It wasn't *my* Judgment that was in question.

A stack of papers on Minos's desk caught my eye, and I stepped forward to retrieve the top piece. Form-5 was emblazoned across the top followed by a ridiculous number of tiny blocks to fill out. It looked like a catch-all form with a section reserved for Minos to mark his Judgments. Though blank, the form was pre-signed, as was the remainder of the stack.

Signed by the Auditor.

I dropped the form like it was poisoned. The Auditor? Why would my nemesis sign forms in Minos's place? Hell's final arbiter of the Rules had no authority in Purgatory! The Rules governing soul management strictly forbade Hell's interference. Those Rules were all that stood between Heaven and Hell going to Armageddon, and if the Auditor was blatantly circumventing the Rules...

I spun on my heel and stomped back out. Only when I saw Frank chatting amicably with Lovetta did I realize that he hadn't followed me inside. I still wasn't used to having an apprentice again.

Lovetta smirked at something Frank said. They leaned

toward each other as though sharing a secret.

"Lovetta," I said, rejoining them, "where is Minos? And why are there forms in there with the Auditor's signature?"

The wolf-spirit's expression blanked, and she straightened. Her shrug oozed contempt and sarcasm. She pulled a nail file from somewhere in her white robes. It made a quiet *shick shick* noise as she sharpened her claws.

"When will Minos return?" I asked.

Lovetta shrugged again and picked at imaginary dirt under one claw.

I ground my teeth. It galled to ask but... "Can I make an appointment?"

She tapped a well-manicured claw on the desk, staring hard as though willing me to just go away, then snatched a blank form and handed it to me. The same form I'd seen on Minos's desk, but unsigned.

"Submit your Form-5 to Leandros and Chiti," she said and waved to my left toward the Soul Processing Desk's far end where two more spirits lounged. Leandros and Chiti were the lion and cheetah to Lovetta's wolf, chatting cheerfully together and not processing any souls. Frank and I were the only ones forward of the ropes separating

Purgatory's masses from the Soul Processing Desk.

"Fine," I said. "I hope the rest of your shift is as pleasant as you are." I snatched the Form-5 and a ballpoint pen and stomped halfway down the long desk before stopping to fill out the form. Frank followed and leaned against the desk beside me, his expression quizzical.

"Why's Purgatory staffed by animals? I thought you said animals didn't have immortal souls."

"They're not animals," I said, printing my name in block letters, my mind not really focused on Frank's questions. What game was the Auditor playing? "They're ancient spirits who chose animal form," I explained, knowing that he wouldn't stop asking questions until I did.

"Hold up," Frank said, eyebrows rising. "Spirits can shapeshift? Can I do that too?" He scrunched his face as though trying to rearrange it. He failed miserably.

"A soul's form reflects how they see themselves. You appear in death as you did in life." I waved at Frank's brown tweed suit and black reaper's cowl. He was balding, bearded, and without a single sharp edge. "However, it takes significant willpower to change that appearance. And the change isn't without consequences."

"Consequences?" Frank froze, sounding nervous. He

touched his face, which hadn't changed a bit. I glanced up at him.

"Everything in the spiritual realm is a reflection of willpower. The stronger your will, the more you can change yourself and your surroundings. But willpower is like a muscle. You have to build it over time. Some have strong willpower—like me. Others have none at all. Push too hard, and you'll exhaust yourself, losing your willpower."

"Oh, sure. Like that time I stayed up 48 hours straight and bought basically everything advertised on late-night TV. It was like I had the willpower of a toddler!" Frank chuckled to himself. "Took me months to pay off that credit card bill."

That wasn't the same thing at all, but I just shook my head and refocused on the Form-5. I checked a box marked URGENT then paused at the next block. Blood type? I was Death. I didn't have blood!

"Before Purgatory's reorganization," I said, returning to Frank's original question. "Lovetta, Leandros, and Chiti were its Guardians, charged with protecting the path to Heaven. The beasts of the field were mankind's greatest fears back then, so they took the forms of a wolf, lion, and cheetah."

Frank's gaze flicked between the Guardians before his eyes widened. "Wait, Dante talked about them in the *Inferno*. I *hated* that book in high school. Are you telling me that Dante's *Inferno* was *real*?" He bumped my shoulder, causing the pen to slip.

I carefully crossed out my error and started again. "Yes, though Dante took significant artistic license with that incomprehensible drivel."

"Huh," Frank grunted. "So ... does Hell really have all those crazy circles of boiling blood, tar pits, and demons running around with pitchforks?"

"Not anymore. Six of Hell's seven levels are dedicated to soul management and frankly look like corporate offices. Most of the damned now go to Level Two: The Department of Bureaucratic Torments. Once we're done in Purgatory, we're headed to Lucifer's throne room on Level Three."

Frank nodded, then fell blessedly silent.

I completed what I could on the Form-5 and straightened, holding it up to review my answers. Over half of the blocks were empty, but it would have to do.

Frank tapped the back of the form. "There's more on

the flipside."

I flipped it over. Damn. "I hate bureaucracy," I said, "but we need to see Minos."

"I don't think Minos works here anymore."

I paused. "What makes you say that?"

He shrugged. "Lovetta said he's been out of the office for a few months now."

"*What*? Why didn't you mention that *before* I filled out this bloody form!"

Frank shrugged again. "I assumed you knew what you were doing. I'm just the new guy."

I glared at my apprentice, the flame in my eye sockets flickering. "That excuse grows wearisome. If you truly wish to take on the Reaper's mantle, then you'd best start taking a more active role in your education. Death is certain. Death does not wait. And Death most certainly does not abide incompetence!"

I slammed the form onto the desk.

I'd expected more from Frank when I'd made him my apprentice. He'd demonstrated inordinate cunning and resourcefulness when he first cheated me, cheated Death, but over the past months he'd been more annoying than helpful. Like he was just a happy-go-lucky tourist of the afterlife.

Death is not a tour guide.

I glanced toward Lovetta, who seemed completely absorbed in sharpening her claws. "How'd you get her to talk, anyway?"

A smirk blossomed behind Frank's beard. "I was polite."

"So was I!"

"No, you started with demands. I complimented Lovetta's purple eyeshadow, noting how it brought out the sable in her fur."

"And she just volunteered information about her boss?"

"Yup. At least, she did after I complained about working for you—oh, calm down," he said. "It's how the game is played. It's called gossip. Bureaucrats are the same everywhere, whether they're IRS agents or immortal spirits. You gotta be more personable if you want to get things done." Frank's expression hardened. "And we need help if we're going to get Abigail out of Hell."

I tapped a finger on my scythe's handle. Saving Abigail was Frank's driving motivation these days. He'd dated her mother, Cora, before he died and seemed to feel some responsibility toward Abigail. Or maybe he just wanted to be the white knight. Who knows? He'd been pestering me nonstop for months to come down here. Not that I'd been dithering. It just took us longer than I'd expected to set things right after Frank's first week as Reaper. The week when I'd been trapped in his body and unable to reap any souls and he'd been more focused on playing golf with dying CEOs than doing the Reaper's job.

But we were here now, and Frank's cheerfulness had elicited more information than my demands. Perhaps he was right. Perhaps I'd been a bit heavy-handed. I glanced around, really looking at Purgatory for the first time since we'd arrived. On the surface, all seemed normal. Souls milled about, awaiting Judgment. On either end of Purgatory's Soul Processing Desk stood two archways: Heaven's Pearly Gates to my right and an obsidian tunnel called the Hellmouth to my left, each guarded by bored-looking angels and demons respectively.

"Frank," I said, a chilling sense of dread wriggling through my bones. "Have you seen anybody move through the Pearly Gates or the Hellmouth since we arrived?"

He glanced between the two. "Nope. Not that I've seen."

I nodded, dread solidifying into something almost tangible. "Something's wrong here. Very wrong."

Frank's expression changed from cheerful tourist to keen auditor like he'd flipped a switch. His gaze swept through Purgatory, observing, calculating. Thoughtful.

Abigail had been stolen from Purgatory sometime in the past two years—she hadn't been specific when we'd talked—but that was still a soul traveling into Hell, even if she wasn't supposed to. This was a complete work stoppage ... and nobody seemed to care!

Plus, the Auditor had been tampering with Judgments in Minos's office. Why? The last time I'd seen him, the Auditor said something about a new position in Nigel's New Order. Was his meddling somehow linked to Nigel, King of the Demigods?

Frank broke into my thoughts. "Think it has anything to do with Hell's reorganization into Nigel's New Order? Sometimes you gotta stop everything to get the new processes established."

I glanced at him. I shouldn't have been surprised that he reached the same conclusions. For his faults, Frank the Taxman had spent his life as an IRS auditor. He was smart and knew how to make connections with limited facts.

"Possibly," I said, thoughts spinning into a tight spiral.

Nigel worried me. Half-human spawn of a demon and King of the Demigods—back when there'd been more than just him—he'd been hell-bent on subsuming humanity into his dark army of demon-spawn: demigods, giant Nephilim, and wretched Cambion. Fortunately for humanity, the Heavenly Host defeated Nigel at Megiddo and banished the entire army to Abaddon, Hell's inescapable seventh level. That was over five thousand years ago.

But Nigel had escaped, and now things were going wrong again. It had to be related.

But why hadn't Heaven noticed what was happening in Purgatory? Souls weren't moving in either direction. Sure, the Almighty was aloof and inscrutable, but somebody at the Pearly Gates must have noticed the paucity of souls moving into Heaven.

Unless Nigel got to them too. That possibility sent a chill through me.

I glanced down the long desk toward Leandros and Chiti. Perhaps they would prove helpful if I were more ... personable. It was worth a shot. I strode toward their end of the Soul Processing Desk, Frank at my heels.

They glanced up at our approach. Leandros was well-muscled under his thick amber mane while Chiti was lean. Their snouts were whiskered and tawny with their upper canines poking ever-so-slightly below their lips, like a warning of the Guardians' fierce nature. Both wore white robes and matching wary expressions.

"Greetings," I said in my best conversational tone. "I must say, Chiti, your spots are looking quite, um, spot-on today."

The cheetah spirit twitched one ear at me but didn't smile.

"And Leandros! My goodness, what big teeth you have."

Frank groaned beside me. "You're killing me, Boss." He leaned on the desk and pushed his cowl off his head.

"Hey guys," he said, scratching at the short-cropped ring of gray hair above his ears. "Any idea when Minos will be in?"

Leandros pointed to the other end of the counter. "That's Lovetta's department," he growled.

"Yeah, but she sent us down here to make an appointment," Frank said, much calmer than I felt. Death did not ping-pong between bureaucrats for their amusement!

Leandros assumed the put-upon look of someone forced to do actual work. He extended a clawed hand. "Form-5, please."

Frank waved dismissively. "You know and I know that making an appointment is a waste of time. Where can we find him? Visiting the Almighty? Or perhaps he's down below with Lucifer?"

Leandros's expression froze at the Devil's name. He didn't say anything, but I saw the truth in his eyes. Frank had guessed right.

The Taxman smacked the counter cheerfully. "Then that's where we're going. Thanks for the lovely chat, fellas!"

Leandros narrowed his eyes. "The Hellmouth is closed."

Which was not a denial of Frank's guess. I leaned forward. "You think mere guards can stop me? I am Death!" I straightened and cracked *Grace*'s butt on the floor. Enough of this bureaucratic nonsense. "Frank, we're leaving."

He placed a hand on my shoulder. I twisted *Grace*'s ebony handle, willing the scythe to send us straight into Lucifer's office.

Nothing happened.

I tried again. Still nothing. I stared at my scythe. This was impossible; a violation of the Rules governing all spiritual matters. The Rules that were burned into my very soul. None could interfere with Death.

My gaze flicked to Leandros. What had changed in the past twenty minutes? My scythe had worked perfectly well bringing us into Purgatory. But now ... nothing.

Leandros's lips curled into a toothy grin, and I felt like a mouse on the wrong end of supper. "Nobody enters Hell right now," he said. "Not until Nigel says."

"Lucifer will hear of this," I told him.

"No," Leandros rumbled. "The Dragon will die."

Chapter 2

THE FERRYMAN

THE DRAGON WILL ... *what?*

I stumbled back from Leandros in shock. The lion-spirit eyed me, smiling his toothy smile, but offering no further comments. I pulled Frank away from the desk, my mind reeling.

He found his voice before I did. "The Dragon," he whispered, "as in, the Devil? Someone's gonna try to kill Lucifer?"

"Yes. He's often referred to as the Dragon, wily and cunning," I said, kicking myself for taking so long to put the pieces together. "Lucifer is in grave danger. Nigel's

New Order isn't just reorganizing Hell's Bureaucracy. It's a coup."

Frank's nose wrinkled. "Bold move. How would that work, killing the Devil? Is there some deeper, darker Hell to banish his soul to?"

My grip on *Grace*'s handle tightened. "There is such a place," I said, considering my words. I hadn't shared with Frank all the details of my brief time as a human. I hadn't told him about finding Evelyn again—Captain of the Heavenly Host, and the only other soul I'd ever loved. Evelyn, whom I'd trapped in Abaddon for five thousand years with Nigel the Demigod and Hell's darkest creations. She and Nigel had worked together to escape, a sin I doubted Heaven would forgive, and returned to the mortal realm twenty years ago. I only learned of their escape six months ago. And Evelyn was now suffering for her sins, I was sure, banished to Heaven by a cursed blade while I watched, unable to help.

Frankly, I would much rather have been in Heaven looking for Evelyn than navigating the morass of Purgatory's bureaucracy. To provide what comfort I could as she'd done for me all those millennia ago when I fell from grace and become the Reaper. It was my fault she'd been banished. My fault she'd failed her duties and was subject to Heaven's punishments.

No, I hadn't told Frank any of that. Some memories were too painful to share.

"Abaddon is Hell's seventh and lowest level," I said. "It's the realm of eternal darkness and ultimate suffering reserved for Lucifer alone after Armageddon—assuming he loses." I turned my scythe, so the curved blade glinted. "But Nigel can't send Lucifer to Abaddon without *Grace*. My scythe is the key to opening Hell's sealed lowest seventh level." We had to reach Lucifer. Warn him.

"Okay, so ... what's the problem with sending Lucifer off to early retirement?" Frank glanced at the souls nearby and lowered his voice even further. "Wouldn't the world be better without the Devil?"

"Not if Nigel's taking over." I ducked under the rope separating the souls from the Processing Desk and pushed into the bored crowd awaiting Judgment. Frank followed. The crowd parted before me like the Red Sea before Moses. Whenever gazes fell on me, eyes widened in fear and souls stepped from my path. Death tends to have that effect. To Frank, I said, "The war between Heaven and Hell has achieved balance over the millennia because everybody plays by the Rules governing spiritual matters. Rules emplaced after Nigel was trapped in Abaddon and—"

"Rules that I'm only partially subject to, right?" Frank said. "I remember you saying something about that."

"Correct. You are subject to all Rules governing souls and soul management," I growled, annoyed at the interruption. My path was abruptly blocked by a lane rope. I ducked under it, barely pausing. "The special Rules governing Death have not—yet—been burned into your soul. But that's not today's problem. My point," I said sharply, "is that without Lucifer's institutional knowledge and respect for the Rules, Nigel will bring chaos to soul management. He might even trigger Armageddon early."

"Ah," he said, nodding with a keen look. "I get it. Better the devil you know, right?"

"Something like that. But the problem goes deeper. Leandros said, 'the Dragon will *die*.'" I glanced sideways at Frank as we wove through Purgatory. "Only one thing can kill Lucifer: *Mercy*, the black blade of unmaking. The sword which Nigel now holds." Stolen from Evelyn as she was struck down by one of the Auditor's minions. Her anguished scream still haunted me.

I lengthened my stride and Frank had to jog to keep up.

"Where are we going?" he asked.

"To see your predecessor."

"Woah, wait a minute!" Frank stopped, but I did not slow my pace. "You had another apprentice? Who?"

"Charon the Ferryman," I called over my shoulder. "We are going to cross the river Acheron."

***

The river Acheron lay beyond Purgatory's western wall. It had once flowed just inside the Hellmouth, but everything shifted when Hell reorganized into a bureaucratic model four hundred years ago. A corporate interior redesign meant to streamline the soul management process.

A process that no longer required the river Acheron and Charon the Ferryman.

After what felt like an eternity of weaving through Purgatory's milling masses—and ducking at least five hundred lane ropes—I led Frank toward an unassuming door simply labeled TOILET. A door no souls entered because the dead do not defecate.

I shuddered and pushed the door open. Of the human body's incessant needs, defecation was, by far, the worst.

An embarrassing aspect of my brief mortality I wished I could forget.

Unfortunately, Death does not forget.

Beyond the threshold, however, we found no tiled room or appalling smells. Instead, we stepped from sunlight into an immense rocky cavern shrouded in mist at the far end. Cool air wrapped around us with the sickly-sweet musk of death. A path lay before us, lined with torches on posts whose flames flickered in small iron cages.

Frank whistled and glanced behind us. The dense crowd of souls wandering aimlessly about Purgatory was still visible through the doorway. "Where'd the bathroom go?"

I shook my head. "It was never there. What you saw was nothing more than a bit of stage setting to disguise the portal to Charon's little corner of Hell. You are in the spiritual realm now. Applying the laws of physics to what you see is a recipe for madness."

Frank nodded and shut the door. It disappeared, swirling into nothingness, leaving only a blank rock wall behind us.

We strode forward, shrouded in mist within moments. The torches cast just enough light for the path ahead while the darkness dogged our heels to obscure what lay behind.

The world reduced to a small path of torchlight hemmed in by oppressive gloom.

After we'd walked for several minutes, the mist thinned again to reveal the languid black waters of the river Acheron. It flowed imperceptibly from left to right, from darkness to deeper darkness. A half-rotted gondola bobbed gently at the water's edge tied to a large iron brazier that crackled heartily with orange flames.

Charon lounged beside the dancing fire in a bright pink fold-out camp chair, reading a paperback. Something with a buxom brunette on the cover melting into the arms of a hero who'd managed to lose his shirt.

Charon was a gaunt old spirit with cadaver-gray skin, wispy hair, and a pocked face. His reaper's cloak, tattered and torn, was hooked over the top of the chair and draped him like a blanket. One hairy leg and bare foot hung over the chair's fabric arm.

He didn't notice our approach, his gaze riveted on the trashy romance. The mist pulled back as we neared, revealing an open steamer trunk at the edge of the brazier's flickering light. It overflowed with battered paperbacks.

Frank and I stopped near the brazier. Charon turned a page.

"What is this?" I said. "No greeting for your old boss?"

Charon shrieked in surprise, practically levitating out of his camp chair. It overbalanced, and he fell backward in a tangle of limbs and cloak. The chair half-collapsed on him before he scrambled up, eyes wide. He clutched the book, place kept with a finger, but his cloak fell to the cavern floor, revealing the Ferryman in all his naked glory.

It was not very glorious.

"You..." Charon's wild gaze flicked between Frank and me, trashy romance pointed accusingly. "You shouldn't sneak up on folk like that!" His voice was high and sharp.

I cocked a bony eye ridge. "Death is often unexpected. You know that."

He swore in Greek and grabbed a black robe more tattered than his cloak from beside his chair. "It ain't like I get visitors these days," he said. His voice became muffled as the robe went over his head like a poncho. "Not since you *fired* me as your apprentice." He wriggled before his head popped out of the top, hair even more askew. "Hell's Bureaucracy shoved me aside like yesterday's trash." Charon snatched his Reaper's cloak from atop his pink chair and swung it around his shoulders.

Frank's face scrunched at me. "You fired *the Ferryman*?

Why? I'd figure he was pre-qualified for the job."

My grip tightened on *Grace.* "Death is not to be taken lightly. Charon was relieved of his apprenticeship duties after he circumvented the Rules and started taking people before their time."

Frank's brows shot up. His mouth formed a silent O.

Charon eyed me sideways. "So, I got a little ... overenthusiastic. Big deal."

"Overenthusiastic?" I said. "You started London's Great Plague! Humanity had wiped out the Black Death before you reintroduced it."

Charon hunched into his cloak. "I said I was sorry."

I shook my head. This wasn't how I'd hoped to start this conversation. "Let us leave the past in the past. I didn't come to revive old grievances. Frank and I need entry into Hell, but the bureaucrats have taken over Purgatory. Somehow, they've stopped me from traveling there." I twisted *Grace's* handle as proof. As before, nothing happened.

Charon's eyes widened. He took an involuntary step forward. The sickly-sweet smell of death came with him. "But ... the Rules forbid *anybody* from interfering with Death. You should be able to go wherever you want!"

"Agreed." I nodded. "And that's not all. Hell is bypassing Judgment and stealing souls. I found blank forms in Minos's office signed by the Auditor. What do you know about Nigel's New Order?"

"Who?" Charon shook his head and gestured with his book. "I don't get out much."

Frank glanced at the steamer chest. "Then where'd you get the books?"

A wry grin creased Charon's face. "The occasional lost soul still wanders in from Purgatory. But nobody carries a gold coin to pay the Ferryman these days, so I send 'em all back to await Judgment. Then, about ten years ago, this lady offered me her entire library as payment for passage. I just had to retrieve the books before her kids tossed them out. I was going mad with boredom down here, so we struck a bargain."

"Fascinating," I said, deadpan, "but unrelated to the problem at hand. Frank and I require transit to Hell." I gestured to the half-rotten gondola.

Charon's wispy eyebrows rose. "You got coin for passage?"

"No. I—"

"No payment, no passage."

My fingers drummed on *Grace.* "Nigel is trying to overthrow Hell's Bureaucracy—"

"Sounds like a fine idea to me."

"—and humanity is suffering for it! You may have a grudge against me, but for the sake of the souls—"

Frank stopped me with a hand on my shoulder. To Charon, he said, "How about a trade, like you gave the lady?" The Ferryman perked up at that and Frank asked, "What do you want? More books? A TV? I bet you'd *love* soap operas."

Charon considered Frank's offer, but then his gaze drifted to my scythe. A hungry gleam lit his ancient eyes. "I'll take *Grace* as payment for passage."

"No," I said with finality.

"Aw, come on. Not forever. Just while you're visiting Hell."

"Absolutely not!" I glared at the Ferryman, but then an idea occurred to me. "However, considering the obstacles we've already met, I suspect that our journey will take longer than anticipated. And I need someone to shepherd souls while I'm gone. If you're interested."

Charon's eyes practically bulged out of his head. "Deal!"

I raised a forestalling hand. "Only while I'm away, and

only if you swear to uphold the Rules and treat every soul with the utmost respect. We cannot have a repeat of last time."

The Ferryman raised both hands like a soul repenting their sins. "I swear on my immortal soul. I'll do your job so well that nobody will even miss you."

That would do. I nodded. Charon grinned and flung the romance to land amongst its fellows near the steamer trunk.

"Hold on," Frank said, looking confused. "How's he gonna play Death without a scythe? Doesn't he need *Grace* to send souls to Purgatory?"

Charon inhaled sharply, an offended hand pressed to his chest. "The Ferryman does not 'play Death.' I am a guide with eons of experience transporting souls the old-fashioned way: by hand." He looked at me and hooked a thumb at Frank. "Who's the new guy?"

"This is Frank the Taxman, the first soul to ever successfully cheat Death. He also helped me put the Auditor back in his place. In return, I made him my apprentice."

"What? A *human* Reaper? What were you think—"

I slammed *Grace*'s handle into the stone floor with a *crack* that reverberated through the cavern. "Frank is my apprentice. End of discussion. Did you want to escape the tedium of your life? Or would you rather return to your reading?"

Charon raised both hands defensively. "Forget I even asked." He stepped aside and gestured grandly to his gondola. "Bring her back in one piece."

"Of course." I nodded with gravity. Charon took that as his cue to leave and practically scampered up the torchlit trail. The mist swirled and swallowed the Ferryman.

Frank watched him go. "Aren't you worried he'll start another plague?"

I shook my head. "The world population has increased exponentially since Charon last reaped a soul. He has no idea how busy he's about to be. Mischief born of boredom will not be an issue." I gestured toward the gondola. "The way to Hell is now open."

"Let's do this!" Frank said, jumping into the gondola. It creaked and swayed alarmingly. "I'm steering."

I stepped aboard and moved to the front of the craft where a small lantern dangled from the gondola's upswept prow. Frank untied the ragged little boat and then pushed us into the Acheron's languid current using the gondola's long pole.

Frank grunted and muttered a few curses while figuring out how to steer using nothing but a pole. The Taxman's skills lay in cunning and sarcasm, not athleticism. While he'd been alive, I doubt Frank ever did anything that reeked of exercise, and the lack of skill showed now that he was a spirit. But he eventually found his rhythm, and the shore faded behind us.

I gazed into the gloom, straining to see the far shore, to catch my first glimpse of Hell where Nigel's New Order was sowing chaos and stealing souls. What was his intent? Did he merely seek power in Hell, or would he try to raise another dark army to subsume humanity? I had to stop him, restore the balance and set things right before Heaven found out what was happening and launched Armageddon early.

As the gondola creaked beneath me, I worried about Abigail, somewhere in Hell amidst all that was going wrong. I'd sworn to right the wrong of her soul's damnation without Judgment. I would make good on that promise.

Nothing is more certain than the promise of Death.

Chapter 3

THE LABYRINTH

THE SILENCE OF OUR crossing was broken only by the soft lapping of the Acheron's black waters against the gondola's prow, like the gentle promise of Death, but with an undercurrent that was deep and unknown. Darkness enveloped us, pushed back only slightly by the lantern's dim glow. Floating on the river brought memories of a rafting trip I'd taken before I became Death.

I'd been a guardian angel back then and had taken Evelyn—the only other spirit I'd ever loved—on a, well, I guess you'd call it a date, though we didn't use those terms at the beginning of time. We'd rafted a river in central Asia in search of a waterfall. Evelyn had loved waterfalls, and I loved to make her smile. That journey had been warm and glorious, full of sunshine and the mingled scents of spring in bloom and of a river full of life.

In comparison, the darkness here felt dismal, dank, and oppressive. And I would have much preferred Evelyn's company over Frank's. I glanced down at the water.

"Frank, I think you've gotten us turned around. We should be crossing the Acheron, not moving downriver."

"This isn't as easy as it looks," he grunted, straining to guide us with the pole. It splashed as he dragged it through the water. "Feel free to take over at any time."

"You volunteered." I gestured into the darkness. "Now turn left."

"I'm trying!"

The current picked up speed. A low rumble sounded in the distance.

"Frank. We need to turn."

"I know!"

The rumble intensified, ominous and echoing in the darkness. I turned back to Frank and extended my hand. "Fine. Give me the pole."

Frank half-pulled the pole from the water and tossed it

toward me.

He missed.

The Ferryman's pole bounced off the gondola's edge. I lunged forward, scrambling to catch it. My knees thumped the bottom of the boat. A board cracked under my weight, dropping my right knee into the cold water. I lurched awkwardly, straining to reach the pole as it arced toward the inky depths. The gondola rocked wildly with me, dipping the boat's edge under the water. Frank shrieked and lunged for the gondola's other side to counterbalance us. We rocked the other direction, pulling my fingertips away from the pole.

The Ferryman's pole splashed into the Acheron. It sank from view, consumed by the black water.

"You fool!" I rounded on Frank.

"It's not my fault!"

"How is this *not* your fault?"

"You didn't catch the pole!"

"Why'd you throw it?"

"So, you could catch it!"

"What in Heaven's name would possess you to throw our only means of steering? I have half a mind to make you swim!"

Frank pointed at the hole my knee had made in the gondola. Water bubbled in. "If we don't start bailing soon, we both may end up swimming."

I glared, the blue flames in my eye sockets flaring with heat. "Oh, yes. That sounds like a marvelous idea. Let me just grab this ... oh wait, we don't have a bucket," I said sarcastically. "All the Ferryman gave us was his gondola, a lantern, and the pole which you threw away!"

My words surprised me. Not my annoyance at Frank, that had been building for months, but the sarcasm that laced my rebuke. It seemed I'd picked up a bad habit from my new apprentice.

The rumble we'd heard was no longer distant. Frank's petulant expression disappeared, replaced by pale terror. "Um, Grim…"

He pointed, and I spun. The river fell away before us, a waterfall appearing at the edge of the lamplight.

Since when did the river Acheron have a waterfall?

I gripped the gondola's prow as it slid forward, tilting into the empty nothingness. "Hold on!" I yelled.

Frank cursed behind me, but it turned into a rising scream whose pitch climbed the scale far beyond tones I would have expected from the Taxman.

***

When I regained awareness of my surroundings, I lay upon a rocky shore, Frank an oversized lump beside me. Our cloaks were twisted around us like we'd been through a tumble dryer. The shattered remains of the Ferryman's gondola lay scattered among the rocks.

Well, so much for bringing that back in one piece.

Grace lay nearby. I grabbed my scythe, dragging it toward me through the rough gravel. The thought that I might have lost *Grace* sent a shiver through me. Never again. I leaned heavily on it and climbed to my feet.

The waterfall rumbled behind us, a black curtain that flowed into a matching pool of darkest midnight. We lay in a small cave that ended abruptly several yards in front of us. A white plaster wall split the cavern, set with a simple open doorway like you might see in a corporate building: simple and unobtrusive. It was as though the cave had been sliced from somewhere else and tacked onto an office. Our only light came from that doorway, which led into a hallway that also looked very corporate—if corporate hallways had gray flagstone floors. White walls marched into the distance, inset with brown doors and lit by unobtrusive florescent lighting in a tiled ceiling.

Frank rubbed his head and slowly clambered to his feet. He adjusted his cloak and brown tweed suit and looked around. "Where are we?"

"I'm not sure," I said, "some liminal space. A bit of 'in-between' left over from Hell's reorganization, I'm guessing. Much like the leftover section that held Charon and the Acheron."

"So ... we could be anywhere? Even right outside the Devil's office on Level Three?"

"Throne room, not office. Once you see it, you'll never confuse Lucifer's seat of power with a mere CEO's. But I doubt we've made it that far. There would be guards. No, I'm guessing from the décor," I gestured to the welcoming hallway before us, "that we're either on Level One with Reception or Level Two with the Department of Bureaucratic Torments. At least there's a clear path."

A distant scream reverberated from somewhere down that hallway before it cut off abruptly. Frank cocked an eyebrow at me. "In there? Where it sounds like somebody's being murdered?"

"We *are* in Hell. What did you expect, garden parties

and scones?"

"What happened to Hell having a bureaucratic model?" Frank said. "I've known a few nasty bureaucrats in my day, but actual murder was usually off the menu."

"Usually?" I asked.

Frank smirked at me, but the expression faded as his gaze returned to the white hallway before us. Brown doors and bulletin boards broke up the hall's monochromatic progression. Frank drew a steadying breath, hitched the shoulders of his cloak forward, and strode confidently through the doorway.

I followed, pleased that my apprentice hadn't succumbed to his fear. I was still annoyed about his handling of the gondola, but at least Frank was headed in the right direction. I decided to let him take the lead to see how he coped with ... whatever we found.

Frank stopped at the first doorway and tried the knob. It didn't turn. I considered offering advice about how spirits don't *have* to use door handles but remained silent. How would he solve the problem?

Frank glanced back at me, brows furrowed quizzically. Then his gaze flicked over my shoulder. Frank's eyes bulged. There was a moment of silence, of indrawn breath before Frank loosed a rattling scream that rivaled the one we'd heard earlier.

I spun. A minotaur's snarling visage filled my vision, the heavy brass ring in its wet nose mere inches from my face. The beast had a bull's shaggy brown head, broad horns, and narrowed black eyes. Muscles bulged under a loose goat-skin tunic. Fetid breath huffed into my face. The doorway we'd entered was gone, replaced by a labyrinthine hallway that stretched to eternity.

Well, that answered the question of where we were: Hell's First Level. I read the minotaur's soul through its eyes and my eye ridges rose in surprise.

A nightmare? But ... weren't they confined to Hell's Basement?

The minotaur nightmare roared, shaking the walls and blowing my cowl off my skull. Behind me, Frank screamed his high-pitched warble and bolted.

I glared at the minotaur. "Was that really necessary?"

Amusement sparkled in the beast's eyes, saying 'yes, scaring the living daylights out of Frank was indeed necessary.' The minotaur stepped around me and thundered after Frank, roaring like the hellion it was.

I ran after them. "Frank, stop!"

Frank did not stop. He scrambled forward, slamming into doors, trying to force them open. He may as well have been slamming his shoulder into stone walls. He bounced like a pinball across the hallway, stumbling and screaming with the rising pitch of pure panic.

"Oh, for heaven's sake. Frank!" I yelled again as I kept pace behind the minotaur. "Calm down! It's just a nightmare. Frank! Come back!" My pleas were lost beneath another roar.

"Do you mind?" I yelled at the beast. The nightmare threw a wink over its shoulder and roared again. The creature kept pace behind Frank's mad scramble, staying close enough to terrify the Taxman, but never quite catching him, as though it were herding Frank.

Toward what?

We neared another hallway and Frank dashed to the right. I cut past the minotaur, getting in front of it, and snatched at Frank's cloak. I missed.

We turned the corner and crashed into a young woman. I barely had time to register her shocked expression before the three of us tumbled to the flagstones and slid to a stop.

The minotaur loomed over us, muscles bulging. It roared loud enough to shake my bones.

I threw up a skeletal hand. "Stop! You've had your fun, but the chase is over."

The beast cut off in mid-roar and deflated a little. "I'm just doing my job," it—no *she*—said in a distinctly feminine rumble.

"And a wonderful job you've done." I climbed to my feet, trying to regain my dignity. "My apprentice was duly terrified."

"Me too," said the young woman we'd crashed into. She rose with limber grace then extended a hand to Frank. He accepted it, and she pulled him upright with a grunt. Then she turned to me, and her eyes widened in recognition; a common occurrence for Death incarnate, though that recognition was usually followed by pleas of 'No, not yet. I'm too young to die,' and other such drivel.

But she surprised me. "Grim?" she said.

I recognized that voice. "Abigail?" I read her soul and confirmed my suspicion. Abigail Knowles, death two years and seven months ago. We'd found her.

Abigail was shorter than Frank and had violently rainbow hair. Blue roots blended to hot pink tips that hung over the shaved sides of her head. She wore black pants, heavy boots, and a purple shirt with fish-net sleeves. The stylized skull on her shirt was a collection of sharp slashes, as though the artist was working through severe anger issues. Emblazoned beneath the skull in the same slasher design was the word REAPER.

Abigail hooked her rainbow hair behind an ear lined with spiked earrings. She had a determined set to her jaw. "It's been months, Grim. I didn't think you'd come."

"I promised I would," I said, "and nothing is more certain than the promise of Death." I eyed Abigail as fiercely as she eyed me. "What are you doing in the Labyrinth? I thought you were in Torments working the call center?"

That was how I'd learned of Abigail's predicament. I'd called the IRS's IT help desk hoping to reach the head of Hell's department of Bureaucratic Torments, Alvin Bureaucracy. Most help desks are subcontracted to Torments. Abigail had answered. Once she figured out who I was, she told me about being condemned to Torments without Judgment, and I'd sworn to investigate her case.

Abigail shrugged. "You never came, so I'm breaking out of Hell on my own. It wasn't that hard reaching the Labyrinth but finding my way up from here has been ... difficult."

I shook my head. "That's by design. I told you, human

souls only travel in one direction. You live, you die, and you move on to your final destination after Judgment." I raised a forestalling hand. "Yes, I know you were never Judged. That's why we're here. But I believe your case is merely a symptom of a larger problem."

She cocked an eyebrow.

"Nigel is staging a coup," I said. "He intends to kill Lucifer."

"*What?*" she squeaked.

Wait, no. That wasn't Abigail. I opened my mouth to respond but froze when I realized that the squeak had merely come from her direction.

A puppy-sized dragon poked its head over her shoulder. It had small horns, shimmering blue scales, and sharp silver eyes that flicked nervously around the hallway, as though searching for danger. The little dragon considered the minotaur looming over us before climbing onto Abigail's shoulder. He must have been hanging off her like a backpack. Leathery blue wings draped the dragon's scaled body like a tiny cloak.

"Grim," Abigail said, "meet Conrad. He's a nightmare." The flames in my eyes sputtered in surprise. Usually, nightmares resembled the minotaur: overbearing and terrifying. This one inspired images of small yappy dogs and was ... cute.

"Conrad," Abigail said to the dragon, "meet Grim and...?" She arched an eyebrow at Frank.

"Frank Totmann." He extended his hand. "Good to meet you! I, uh, dated your mom Cora for a while."

Abigail's expression hardened. She did not shake Frank's hand. "Yes, I'd heard." Frank froze for an awkward moment before lowering his hand. Abigail glanced at me. "What's he doing here?"

"Frank is my apprentice."

"Your *what?* Last I heard, he'd stolen your scythe and 'scurried off like a school yard bully,' I think were the words you used."

I nodded. "A lot has happened since last we talked."

Abigail's jaw worked, and her eyes narrowed at Frank. He looked like he wanted to say something in his defense, but just shoved his hands into his pockets.

The minotaur broke the tense silence, waving a clawed hand. "And I'm Teri. So nice to meet everyone!" Teri's broad smile revealed yellow teeth. Then those beady eyes swiveled toward me. She looked me up and down like I was some delectable treat. "Especially you, handsome. Hubba

hubba!"

Hubba ... hubba? I leaned away from her. "The pleasure's all mine," I said uncertainly. "I intend no discourtesy, but why is a nightmare all the way up here on Hell's first level? Last I heard, nightmares were restricted to the Basement on Level Six."

Teri's enthusiasm dimmed. "The number of souls roaming the Labyrinth has slowly climbed for decades. Too many for Asteron—the real Minotaur—to herd into Reception alone. So, Hell's Resources brought some nightmares in to help."

I nodded in understanding. I too had felt the strain of shepherding so many souls as humanity's population increased. I gestured down the hallway. "Well, then. Now that we're all acquainted, perhaps you could take us to Reception? We need access to the lower levels."

"Anything for you, handsome," she said, giving me a look that I think was supposed to be sultry.

Conrad waved goodbye, his voice high and saucy. "Have fun, Bones!"

Bones? "You're not coming?"

"Abi and I are headed up, not down," he said, pointing one claw upward, one downward. "We're blowing this joint!"

Abigail shook her head. "We've been trapped in the Labyrinth for weeks. Grim's our best chance of escape, so we're sticking with him." Conrad cracked his jaws to argue but then snapped them shut when Abigail's eyes narrowed. What was he to her? Not her nightmare, surely. I couldn't imagine a cute blue dragon being Abigail's greatest fear. He wrapped himself in his wings, clearly settling in for a good sulk.

I inclined my head toward Teri and said, "Lead the way."

"Sorry, sexy, can't do that," she said.

"But you just said—"

"I can point you in the right direction, but I have to *chase* new arrivals to the center of the Labyrinth. And you have to scream. It's in my contract."

"Death does not run helter-skelter, screaming." I appreciate dramatic flair as much as anyone, but not at the expense of my dignity. I made a mental note to discuss this with Frank, considering how he'd reacted to the minotaur.

Teri's brows furrowed. She considered me carefully before nodding. "This way." She turned toward the nearest door and placed a palm on it. It flashed once then creaked open with a properly ominous creak, as though the simple office door was actually a rusty dungeon gate. A stone staircase spiraled downward into darkness. "We'll take a shortcut backstage," Teri said, slipping through the door and descending down the spiral.

Backstage? I wasn't aware that Hell had a 'backstage.' But at least we were headed in the right direction: into the depths of Hell. What terrors would we find?

I didn't expect the answer to that question to be cats.

Chapter 4

BACKSTAGE

WITHIN HALF A TURN, the stone wall encasing the spiral stairs ended without a railing, presenting a broad rough cavern underlit by lava pools that spread like flicked droplets of torment. Stalactites beside us strained to reach matching stalagmites on the uneven stone floor. Crisscrossing paths connected more staircases that spiraled to the ceiling. The air was hot and dry and bore Hell's distinctive rotten egg undertone of brimstone.

There were cats everywhere. They slept on stone shelves, paced quietly along paths, or watched us with piercing, judgmental eyes. These weren't spirits. Cats have no immortal souls. They were real. One hundred percent flesh and blood and disdain for we mere spirits who dared walk among those who had once been worshiped as gods.

The cats glowed with vibrant life. It wasn't a visible glow, no halos on these kitties, but they had a presence, a solidity that defied the eye and the imagination. They were more real than the rocks they slept upon.

Frank whistled. "Now *this* is what I expected Hell to look like. But what's with the cats?"

Abigail gave an echoing whistle from between us. "There were cats in Torments too, but nowhere near this many." She glanced back at Frank. "Let me guess, you hate cats?" Her tone was sharp and judgmental.

"Nah, I love 'em!" Frank said cheerily, ignoring her tone, "My cat's name was Diana. A long-haired Persian with the cutest little scrunched face. Man, I miss her. But where'd these cats come from?"

I glanced back as we spiraled down the stairs. "Cats and crows can transit realms at will, a remnant of times when spirits used them as messengers. They must feel that this is a safe haven."

"Okay," he said. "So why aren't there any crows here?"

Conrad answered, rousing from his sulk on Abigail's shoulder. "Crows are jerks." His high-pitched voice dripped with scorn. "Hell stopped using them as messengers because they thought it was grand fun to change the messages. A game. Remember the burning of the library at Alexandria?"

"Sure," Frank said, though I know for a fact he hadn't been there.

"Totally a crow's fault! Changed a message from 'incapacitate' to 'incinerate,' and then he and his buddies watched and cackled from the rooftops as the library burned!" Conrad harrumphed.

Abigail made shushing noises at him then asked Teri, "Why'd you call this backstage?"

"Before the reorg," the nightmare minotaur said, "this was part of the Pit. But when the corporations moved into Level Four, they didn't need this section, so it got closed off. There are all sorts of lost bits of Hell that only nightmares use as shortcuts between levels." That explained the pool where Frank and I had landed. We reached the bottom of our spiral stairs, and she led us along a winding trail between lava pools and ledges.

A battle-scarred black tomcat leapt past me from a shelf to our right. He was so close that I smelled his musk. I jerked back in surprise, bumping into Abigail and Conrad as the cat landed on Teri's broad shoulders.

The little dragon squawked in my ear. "Hey, watch it Bones!" His wings flapped against my head.

I stopped and turned. "I am not 'Bones.' I prefer Grim as a name, Death as a title."

"Yeah, whatever Bones."

I eyed the dragon, who turned away from me in haughty disdain, then I glanced at Abigail. "How did you end up with such a charming companion?"

She smirked and reached up to scratch Conrad under the chin. "He's a nightmare messenger, a rather dangerous job down here."

Conrad's eyes closed under Abigial's ministrations. A happy growl rumbled free, and he muttered, "Hell takes the phrase 'kill the messenger' very seriously."

"Um," Frank said from the tail of our little band. "You mean '*don't* kill the messenger,' right?"

"Nope." Conrad shook his head, but only slightly so he didn't move away from Abigial's scratching fingers.

I turned to follow Teri again, who was now several yards away down the twisting and uneven path. She hadn't even paused when the tomcat landed on her, but, like Abigail, reached up to scratch under his chin. He rode her broad shoulders like a surfer, catching the rhythm of her pace before laying down.

Abigail said, "I met Conrad in Torments. He'd just delivered a NOTICE from the Office of Micromanagement to my boss Kevin."

"Notification of Torment Instruction Coach Assignment," Conrad chimed in. "Getting a NOTICE is pretty standard when your section falls behind its call quotas. But Kevin didn't take the news well. Tried to tear my wings off."

"Anyway," Abigail said, "I let Conrad hide in my desk drawer. Afterwards, we hatched our plan to escape Hell together."

I glanced back. "By waltzing out the front door?"

"Basically." Abigail shrugged.

I shook my head and trudged onward. "The Hellmouth only works in one direction. Your soul wouldn't have passed back into Purgatory."

Silence fell after that. We wound past staircases and stalagmites, flaming pools, and cats. So many cats. We neared a spiral staircase much broader than the others, and rough voices broke the silence. Voices engaged in a cheerful argument.

Four minotaur nightmares who could have been Terri's doppelgangers huddled around a stone table at the base of the stairs. Dice rattled.

"Five sixes!" one yelled. "Beat that!"

A groan went up from the others. One snarled. "You palmed the dice."

"Did not."

"Liar!" There was a small scuffle before the second minotaur raised a hand in triumph, dice on his palm. "Ah, ha!"

Teri strolled up and slapped the cheater on the back of his scruffy head. "I told you, Niko, the name of the game is cheating *without* getting caught."

Niko rubbed the back of his head and scowled at Teri. "I'm trying, but I'm not as strong as you." His beady eyes widened when he saw us. "Hey, who're they?"

"Visitors headed to reception."

That got everybody's attention. Niko's voice lowered to a rumbling whisper. "What are you doing, Teri? You're supposed to chase 'em there, not lead 'em backstage. You'll get tossed back in the Basement!"

"Only if somebody tells." Teri grinned. "Now scoot

over and let me show you how to properly cheat." She scooped up the dice and rattled them in the cup. The cat on her shoulders leapt to the table and sniffed at Teri's companions. Niko gave him several heavy pets. The cat flopped onto his side in the center of the table and started purring.

I raised my hand. "Pardon, but we really are in a hurry. We don't have time—"

Teri waved absently, still rattling the dice. "Keep your pants on, handsome. This is Hell. We have all the time in eternity."

"If only that were true," I said, slightly off-put by her casual flirting. Flirting with Death doesn't usually end well for the soul that tries it.

The dice cup paused, and Teri half-turned to meet my gaze. "The Nightmare Council negotiated mandatory breaks as part of our contracts. I have to sit here. You can join me, sexy"—she gave me that terrifying sultry look again—"or head up on your own." She pointed the dice cup at the broad spiral stairs. "Reception's through the door at the top."

Teri slammed the cup down. She eyed her minotaur compatriots as though we no longer existed. "Any guesses what I got?" There were a few grunts, but no takers. "Full house," Teri said, then lifted the cup to reveal three sixes and two fives. The others roared in disgust, and Teri chortled.

I shook my head, amused at their game even as annoyance surged through me. Nightmares were unpredictable and fickle, just like the human souls they were cut from. Yet they retained the *potential* for great power. That potential terrified Hell's leadership. It was why nightmares were restricted to the Basement.

Despite the dice, the minotaurs' game was not one of chance. It was one of willpower. In the spiritual realms, one can change the appearance of anything with sufficient willpower. If I wanted, I could waltz into Reception looking like Teri. Not that I would, but I *could.* Very few souls possessed my level of control and willpower. However, such an extreme change would be exhausting, even for me, and I needed to keep my strength for the unknown troubles ahead.

"Let's go," I said to Frank and Abigail, heading up the stairs. "It's time we talk to Hell's Receptionist. I hope his third head is taking a nap today, or this could get ugly."

"His third ... what?" Frank asked as he climbed beside

me. He glanced back at Abigail as if to confirm that he'd heard correctly.

She sighed but nodded. "His third head. Hell's Receptionist is Cerberus, the three-headed dog."

***

At the top of the stairs, we pushed through the door into a scene of pure chaos. Hell's Reception was so tightly packed with souls that I could barely squeeze through the door.

The domed room was expansive. Not as expansive as Purgatory, but massive enough that the sea of souls defied counting. Yet despite the dense press, none flowed into the dozen archways evenly spaced around the perimeter, hallways that emptied in from the Labyrinth. Well-muscled demons with drawn blades braced each entry. A few small wooden doors like the one we'd just pushed through also lined the perimeter but without guards.

At the room's far end sat Cerberus behind a desk sized for his twelve-foot-tall frame. All three heads were awake and looked—from left to right—cheerful, resigned, and annoyed. Several cats lounged upon his desk, furry gods awaiting worship. Behind Cerberus was a bank of elevators, our ticket into Hell's lower levels ... if we could get through this crowd.

Which might prove troublesome. Perhaps we could go backstage again and come out through one of the doors closer to Cerberus. I reached past Abigail and pulled on the door. Locked.

Of course it was.

A large number board above Cerberus's head glowed red with the words NOW SERVING and a string of numbers and letters. The number changed to something not in sequence. Cerberus's righthand head—the annoyed one—growled, "Now serving number 50-10N6-5UC43R!" As one, the packed souls glanced at little slips of paper in their hands. None responded and Cerberus growled again, "50-10N6-5UC43R! Come forward or lose your place in line!"

Still, no soul came forward and Cerberus slammed a paw onto his desk. A sleeping tabby jumped to its feet and hissed. His annoyed head ignored it, but the cheerful head dipped down to lick the cat affectionately. This seemed to placate it, and the cat flopped down again.

The number board flickered and displayed a new number, also not in sequence. Annoyed Cerberus growled, "Now serving num—"

The number board flickered and went dead. A collective groan rose from the crowd as Cerberus's central, resigned head twisted to growl up at the board. A soul just past Abigail groaned, "Not again..." He was an obese gentleman with wheezing breath whom I'd reaped nearly five years ago.

Cerberus reared up to his full height and slammed a forepaw on the dead number board above him. It flickered, random numbers and letters dancing across it until they disappeared leaving a solitary number one. The annoyed head's growl turned deep and menacing while the resigned head gave a heartfelt sigh. It spoke to the crowd in a drone that wasn't quite conciliatory.

"I'm sorry, but we appear to be experiencing technical difficulties. Please collect a new number from the dispensers along the wall, and we will process you in the order indicated on your new ticket."

The obese gentleman pulled a ticket from a manual dispenser near the door we'd entered and glanced at it. He snorted in disgust. Over his shoulder, I read a string of random numbers and letters.

That was it. Our literal ticket up to Reception and a conversation with Cerberus. I just need to change that ticket's number the same way Teri had changed her dice. The Rules restrained me from actively lying—truth in death and all that—but changing a spiritual item's appearance was perfectly acceptable.

"Abigail," I said, pointing, "I need that ticket."

She cocked an eyebrow, gaze flicking over the man's shoulder to the ticket, then to Cerberus. A smile blossomed on her face. She'd made the same connection I had. Abigail reached over the man's shoulder and snatched the ticket.

"Hey!" the man said, spinning, hand outstretched. His gaze fell on me as I, admittedly, loomed over Abigail's shoulder. His grasping hand froze mid-motion. His eyes widened.

Abigail passed the ticket back, and I took it. I pushed my willpower into—

I stopped. The number had already changed, eight digits replaced by a large number one.

My gaze flicked to Abigail. She'd made the change in passing? Imbued the ticket with her willpower without any apparent effort? That was ... impressive.

Conrad wore a knowing smile on Abigail's shoulder. Was *that* why the little nightmare stayed with her? To benefit by proxy from her power?

I shook my head. No time for that now. We had to reach Cerberus. I slapped the changed ticket back into the man's still outstretched hand and then grabbed his wrist and thrust the ticket into the air. He yelped, and I yelled above the crowd.

"Coming through!" I slid past Abigail and shoved the man forward with my scythe's handle. We waded into the crowd, Frank and Abigail tight on my heels. There were grunts and grumbles, but the crowd reluctantly let us pass. I felt rather proud of myself. This plan was flawless in its simplicity.

Across the room, another hand shot up. "Ticket one, right here!" a woman's voice yelled.

I glared in her direction. Okay, so there was *one* flaw in my plan. I pushed the condemned soul ahead of me, and the crowd parted like ice flows before a ship. He glanced back, lips pursed, but Death's flaming stare forestalled complaints about his rough treatment as our ship's prow. I would apologize when we reached Cerberus.

I never got the opportunity.

Chapter 5

THE COUP

THE DOME ABOVE CERBERUS peeled back like two sides of an unrolling scroll, revealing a live projection of Lucifer's throne room. A projection that I suspected was visible in every office, cubicle, and torture chamber in Hell.

That took a *lot* of willpower. Lucifer-level willpower.

"This can't be good," Abigail muttered, running fingers through her rainbow hair.

I couldn't agree more. An unconscious wave of fear rippled through the souls pressed against me, a reasonable response to seeing the four most powerful spirits in the underworld. The Auditor, the Keeper of Records, Nigel the Demigod, and Lucifer himself.

The Auditor—my nemesis whom I'd recently kept from claiming my title as Death—loomed behind Lucifer's left shoulder, tall and thin like stretched dough. He had curled horns, a rumpled suit, and wore gold-rimmed glasses. His oversized clipboard was clutched before him like the infernal shield it was.

Lucifer stood proudly before his golden throne clad in white robes, glowing like an angel of light. Olive skin, perfect hair, and eyes so silver that they practically glowed. White wings flowed behind him like a cape. Despite the millennia since Heaven cast him out, Lucifer still maintained that *he* was the rightful heir to the Almighty's throne. Rarely did he appear in public as anything less than the Morning Star.

Behind Lucifer's throne and to the right stood the Keeper of Records. I'd had few dealings with the Keeper, who looked more like an Amazon than a demon. She had no visible horns poking through her braided black hair and was clad in leather armor, strappy sandals, and seething rage.

I'd never understood the Keeper's anger, and she'd never bothered explaining it to me. She was an unmatched administrator and seemed to enjoy her job. Especially when she got to—literally—eviscerate someone who misfiled something. In addition to maintaining the records for Hell's Bureaucracy, the Keeper also maintained Hell's half of the Rules, the unbreakable restrictions burned into every angel's and demon's soul. The Rules had created parity after the battle of Megiddo and Nigel's imprisonment in Abaddon.

There had been ... excesses. On both sides.

Yet, Nigel the half-human King of the Demigods now stood before the throne at Lucifer's right hand. The place of honor. My jaw clenched. Nigel wore a heather-gray Armani suit, a politician's easy smile, and a curved sword at his hip.

Mercy. The black blade of unmaking.

A shiver of rage washed through me. That was Evelyn's blade, not Nigel's.

Lucifer waved a hand as though silencing a crowd. "Denizens of Hell, a glorious day has come! A day I have long awaited." He clapped Nigel on the shoulder and smiled broadly. "Nigel, last of the demigods, has risen quickly through Hell's ranks since his return from Abaddon. He has proven himself time and again since that unprecedented escape, embodying Hell's values as few others have.

"However"—Lucifer's cheer disappeared as though it had never existed—"some have questioned Nigel's right to hold power in Hell. He is, after all, half-human." The Lord of Lies glared out at us, but then his expression blossomed once more into a brilliant smile. "He is also my son. My prodigal son who has returned to rule at my side." Lucifer threw an arm around Nigel's broad shoulders.

"Damn."

It took me a second to realize that *I* had spoken. Nigel was Lucifer's son? That changed everything.

Nigel pulled away from his father, his broad politician's smile warm and guileless. His gaze flicked to the Auditor's.

The Auditor grinned. It's a terrible thing to see an auditor smile, to see them filled with vicious anticipation. A shiver crawled through my bones.

The Keeper and the Auditor leapt forward, palms slamming into Lucifer's shoulders as they grabbed him. The Keeper swept the Devil's feet backward while she and the Auditor dropped him to his knees. Lucifer's surprised yell cut off when the Auditor cracked the back of his head with that infernal oversized clipboard.

Nigel drew his curved sword slowly. *Mercy*'s midnight blade made a gentle *shing* as it cleared the scabbard. It didn't reflect light but seemed to absorb it.

The silence in Hell's Reception deepened, all of us watching the tableau in horrified fascination. Lucifer surged against the demons holding him. He was powerful, incredibly so, and he nearly threw them off.

"You fools!" he bellowed. "How dare you betray—"

The Auditor again slammed the edge of his clipboard into the Devil's head, this time on his temple. Lucifer sagged, dropping to his hands. He shook his head and blinked vacant silver eyes.

Nigel swung *Mercy*. The Devil's head left his shoulders as easily as if they'd had a guillotine.

Lucifer, the Lord of Darkness and the Morning Star, wisped away like smoke.

I staggered back in shock. Lucifer had ruled Hell since the beginning of recorded time. I tried to wrap my mind around a world without the Devil in it.

Nigel sheathed *Mercy*. He gazed out upon us, and I swear his eyes bored into my very soul. His lips curled into a smile. "I rule at nobody's side. The Dragon is dead."

***

There is nothing more frightening than the unknown, than having your entire world flipped upside down. For the souls around us, the bureaucratic tedium of Hell's Reception had been familiar. Bureaucratic abuses that they'd grown accustomed to in life continued in the afterlife.

That all changed when the Devil died.

The window into Hell's throne room rolled shut, and a shocked hush fell over the crowd. Then somebody screamed a terrified, horrified scream. The crowd surged into motion, panic spreading faster than wildfire, and they jostled us like a mosh pit. Souls pushed and pulled and ran in every direction, but the room was packed. There was nowhere to go.

They tangled in my robes. A shoulder slammed into me. A knee hit my leg. I spun. Dropped to one knee. The crowd closed in.

I experienced something new in that moment, an emotion I'd never known.

Panic.

It wasn't my panic. I was Death incarnate. I had nothing to fear because nobody in this room was powerful enough to harm me. It was the mob's panic. It suffused the air with a scent like mingled sweat and burning metal. The roar of voices filled my head. Yelling, hysterical, violent. I felt my will subsuming to the mob's.

I surged to my feet and became one with the ebb and flow of souls. I lost sight of Frank. Of Abigail. Of myself. It was only through millennia of habit that I retained a death grip on my scythe *Grace*. We-the-mob cast about, looking for escape. The Labyrinth. Souls near the edges of the domed room scattered toward the archways.

Gates dropped over the doorways. Souls crashed into them in waves. Some, in their panic, attacked the demons bracing the Labyrinth's entries. They were beaten back with such savagery that tiny islands of calm formed around the guards. The crowd surged back on itself. Tightening. Compressing.

A hand caught my jaw and jerked my face downward.

Abigail stared into my flaming eye sockets. Her brown eyes were clear. Stern, but not panicked. "It's a lie!" she yelled over the crowd.

"What?"

She pointed at Conrad, who clutched her shoulder with all four paws, his tail wrapped around her throat for balance. The little dragon cast about fearfully, but his silver eyes were not panicked.

"Lucifer is not dead," Conrad said.

"*What?*" I said again, then shook my head. I pulled myself together. Forced the mob's emotions away. It wasn't easy, but clarity returned.

"The Dragon is not dead," Conrad said.

"How do you know?"

"I just ... know." He looked supremely uncomfortable and cast his silver-eyed gaze downward.

"Not good enough." I leaned forward. "I've been in Lucifer's presence more times than you can count. That *was* the Prince of Darkness who died."

Conrad's voice lowered to a whisper. "I know because I am still alive."

I arched a bony eye ridge.

"I am Lucifer's greatest fear."

"Why would the Lord of Darkness fear a scrawny little nightmare like you? You're not even..." And that's when realization slammed into me. His silver eyes. "No," I said, grabbing Conrad's chin to gaze deep into those silver eyes, and I read his soul for the first time. I read the truth.

My jaw dropped before I caught myself. "You're not just

any nightmare. You're the *Devil's* nightmare?"

He nodded. "Lucifer fears being weak and ineffective. Being nothing. A powerless little wyrm who is easily forgotten."

"But..." My gaze flicked to Abigail.

She pushed her rainbow hair behind one ear, her eyes tight. "Lucifer is alive," she said, "and nobody else knows."

I gazed over the crowd, though I didn't really see them as the implications rolled over me. We could still stop Nigel and his New Order. Restore the balance between Heaven and Hell that kept Armageddon at bay.

Death was supposed to be impartial, but humanity's very souls were at stake. My gaze flicked back to Conrad. My grip tightened around *Grace's* ebony handle, and I spoke with the finality of Death.

"We're going to rescue the Devil."

Chapter 6

THE PROPER PAPERWORK

I EXPECTED SOME SORT of protest from Abigail, but she merely clenched her jaw and asked Conrad, "Where is Lucifer?"

He pointed downward, his voice nearly lost in the jostling mob. "Don't know exactly. That way."

I'd figured that much out. But at least we had confirmation. I pointed at the elevators behind Cerberus. "That's our exit!" I yelled.

The three-headed dog stood upon his desk, scattering

paperwork with his oversized paws. All three heads barked at the crowd. They ignored him and surged around his desk, seeking to escape via the elevators. But those shiny silver doors didn't open for them. Condemned souls had no transit access through Hell.

I realized two things at that moment.

First, Cerberus was not panicked. His heads were by turn scared, frustrated, and—still—annoyed, but not panicked. He barked and snarled but seemed more surprised than anything. Which brought my second realization: Cerberus was not part of the coup. Perhaps he'd be an ally?

I glanced around. Abigail hung close to my elbow. Where was Frank? There, only feet away. I pushed against the crowd, trying to reach him. The crowd pushed back. No matter how I struggled, the ebb and flow of the mob eliminated any headway.

I stopped, becoming a rock in the turbulent sea of humanity. What was I doing? Why struggle and fight like a human? I was Death, the terror of men's souls! The mob feared Nigel and his New Order?

They'd feared me first.

I slammed my scythe's handle into the floor. "Silence!"

I bellowed, putting enough willpower in my voice that stillness rippled outward like waves in a pond.

That was better.

Yet the power of the mob pushed back, shrinking the stillness.

"Move!" I intoned. A path parted like the Red Sea before Moses. Pressure from the dense crowd kept the path narrow, but I strode forward and grabbed Frank's shoulder. He jumped as I pulled him close. With him and Abigail in tow, I pushed toward Hell's Receptionist.

"Cerberus!" I yelled. "We need passage!"

The three-headed dog saw me. His frustrated center head's eyes widened in surprise. The annoyed head growled. But the cheerful head barked excitedly. "Grim! It's been ages! How you been?"

"You know how it is. Stop time, reap souls, rinse and repeat for eternity," I said with exaggerated calm. "I need access to the lower levels." I waved toward the elevators. Frank half-collapsed onto the desk, his eyes wild with shared panic from the crowd.

"Not happening," Cerberus's frustrated head said. "Not without the proper paperwork."

Bloody bureaucrats. So much for my ally.

Abigail leaned in and pointed toward the ceiling where we'd seen Hell's throne room. "Did you not see that? The rules of the game just changed."

"But not the Rules," all three heads growled together, their emphasis clear. The resigned one said, "Those never change."

Abigail rolled her eyes. "Don't you care that your master was just murdered?"

Cerberus's cheerful head waggled from side to side, seeming unconcerned. The resigned one scowled, and the annoyed head examined Abigail like she was a snack. "That's echelons above my pay grade," cheerful said, sounding flippant. "My problem is calming this crowd. Take a number, and I'll get to you."

Unbelievable. I just stood there, unsure what to do next. Frank regained his composure and slipped from my side to join the souls near the elevators. At the same time, Conrad whispered something in Abigail's ear. Her head snapped up, and she leaned toward me.

Before she could pass her message, Frank waved a piece of paper at us. A form he'd filched from Cerberus's desk.

So, he had a blank form. Big deal. What we needed was—

Frank slapped the form against an elevator door. It slid open.

The proper paperwork. Frank had stolen the proper paperwork.

I dashed around the desk, Abigail at my heels. Panicked souls surged forward, pushing Frank into the back of the elevator. Cerberus barked at us, yelling at the escaping souls to stop. They didn't stop, and we squeezed in. The doors slid shut on my heels.

***

Tense silence flowed over us as the elevator jerkily moved downward. The elevator was simple, though large, with wood-paneled walls. The compressed souls relaxed a bit as we descended, even going so far as to clap each other on the shoulder and exclaim about their narrow escape. They clearly didn't know where we were going.

Tinny music filled the air, its volume low enough that I hadn't heard it at first. I strained to hear the catchy tune. It was slightly off-key but repeated as though designed to stick in your head for days.

From the back of the elevator, Frank glanced up at the

speaker in one corner. "Huh. I guess it makes sense that Hell would invent Musak. Torture by earworm."

Trapped by the door with Abigail, I shook my head. "No, Hell merely imported Musak. Sometimes humanity devises its own worst torments."

Frank grunted. "Yeah, sure, but of all the music for Hell to import"—he jabbed an irritated finger at the speaker—"'Never Gonna Give You Up'? I hate that song!"

Abigail chuckled. "You got rickrolled in Hell."

"What?" I said, completely lost. Abigail shook her head and glanced up at me.

"You keep up with pop culture and music, Grim?"

"Not in the slightest. Though I did catch one of Frank Sinatra's performances." I'd been reaping the soul of an elderly attendee and stuck around for the encore. "Does that count?"

"Not even close."

Conrad leapt from Abigail's shoulder, flapped once to reach the back of the elevator, and landed on Frank's shoulder. The elevator was too packed for the Taxman to do anything more than flinch. The dragon snatched the form Frank had stolen and waggled it in front of his wide eyes. "You know, Tubby, I could have gotten us in here without you stealing a Form-5. I'm a nightmare messenger, remember? Full access between levels."

Frank's expression drew down into a scowl. "Lay off the nicknames, *Sparky*. My name's Frank."

Conrad looked pointedly at Frank's gut, then back into his eyes. "I call 'em like I see 'em, *Tubby*." Frank's lips pursed, but Conrad ignored him. He scanned the Form-5 then addressed the elevator at large. "Is there an Analisa Agonos here?"

The souls glanced at each other, shaking their heads, but I rocked back in shock. Analisa? I hadn't seen her in years. Not since she'd challenged me to a game of twenty questions for her soul. I won—barely—and reaped her soul. Yet, she'd shown herself quite resourceful in avoiding Judgment. If her access form to Hell was still sitting on Cerberus's desk after all these years, I wondered where she was now.

When nobody identified themselves as Analisa, Conrad shrugged and blew a tiny yellow flame over the corner of the form. It lit in a crackling flash. Conrad held the form as it burned, twirling it slightly. Ash settled on Frank's balding head. He brushed himself off, flipped up his cowl, and glared at the dragon.

Conrad leapt back to Abigail's shoulder and silence descended once again, filled only with the grating, repetitive tones of Musak. Slowly, Frank's scowl faded. Never one to handle long silences well, he asked Abigail from across the elevator, "So, how'd you die?"

Her lips pursed. "Flash flood two years ago." Her eyebrows pinched. "At least, I think it was two years ago. Time blends weirdly down here, so it's hard to keep track. Anyway, my car was swept off the road and buried in mud." One eyebrow cocked at Frank, and her tone turned sharp, "But you already know that ... since you dated my mom."

Frank raised his hands in surrender. "Just trying to be cordial. I don't know what your deal is with me. We came down here to rescue you!"

Incredulity washed over her face. "Like I'm some princess, and you're the white knight?"

"No! Well ... Okay, I can see how it might look like that. But Grim promised to come, and I'm here to help. And your mom was, well, Cora was amazing and I couldn't imagine her daughter being stuck down here. So, yeah. We came to rescue you. Is that a crime?" Frank crossed his arms.

All eyes swiveled to Abigail like spectators at a tennis

match. Her lips pursed, and her cheeks flushed at the attention. She muttered something that may have been an apology, but I doubted it. Frank, however, took it as an apology.

"Not a problem," Frank said, unfolding his arms. Then a half-smile creased his face. "Cora really was great. Helluva woman. It had been years since anybody showed interest in me. She was kind, sweet, and totally out of my league." The smile grew. "Good kisser, too."

"Oh. My. God! I did *not* need to know that." Abigail's voice reverberated off the walls.

Snickers filled the elevator, hidden behind hands, and the grin dropped from Frank's face. "Oh. Uh, right. My bad." He glanced nervously at Abigail, then me, then at his shoes, seemingly unable to figure out what to do with his hands.

Abigail ran her fingers through her hair, pushing it over to the right side of her head. It fell like a shield between her and Frank. The souls packed in around us swiveled their attention back to Frank.

After an awkward silence, Frank drew a deep breath, and—not taking the hint to stop talking—said, "Look, I'm not going to apologize for dating your mom. I only

... I'm just ... making conversation." He trailed off into a mumble, for once at a loss for words.

Abigail's shoulders tensed for a long moment before sagging. Her eyes turned on Frank like twin lasers. "Fine. How did *you* die?" Her words had a cheerful upward lilt at odds with her expression.

"Heart attack," Frank said, "after the Auditor tried to rip out my soul."

That wasn't quite how things had happened, but I didn't interrupt. I suspected Frank was trying to make his death sound more exciting. Which, to be fair, it had been, just not how he'd described. The Auditor had been ripping out *my* soul, not his.

Abigail ran a discerning eye over Frank's hefty frame and cocked an eyebrow. I could see the snarky response dancing behind her teeth, but she held it in.

Conrad didn't. He snorted and said, "The Auditor didn't kill you, Tubby. It was the donuts!"

Frank shoved a finger toward Conrad. "Look, you little blue-scaled twerp! I could do without the commentary."

Conrad leaned back and made an expansive gesture with his forelegs. "Welcome to Hell! Everyone suffers for their life choices here, not just you."

Frank glowered and opened his mouth to respond. Conrad did the same, but Abigail raised a hand to forestall them both. She glanced at the dragon. "Conrad, don't be rude." Surprisingly, both he and Frank snapped their jaws shut.

The elevator stopped with a slight bump. The doors slid open with a cheerful *ding*.

Thank heavens! I didn't know how much more of that I could have taken.

We stepped out into Hell's Department of Bureaucratic Torments.

Chapter 7

CUSTOMER ANNOYANCE

THE DEPARTMENT OF BUREAUCRATIC Torments looked much the same as the last time I had visited. Not much changes in four centuries.

Which was odd. Chaos had exploded upstairs after Nigel executed his coup. Yet here in Torments, Hell's second and most populous level, all appeared normal. It was as though the coup hadn't even happened.

Low cubicle walls stretched as far as the eye could see, retrofitted into one of Hell's original caverns. Hell had invented cubicles centuries before the corporate world adopted the concept, and the Department of Bureaucratic Torments had refined the tedium of cubicle life into an art form. Miserable-looking souls hunched over their computers, muttering into headsets. Fluorescent lights hung on long chains from the rough, uneven stone ceiling. Wide towers that looked like melted wax dominated the hellscape, inset with windows and rising to blend into the ceiling's dripping stalactites. Those were the senior offices of Hell's Department of Bureaucratic Torments. Offices like Records and Micromanagement.

Hell reorganized into its bureaucratic model because hellfire and brimstone had lost their efficacy at breaking the human spirit. There was only so much pain the soul could suffer before the gnashing of teeth became glassy-eyed apathy. Hell's primary charter was to punish souls condemned by Judgment, so new tortures were devised. Methods most insidious and cruel, yet infinitely more effective than mere pain at breaking the soul:

An eternity of customer service.

Lucifer, never one to pass up an opportunity for profit, then offered cut-rate customer service to Earth's corporations, with the appropriate 'signing your soul' addendums hidden in the contracts. The corporations leapt at the opportunity. Government agencies quickly followed, and

Hell's customer services have remained in high demand ever since.

Demons patrolled the aisles. Some had whips—old habits die hard—but most brandished clipboards and cheap ball-point pens. Cats also roamed the aisles or slept sprawled atop whatever flat surface was handy, like computer towers and cubicle walls. Though, as Abigail had noted earlier, there weren't nearly as many as we'd seen backstage.

The elevator emptied onto a semi-circular landing contained by a waist-high plaster wall. A heavy wooden reception desk in the center of that wall had the large words CUSTOMER ANNOYANCE engraved on it. We'd arrived at the department dedicated to extended warranty calls, political polls, and credit card scams.

I strode confidently toward the desk bracketed by Frank and Abigail. A hulking horned gorilla of a demon sat behind the reception desk, petting an orange cat who lounged amidst her paperwork. Her nameplate read CLARISSA BUREAUCRACY. She waved a clawed hand, and her face split into a broad toothy smile.

"Mr. Grim! So nice of you to visit, and with guests too!" She looked past us at the crowd surging out of the elevator.

"Welcome to..." She trailed off as I swept past the reception desk without slowing.

"Sorry, Clarissa," I said. "I've been received enough." I strode swiftly past as though late to an appointment and didn't look back.

I didn't have an appointment, but I knew where I wanted to go. The largest tower held the office of Alvin Bureaucracy, head of the Department of Bureaucratic Torments. We weren't friends, exactly, but he still owed me a favor, and Alvin had his fingers in everything. If anybody knew where we could find Lucifer, it was him. There was no direct route to Alvin's tower, so we would have to weave a zigzag path through Customer Annoyance.

Once out of earshot, I glanced at Conrad and asked quietly, "What's Clarissa doing?"

He craned his head to look back from his parrot-like perch on Abigail's shoulder. He chuckled a growly little chuckle. "We just dropped twenty undocumented souls on her desk. Old Gorilla-Face isn't paying us any attention at all."

"Good," I said. "Clarissa is nice enough, one of Alvin's many cousins, but entirely too nosy."

Frank sauntered up beside me and wrinkled his nose. "A

nice demon? I thought evil was part of the job description."

I shook my head. He had so much to learn. "Consider the IRS where you worked. From the outside, it's a soulless den of evil auditors hellbent on destroying people's lives. However, that wasn't what I found during my week stuck in your body. Most of your coworkers were gracious and kind. Humans who just wanted to do their jobs and go home. Remember Lucy?"

Frank nodded. Lucile Pembrook had been a charming octogenarian IRS auditor and an inveterate gossip. She'd been the first soul Frank reaped after becoming my apprentice.

"She worked until her literal dying breath to get the Lisle family their refund," I said. "Yet from the outside, many would call her evil simply because of her job title." I caught Frank's gaze. "Do not be so quick to judge Hell's denizens simply because they are in Hell. One's actions are what matter."

Chastened, Frank dropped back to walk behind me, his expression thoughtful.

The drone of voices washed over me as we wove through the aisles, snippets of one-sided conversations floating past.

"...been trying to reach you about your extended warranty."

"...card has been compromised. Can you confirm..."

"Have you considered voting for Damien Nigel?"

My teeth ground. Right. Nigel was also running for political office. Independent candidate for United States President if memory served. What was he playing at? He'd already conquered Hell. Why seek power in the mortal realm too? It was so ... fleeting.

Power. My thoughts spiraled back to the coup. "How did Nigel do it?" I muttered as we turned down yet another aisle between cubicles.

"Do what? Take over Hell?" Abigail asked, stepping up beside me. "Lopping off the Devil's head seemed to do the trick."

"But that's the problem. Lucifer lives. So, who did Nigel kill? They had to have been a willing participant. At least, initially. It takes a *lot* of willpower to transform one's own appearance. Changing someone else's is exponentially harder. And then to overwhelm their free will enough to put on such a convincing act?" I shook my head. "Even if he is Lucifer's son, not even Nigel has that kind of power.

Not even the Devil himself can overcome free will through brute force."

Abigail chewed her lip as we mulled the problem. We turned a few more corners on our zigzag path, but no answers came. She fell back to walk beside Frank.

"So," she asked in a strained voice, clearly trying to breach the divide between them, "how did you and my mom meet?"

Frank chuckled. "Funny thing that. We'd worked in the same building for years. I'd seen her in the halls. But we actually met through her online black magic supply shop."

"Her ... what?"

"You know. Cordelia's Apothecary Supply?"

Abigial swore. "She always did dabble in that crap."

Frank said, "I was, uh, working on my spell to swap souls with Grim here. Needed some special ingredients. Cordelia's Apothecary Supply had them, but man they were expensive! Way outside my budget. But then I realized that Cora *was* Cordelia, so I asked her to dinner."

Abigail's voice lowered dangerously. "You asked my mom on a date just to weasel a better price out of her for black magic?"

"No!" There was a pause. "Well, sort of. It was just a

dinner meeting. You know, between colleagues."

"Did *she* know it wasn't a date?"

"Uh…"

"Men are unbelievable!"

"But the dinner was fantastic! And, well, I kinda fell for her."

I made another right-hand turn down our zigzag path, only half-listening to the conversation behind me, my mind picking at the problem of Nigel's political campaign. He'd been trapped in Abaddon with Evelyn for millennia. The world changed while he rotted in Hell's inaccessible lowest level, but from my brief glimpses of Nigel in the mortal realm, he'd adapted well. He looked every bit the politician he pretended to be.

Perhaps Evelyn knew his plans. They were blood enemies, but she'd admitted to working with him during their escape. Perhaps he'd confided in her.

If only Evelyn was around to ask. But she was stuck in Heaven, banished from the mortal realm by a cursed blade.

Frank was still talking. "…then Cora asked me on a second date—"

"Aha!" Abigail said. "You admit it was a date!"

"Well, yeah, but—"

A braying voice from behind us interrupted Frank. "There you are!"

We spun. A small, sallow-faced demon bore down on us with the righteous indignation of a middle manager on a mission: lips pursed, gray suit rumpled, chest thrust out with self-importance. Thin goat horns spiraled upward from his narrow head. A pair of twin demons followed in his wake, clipboards held at exactly the same jaunty angle, ballpoints poised. They looked like bureaucratic drones—tall, thin, and mustachioed with perfectly coifed hair that hid small horns.

Abigail swore under her breath and slid behind me. She whispered, "That's Kevin, my section's demon overseer."

"What's the meaning of this?" I said to Kevin, stopping the demon with a hand to his chest. The twins behind him marked their clipboards in unison.

Kevin leaned around me and jabbed a claw at Abigail. "My section fell behind after this one disappeared. I barely made my call quota!"

I cocked my head to one side. "Hell is in the middle of a coup, and you're worried about your call quota? There are bigger issues at stake." I did my best to loom, hoping to intimidate him. It didn't work.

"Not for me," he said. "We got a reorg coming, and I gotta report good numbers for Nigel's New Order. That's the only way to get these damned torment coaches off my back!" Kevin's thumb hooked over his shoulder at the twins, and he growled, "Dave and Dirk are the worst."

Dave and Dirk made more notes.

"You'll have to make your quota without Abigail," I said. We didn't have time for this.

Kevin shook his head and eyed me up and down. He was short, so it was more up than down. "Not your call, Reaper. You got no authority here. What are you even *doing* in Hell anyway?"

That was ... tricky to answer. I couldn't lie, but I couldn't exactly admit to plotting against Nigel on my quest to rescue Lucifer. I sidestepped the question.

"The Rules forbid interfering with Death's duties. Now move along and—"

"The Rules?" The demon brayed a laugh, revealing entirely too many sharp teeth. "The Rules don't apply in Nigel's New Order."

"Don't be ridiculous," I snapped. "The Rules are not a matter of choice. They are burned into our very souls."

That toothy grin widened impossibly wide. "The Dragon is dead, and all things are made new. Even the Rules."

I stared at the cretin. Lovetta the Guardian had said something similar in Purgatory. But judging from Kevin's confident expression, this goat-horned nuisance truly believed that the Rules didn't apply. Or worse, that they no longer existed.

Which, though highly improbable, was ... possible.

At the Great Parley between Heaven and Hell, after the debacle at Megiddo, the Rules were written in two halves: one governing Heaven, the other for Hell. Sure, there had been some basic Rules before then, such as 'Truth in Death' which kept me from lying, but those first Rules were rolled into the final document which spanned volumes. Each realm maintained its own half of the Rules as a bit of mutually assured destruction. If one side destroyed their Rulebook, the other could do the same and the bad old days of unchecked spiritual warfare would resume. Cue Armageddon.

Would Nigel dare attempt such a thing?

Yes. Yes, he would. I'd imprisoned Nigel in Abaddon before the Rules were even written. To him, the Rules would be nothing more than a hindrance to his quest for ultimate power.

Hell's Keeper of Records was the key. She'd helped Nigel stage his coup, so it was *possible* that he'd convinced her to destroy the Rulebook. The Rulebook that had limited Hell's power and influence for the past five thousand years.

What a terrifying thought. Yet, it explained why I could no longer travel through Hell simply by twisting *Grace* and willing it so.

For the first time in millennia, the Rules had changed.

An ember of inspiration came, smoldering and burning. I served both Heaven and Hell yet was beholden to neither. As such, the Rules governing Death were evenly split between each realm's Rulebooks. If Nigel had burned his Rulebooks ... was I free too?

Could I lie?

There was only one way to find out. I leaned toward Kevin and lowered my voice to a conspiratorial whisper.

"We are on a mission from Nigel himself. Sent to evaluate mid-level managers for positions of higher authority within Nigel's New Order."

I'd done it. For the first time since Cain killed Abel, I'd *lied!* Excitement tinged my voice. "How should my report about *you* read ... what was your name again?"

The demon's eyes widened. He abruptly stepped back and pressed at the wrinkles in his suit. It didn't help. "Uh, I'm Kevin. Kevin Bureaucracy. Customer Annoyance Manager, Grade 3."

I turned back to Frank. "Make a note for Nigel's special attention. This section's calm continuance of operations during this time of turmoil indicates that Kevin Bureaucracy is a middle manager with the *highest* potential." Okay, perhaps that was a bit over the top, but I was swept up in the excitement of *lying*.

Frank nodded with gravity and a badly hidden smirk. He'd caught onto my ruse. Had he realized the import of my newfound mendacity?

Kevin's demeanor completely changed. His red eyes widened, and he wrung his hands. "You mean it? You'll mention me to Nigel?" Behind him, Dave and Dirk scribbled furious notes.

I gazed deep into Kevin's beady red eyes.

"Absolutely," I lied. "But first we must speak with Alvin Bureaucracy on a matter of gravest importance." I turned away, but Kevin leapt ahead of me.

"Follow me!" He scurried toward Alvin's tower.

"That's really not necessary," I said, striding to keep

up with him. Abigail and Frank fell in behind me, the bureaucrat twins behind them.

"My cousin's a busy guy," Kevin brayed, "but don't you worry, I'll get you to the front of the line!" He broke into a jog.

I hadn't been worried about a line, but I didn't see a way to banish Kevin, so we followed in his wake. My mind spun as we neared Alvin's tower, the black heart of Hell's Department of Bureaucratic Torments. Our mission had just gotten so much easier. I could lie!

What could possibly go wrong?

A Lie Expanded

KEVIN CHATTERED INCESSANTLY AS we ascended the elevator in Alvin's tower, his attempts at ingratiating himself making me like him less and less. Regardless, I nodded along dutifully. Grating Musak provided an appropriate ambiance for the interminable ride; the same tune we'd heard before. What had Frank called it? "Never Gonna Give You Up?" Rickrolling must be a terrible fate indeed if it involved listening to that song over and again. It put my teeth on edge.

Behind me, Abigail and Conrad carried on a whispered argument. I couldn't quite catch what they said over

Kevin's braying monotone, but it ended when Abigail hissed, "No! I'm not leaving," and Conrad fell silent.

Kevin's torment coaches were so quiet that they practically disappeared into the elevator's back corner. Only the scritch of their cheap ballpoints betraying their presence. Which one was Dave, and which was Dirk? They looked perfectly identical.

The elevator opened into a brightly lit and modern reception area. Alvin's suite was the tower's top floor, split in half between reception and his office. All hints of stonework from Hell's original design were covered by gleaming white plaster with unobtrusive gray trim. The curved wall to our right was a single long window overlooking Torments, cubicles viewed past stalactites large and small. Pictures of senior demons lined the curved wall to our left, a sort of chain-of-command display. Nigel's broad politician's smile gleamed from the largest picture, hung behind the reception desk. Lucifer's likeness was nowhere to be seen.

That was fast.

The scent of warm coffee filled the air, which was its own form of torment. Coffee was forbidden in Hell, as were all substances that might bring relief and comfort to the damned. Leave it to Alvin to add an aromatic cruelty to his waiting room. Both Abigail and Frank drew deep breaths, their gazes darting about in search of the coffee pot that didn't exist.

As Kevin had warned, the reception area was full of demons waiting to see Alvin. They were all humanoid but with a dizzying array of shapes and descriptions. Tall, short, muscled, wiry, male, female, androgynous, horned, and winged. Some even appeared human. Their common traits were their beady red eyes, rumpled gray suits, and disgruntled expressions.

Kevin shoved through the crowd toward the reception desk at the front of the half-circle room. As we followed, Frank glanced around with professional curiosity before nodding with approval. "Nice digs! Better than we had in the IRS. But shouldn't a waiting room have chairs?"

From Abigail's shoulder, Conrad said, "Everything in Hell is about power, Tubby. Alvin Bureaucracy can make his subordinates stand, so he does."

Frank's eyes narrowed at the nickname, but he didn't comment further. We soon reached the reception desk, yet another bureaucratic hurdle in Hell's endless entanglement of red tape. Oh, joy. A cat sprawled upon the desk. It was like they were an essential element of Hell's bureaucratic miasma. This one was a mottled gray who was grooming himself.

Behind the desk sat a demon with a face more wrinkled than a prune. Tusks jutted up from his lower jaw and small horns curled off his head. Brutus Bureaucracy according to the nameplate on his desk. His expression belied thin patience with the winged demon looming over his desk. She had voluptuous curves, narrow eyes, and spiky black hair that looked like hedgehog quills. Belted twin daggers sat atop a form-fitting gray suit cut in a modern take on the kimono.

"No," Brutus told her with a voice like crushed gravel, "I don't know details about the reorg. Alvin's in a senior-level meeting right now, so you'll just have to wait like everybody else."

I swear, 'wait like everybody else' was becoming today's mantra. I was done waiting. But before I could say anything, Kevin elbowed past the demon I mentally nicknamed Ms. Hedgehog.

"Hey, Brutus," he said, arms spread as wide as his grin. "How's it going, cuz? I'm about to make your day."

Brutus eyed Kevin, glanced toward me and my companions, and arched an eyebrow. At least, I think he arched an eyebrow. The motion did little more than shift his deep wrinkles to one side. Ms. Hedgehog growled at Kevin, but Brutus cut her off with a raised palm. To Kevin, he rumbled, "Can you clear these whiners out of my office? Or get this damned cat off my desk? Because *that* would make my day." The cat flopped onto its side and lifted its hind leg toward Brutus. Contorting like a gymnast, it resumed licking itself. Brutus leaned away, nose wrinkled even more than normal. "Otherwise," he said to Kevin, "the back of the line is over there." He waved toward the elevator where Kevin's torment coaches had fallen into quiet conversation with another demon.

Kevin eyed the cat nervously. "I ain't touching that cat. You know what happened last time." He shuddered while Brutus grunted in unhappy agreement. Then Kevin's gaze swept the room's gathered middle managers. A grin blossomed on his sallow face. "But I can clear this office. Grim is here on orders from Nigel himself!" Kevin gestured grandly toward me.

Uh, oh. I tried to shush the little prat, but he prattled on.

"He's evaluating us for *special* promotions. Particularly

those who have"—he squared his shoulders and quoted me—"maintained order during the leadership transition while hitting their call quotas." That got everybody's attention. Ms. Hedgehog suddenly looked nervous.

"Actually—" I said, finger raised to interrupt Kevin, to stop this farce from going any further. He rolled right over me. He turned to Ms. Hedgehog looming over him and poked her in the chest.

"Kurayami, why are you here? If my section performed as badly as yours, I'd seek *less* attention. Not more." She puffed up, hands flashing to her daggers, and Kevin leaned forward. In a stage whisper, he asked, "How's your section keeping up, Kurai?" He sneered her name, emphasizing the last syllable and drawing it out like a curse. "You know, with you always gone doing Hell-knows-what instead of actually doing your job."

Murderous rage filled Kurai's eyes. She gripped her daggers, but her red eyes flicked toward me before she drew. Uncertainty warred across her face and her shoulders sagged a bit. "I..." She gulped. "Well, it's been difficult in Customer Annoyance ever since humans invented caller ID. Hardly anybody answers anymore."

Kevin grinned. "Hasn't slowed me down."

And yet he was assigned torment coaches for failing to meet quota. But Kevin didn't seem bothered by inconvenient facts. He spread his arms, taking in the entire room. "How about the rest of you? Would you rather wait around to whine at Alvin, or go prep for your pending evaluation from Death himself?"

Hell's gathered middle managers turned nervous expressions toward me.

Okay, this had officially gone too far. Why had I lied in the first place? I was *not* prepared to evaluate half of Hell's bureaucrats just to keep up the ruse!

"Kevin," I said firmly, "thank you for the introduction, but I can take it from here."

I turned back to Brutus and froze. Alvin's door was open. Two very mismatched demons stared at me from behind the wrinkled receptionist.

Alvin was scrawny, only two feet tall, with small horns that poked through his greasy combover. He ran a surprised gaze over me and seemed at a loss for words.

Beside him towered a brutish demon clad in a tight gray suit whose cut inspired visions of a warrior's armor. Three parallel scars crossed his face, and he was missing his left forearm. A scimitar's handle poked over his left shoulder.

Xandu. The Auditor's right-hand demon. The bastard who'd struck down Evelyn and stolen *Mercy*. He'd then delivered the blade to Nigel as a gift from the Auditor.

My grip on *Grace* tightened so hard that my knuckles cracked. Red flames clouded my vision. I took an involuntary step forward.

Death is supposed to be emotionless, I reminded myself. Calm.

I didn't feel calm. I wanted Xandu to suffer as Evelyn had suffered. To feel the pain of banishment. To become an abject failure, humiliated before his peers, and reduced to nothing!

There are fates worse than Death. Xandu deserved them all.

Xandu eyed me, face expressionless. "Grim," he said, voice flat, but then his gaze fell on Frank. A snarl curled Xandu's lip. His hand absently brushed the stump of his forearm. "Frank Totmann. Welcome to Hell. I'm going to enjoy tormenting you."

Frank grinned and gave a cheeky wave. "Heya, Xandu. Nice to finally meet you. How's yer golf game these days?"

Xandu lunged past the reception desk, his remaining hand shooting toward the scimitar over his shoulder.

"Stop!" I said, throwing up a skeletal palm. "Frank is not here as a condemned soul. He is my apprentice and under my protection." I threw an admonishing glare at Frank. I appreciated his taunts of Xandu, but our position here was tenuous at best.

I was the one responsible for Xandu losing his forearm, not Frank. While I was in Frank's body, Xandu had tried reaping my soul and that of another, a man named Garrick Thorsson. He'd torn Garrick's soul free, but then Garrick surprised us both and fought back. In the end, Garrick and I escaped, leaving Xandu without his left forearm and one scimitar. Garrick had disappeared with the scimitar, a ghost who hadn't—yet—been sent to Purgatory. I wondered where he was these days.

Xandu's hand slowly lowered to his side, and his gaze flicked back to me. He stared hard into my flaming eye sockets and pointed at Kevin. "He said you're working for Nigel?"

Damn. He'd overheard. Behind the desk, Alvin was inching back toward his office.

Xandu's gaze burned into me. I considered telling the truth and to hell with the consequences. The truth had served me well for millennia. But what about Abigail and

Frank? I couldn't guarantee their safety if things turned violent.

The silence stretched, broken only by the slurping sounds of the cat licking itself. Everyone stared at me. No, I couldn't tell the truth, so I expanded upon my lies.

"It's true," I said. "I am here as a consultant to assist Nigel's New Order in evaluating demons for management potential. As a disinterested party, Grim Reaper Consultants can provide Hell's new leadership with an honest and impartial evaluation. Honesty in Death is our motto!"

Frank and Abigail glanced at each other with surprised expressions. I couldn't blame them. Grim Reaper Consultants? Where had *that* come from?

Xandu's fist clenched and unclenched, but his voice remained level. "I wasn't informed of consultants coming in."

"Of course not," I intoned with false indignation. "You're on the list for evaluation. We can't have you shredding files beforehand!" I leaned in conspiratorially. "But just to be sporting, I'll give you a five-minute head start. Once I'm done evaluating Alvin, I'll come find you." That should do it. I just needed five minutes alone with Alvin in his office, and then I could leave this entire farce behind and get on with rescuing Lucifer from ... wherever he was.

Xandu's eyes narrowed. He waggled an accusing claw between Abigail and Frank. "And these two?"

"They're my apprentices." At least that was half-true. "I can't evaluate everybody myself. That would take forever!" He wasn't buying it. I doubled down on my lies.

"Your reputation for violence and cruelty are well-known." True. "But Nigel's New Order is looking for more than mindless thugs." Could be true. Didn't know, didn't care. "The Auditor himself requested that I find him a more ... suitable assistant. One to serve as both his right *and* left hand." A blatant lie that I capped with a small gesture toward Xandu's missing left hand.

The sudden fire in his eyes said I'd hit my mark.

"Your time in the Office of Micromanagement is done," I said. "But where you end up depends entirely upon how I write my report. Now give me a few minutes to deal with Alvin, and then we'll talk."

That was it. I don't think I could have spun a bigger web of lies if I'd tried. I silently congratulated myself on my perfidy while Xandu visibly fought to control his temper. His fingers twitched. A growl rumbled from deep inside his chest.

Did I take it too far?

"Liar!" Xandu snarled and drew his scimitar. "Seize them!"

Damn.

I slammed *Grace*'s handle to the floor and pointed an accusing finger. "How *dare* you? I am Death. Death does not lie!" I lied. "Xandu wants to overthrow Nigel," I yelled to the gathered demons. "Stop *him*!"

There was a brief moment of shocked silence before Alvin's waiting room erupted into pandemonium and violence.

ABIGAIL'S BLADE

Several things happened simultaneously. A handful of demons, led by Kevin who'd bought my lies wholesale, turned on their compatriots with cries of "For Death and Nigel!" I suspected they had the most to gain if Grim Reaper Consultants won the day. Blades appeared, claws slashed, and the waiting room filled with the sounds of battle. Alvin, the eternal coward, ducked into his office with Brutus. The cat scrambled in after them before the door slammed shut.

Kurai spun toward me, twin daggers appearing in her hands. I backed away and whirled *Grace* to block her attacks. Steel rang as our blades connected. Lightning flashed.

A brutish demon nearly Xandu's size seized Abigail. Clawed hands wrapped around her throat. He attempted to throw her to the ground, but she snaked her hands through his and did something to his thumb that broke his grip, reversing their positions. Suddenly *he* was flying headlong over Brutus's desk with a surprised roar. The demon impacted with a thump beneath Nigel's picture and slid bonelessly to the floor.

The twin torment coaches stalked after Frank, clipboards in their left hands, knives in their right. I might have wondered at the sudden appearance of weaponry, but *everybody* seemed to have some kind of blade hidden about them. My apprentice backed away, his hands raised.

"Dave, Dirk, hold on! Attacking me won't look good on your report! You want to be cleaning toilets for eternity?" Not that Hell had toilets—thank *heavens*—but at least Frank maintained my fabrication. He'd always had a keen ability to lie, unbound by Death's Rules. Rules that no longer seemed to matter.

I blocked more attacks from Kurai, backing away, but holding my own. Then Xandu joined her. He attacked with a flurry of strikes: high, low, and center. I barely blocked them, parried one of Kurai's daggers, and dodged the other when she threw it. The blade clattered against the wall behind me and then reappeared in her hand.

That wasn't good. Kurai's willpower was strong. She could bend Hell's reality to match her own.

Xandu struck again, unrelenting. I backed away, too busy defending myself to consider going on the offensive. I consistently lost ground. This wasn't going to end well. Three blades against my one, and I wasn't exactly trained in martial combat. Plus, Xandu was the most formidable fighter I knew. He'd even defeated Evelyn.

"Give up, Grim," he snarled, blade slashing toward my neck. I blocked with *Grace*'s handle but lost my footing when I had to twist away from Kurai's flashing daggers. While I was off balance, Xandu struck again as though chopping a tree. The force of his blow reverberated through my bones.

Grace flew from my grasp.

And just like that, mere seconds into the battle, I'd lost.

Dark satisfaction filled Xandu's scarred face. He swung at my neck one final time. He couldn't kill me—only *Mercy* could grant a true death—but this was going to hurt. A lot.

A silver blade stopped Xandu's scimitar a hair's breadth from my neck. I flinched back, tripped over my cloak, and fell to the floor. The two blades slid along each other, sizzling and sparkling with lightning.

Wait … that wasn't just any blade. That was *Grace*. My scythe! Who would dare—

Abigail stepped over me, *Grace* in her hands. Lightning crackled around her grip on the ebony shaft. A flowing black cloak materialized on her shoulders, hood thrown back, edges snapping behind her in an unfelt wind.

My jaw dropped for the second time that day. That was no illusion, but a genuine Reaper's cloak: darker than midnight and drawn with *Grace*'s power from the very depths of Hell.

How the *hell* had she done that? To truly wield any one of the three great blades, to invoke *Grace*'s imbued magic without breaking a sweat, required a strength of will nonexistent in most humans. Frank had done it with the aid of black magic. Without that magic, he barely had the willpower to change directions while walking.

Conrad roared a tiny roar from Abigail's shoulder. He spread his wings and blew a little curling gout of flame.

Abigail's face flickered, shades of a bony skull peeking through skin that appeared briefly translucent. Flame flashed in her eyes. Her gaze never left Xandu.

"Death cannot be defeated," she said. Her voice boomed through the room. "Stand down."

Xandu flinched back. His surprised gaze flicked between Abigail and me. Then his eyes narrowed.

"No," he said. "You are not Death."

He lunged, sword whipping toward Abigail's neck. Conrad leapt from her shoulder with a shriek and *Grace* spun in Abigail's hands as though it belonged there. She blocked Xandu's attack. Then the next four. Kurai struck from the right, slashing with both daggers. *Grace*'s blade, shaft, and butt snapped out, a blur of motion that pushed both demons back toward Brutus's now-empty desk.

A dagger clattered from Kurai's grasp, knocked loose with a *crack* of the scythe's shaft. It reappeared in her hand, but Abigail slammed the scythe's butt into Kurai's belly. The demon doubled over and Abigail spun *Grace*. Her hands slid to the end of the shaft and the blade chopped into Kurai's back like an axe.

Kurai screamed. The scream faded as she disappeared into the ether, fading like every soul I reaped.

I'd thought my jaw couldn't drop any further. I was wrong. *Grace* wasn't a blessed blade to banish demons, so how…?

Of course! *Grace* was the blade of balance. It had sent Kurai to where she was supposed to be. Whether that was her own office, or the Lake of Fire didn't matter. She wasn't here anymore.

Xandu stepped back. His gaze flicked to me, then swept over Abigail, considering. Calculating. I scrambled up, but stayed back, not wanting to interfere.

Abigail-the-Reaper crouched between us, scythe ready in a two-handed grip. Her black cloak swirled in the unfelt wind of her willpower. Like a tiger lashing its tail. She and Xandu circled each other. A half-smile quirked Abigail's lip. "Give up, Xandu. You're outmatched."

He sneered. "You forget your place, *human*. This is Hell!" Xandu's voice rose above the din of combat, and his gaze swept the room. "Strike her down and you are *all* promoted. Fail, and even the nightmares will shudder in terror at your punishment for *daring* to rebel against Nigel's New Order!"

Abrupt silence fell. Red eyes blinked at Xandu, then swiveled toward Abigail. She eyed them back. Her smirk faded.

Conrad, who'd retreated out of the way on Brutus's desk, shrank in on himself. "Ah, shit."

The demons charged. All of them.

Abigail held her own for longer than I expected, dodging, striking, and blocking. Seven demons fell to *Grace's* implacable power, transported away to wherever they were supposed to be. But in the end, the horde overwhelmed Abigail through sheer numbers. She screamed as they bore her to the ground.

I scrambled forward, hoping to snatch *Grace* from amid the tumble of bodies and blades, of claws and fists. Xandu reached me first.

He clubbed my skull with his amputated arm, driving me to one knee. He hit me again, sending me to the floor. My world spun, and I struggled to push myself upright, to reach *Grace.*

Xandu stepped on my hand, then plucked *Grace* free of the demonic scrum. He raised the scythe and roared; a victory cry echoed by the demons. Xandu sneered down and lifted my chin with *Grace's* blade, which felt cool against my jaw.

"Death has no power here," the demon said. "And you

never will. Enjoy your eternity of torments."

"Torments don't scare me." Okay, that was a baldfaced lie, but bluster was all I had left.

Xandu grinned and waved toward the long curved window overlooking Alvin's domain of cubicles and call centers. "Maybe not *those* torments. But Nigel's New Order is restoring Hell to its former glory. A few centuries of being boiled in blood will change your tune."

My jaw clenched. I had no answer to that.

Chapter 10

THE PIT

HELL'S FOURTH LEVEL WAS under construction, or rather, destruction. No, that wasn't quite right. Reconstruction? Whatever. Things were changing, and not for the better.

The twin torment coaches, who'd volunteered as prisoner escorts, shoved us out of an elevator onto a rocky shelf that half-ringed a massive Pit. The Pit looked like a mining project that got out of control. Sheer cliffs dropped to a rock-strewn valley. Everything was rust-red and crumbling and though I couldn't find any source of light, the Pit was clearly visible despite an oppressive gloom. This used to be Hell's business center, home to countless corporate offices. Now, only the Pit's far end was packed with office buildings. They looked small in the distance, but those monoliths could have rivaled anything in New York or Hong Kong. The architecture ranged from gothic stone to modern glass.

Those buildings were also on the move. The ones closest to us—perhaps halfway across the Pit—rose slowly toward the distant cavern roof. One by one, they followed each other upward like a coiled rope being pulled inexorably into Hell's third level. The Pit's stone roof received its transient offerings with slurping gray bubbles, like an inverted pool of liquid rock.

The rise of Hell-based corporations was inevitable after Hell reorganized into the bureaucratic model. Many corporations were still Earth-based and human-run, but a growing number transitioned to Hell every year for the tax breaks and CEO benefits packages. Packages whose golden parachutes only lasted until death. Hell played the long game, and it paid to read the fine print.

Originally, the Pit had been used to punish the greedy. I supposed that the transition to making money from corporate greed was a natural next step. Yet, the current reconstruction was slowly returning Hell's fourth level to its original heinous glory but with a twist. Level Four's original punishment required the damned to push massive boulders for eternity. Now, the Pit's center was split by a river of boiling blood. The ground beyond the river—where the corporate offices were departing for Level Three—was a swamp, brackish and red, slowly revealed by the rising buildings. Dead trees with whipping vines grew from the bubbling swamp as though pulled upward by the departing buildings before snapping free. My senses were tickled by the coppery tang of blood which overlay Hell's perpetual undertone of brimstone.

The near half of the Pit had returned to its original design with shoulder-high boulders that looked like the Devil's billiard balls. A small cluster of souls struggled amidst the rocks, knocking them together as they pushed them. There was no goal, no end game, just keep the boulders moving. Forever.

I noticed a distinct absence of cats. Even they wouldn't deign to visit the Pit. Guards lined the Pit's edge, centaurs with longbows.

"What's this?" I asked our captors. "No receptionist?"

The torment coach behind me sighed a heavy nasal sigh.

Though I still couldn't tell the two apart, I designated this one as Dave. "Corporate reception moved up to Level Three with the corporate offices."

"But ... how will you keep track of your tormented souls down here?" Was that a note of sarcasm in my voice? Yes, Frank was indeed rubbing off on me.

From behind Frank, Dirk answered with a nasal wheeze that matched Dave's. "Hell's Bureaucracy will burn in the fires of Nigel's New Order." He spoke as if reciting the company motto, but his tone was sad. Disappointed.

I couldn't blame him. I held no love for Hell's Bureaucracy, but I had to admit that things had been more orderly since the reorganization. Now, Nigel's New Order seemed hellbent on chaos and disruption. If he had his way, if we didn't save Lucifer, the entire system might crumble. And who would suffer most? Humanity's eternal souls.

Yes, damned souls are meant to suffer in Hell, eternal torments after Judgment and all that, but the punishment had always fit the crime. Most souls condemned to Hell these days weren't grandly evil and Bureaucratic Torments were sufficient. Oh, humanity still birthed the occasional Ted Bundy and Adolf Hitler, but that was why Hell's Bureaucracy had retained the Lake of Fire on Level Five, the one part of Hell that Dante hadn't toured. A place reserved for the worst of the worst. It was also where banished demons went. Not that I expected to banish anybody anytime soon.

Though, I'd start with Xandu, given the opportunity. He'd ordered us sent down here and disappeared after our capture, presumably to deliver *Grace* to Nigel. My hands clenched, missing the feel of the scythe in my grip.

Abigail's lips were a thin worried line as she took in the Pit's horrid grandeur. She looked very much like her mother Cora in that moment, though with more piercings. Frank, however, glanced around like a tourist, more curious than concerned with our predicament. He practically goggled at the guards around the edge of the Pit. "So ... centaurs are real?"

"Yes," I said, not in the mood for a lengthy explanation. I was trying and failing to find a way out of this.

Conrad, in his customary dragon-parrot position on Abigail's shoulder, felt no such compunctions. "Demons aren't the only spirits in Hell, Tubby," he said brightly. He didn't look worried or frightened. What did he know that I didn't?

Frank's face scrunched. "Are they nightmares? Like the

minotaurs we met backstage?"

Conrad rolled his eyes. "Not even close! Nightmares are bits of a human soul, their darkest fears sliced away to torment those they came from. Spirits are different. Centaurs, phoenixes, Anansi the spider, Basan the fire-breathing chicken—*all of them*—are creatures from the other spirit realms."

Frank missed a step. "Basan ... the fire-breathing chicken?"

This time Abigail rolled her eyes. "He's Japanese. Don't you know *anything* about cultures besides the American suburbia you grew up in?"

Frank's lips flapped silently as the two ganged up on him, but then his expression hardened. The centaurs turned to watch our approach.

"Where do you think humanity's mythologies came from?" Conrad continued. "Sure, there are *some* centaur nightmares, drawn from the human psyche after they saw the real thing. But you'd never mistake a nightmare for the real thing. These centaurs are very much their own spirits."

"How can you tell?" Frank peered up at the nearest centaur. Their captain, I assumed from the small gold circlet he wore. The centaur returned Frank's regard with a glower. "Do different spirits have unique smells?" Frank asked. "Cause these guys smell like sh—"

The centaur captain seized Frank's throat and wrenched him up to eye-level. Frank kicked and struggled, clutching at the centaur's broad wrists. His eyes bulged. The centaur pulled him close until their noses nearly touched. "What'd you say 'bout us?" His drawl was laconic. Self-assured.

Frank gasped. "Nice ... to meet you."

"Nah, it ain't." An evil smile split that broad face. His muscles bulged, and then he flung Frank into the Pit.

The Taxman shrieked a high warbling shriek and flailed as he fell. His cloak billowed behind him. Before he'd even hit the bottom, the centaur turned to me.

"Wait!" I said, raising my hands. I tried stepping back, but the bureaucrat twins blocked me. "Surely there's another way into the Pit. A ramp of some sort?"

The centaur grinned. "Yeah, but my way's more fun."

And then I was airborne.

***

As the saying goes, it wasn't the fall, but the landing that hurt. Unlike my apprentice, I did not shriek like a child.

Yet, when I faceplanted into the stone below, I may have uttered a few choice words about over-enthusiastic centaurs. The ground tasted of blood, ash, and despair.

Yes, despair has a taste. Those who have tasted despair will never forget its lingering twist on the tongue. The numbing burn that makes you beg for release while robbing your will to do anything.

Which, come to think of it, was an apt description for the smell of most bureaucracies I'd visited.

I wiped my face and climbed to my feet. Being a spirit in a spiritual realm, I didn't have to worry about broken bones, but the pain of striking stone after a thirty-foot fall was still very real. I rolled my shoulders to loosen the joints and glanced up.

Abigail was next, her cloak billowing behind her into a half-parachute that slowed her fall. She almost made it, landing with a grunt and a roll that brought her back to her feet. But she had too much momentum and slammed into the nearest boulder. The cloak wrapped around her like comforting arms.

"How are you doing that?" I asked.

"What?" she asked, straightening to roll her shoulders as I had. Her undercut rainbow hair flopped to one side as she popped her neck.

"Controlling your cloak. Even Frank can't bend his cloak to his will, and he's my official apprentice. It just hangs on him like a sack."

Frank groaned, still face-down on the stone.

"And how'd you even get a Reaper's cloak?" I added.

Abigail shrugged. "You said souls can change their appearance. I wanted to intimidate Xandu, so, I made myself look like you." A half-smile lit her face. "Or, at least, a version of you that could fight worth a damn. It almost worked too."

Incredible. There was strain around her eyes, tiredness from exerting so much of her willpower in so short a time, but she was far from exhausted.

"Where'd you learn to fight like that?" I asked.

Abigail considered me for a long moment before she said, "I got bullied a lot as a kid. Dad wasn't in the picture, and the school wouldn't do shit, so Mom signed me up at the martial arts school down the street. I was eight when I finally fought back. Sent the bully to the hospital. The school went ballistic. Mom bought me ice cream. I never stopped training, and the bullies never touched me again."

I nodded. "You held your own against Xandu. An impressive feat."

"Yeah. I'll get him next time," she said as Conrad glided down to perch on her shoulder. At least one of us hadn't entered the Pit via faceplant.

"I'm sure you will," I said, and I meant it.

Frank finally pulled himself to his feet, groaning the entire time. I glanced toward the cluster of damned souls pushing their boulders. They were about twenty yards away. Grunts and gasps echoed across the barren Pit. The uneven ground moved the stones unpredictably, creating a cacophony of *cracks, clunks,* and the occasional scream when someone got caught between stones.

"Grim?" a woman's voice said from behind one of the stones. I caught a flash of red hair before the boulder shifted sideways.

I froze. I knew that voice, but it was impossible. She couldn't be here. Then the woman stepped into full view, and my world turned upside down.

Inez Davidson. My friend and the only immortal human I'd ever met. Granted, I doubted she knew of her pending immortality, but that wasn't the point. Why was she here rolling stones in Hell? She looked gaunt and weary, cheeks sunken like she'd been starved for weeks, yet she still glowed with life. The same indefinable glow we'd seen with the cats backstage. She was more real, more solid, than anything around her.

Inez was here in the flesh.

Matted, shoulder-length red hair clung to her head, and her mismatched blue and green eyes were tight with exhaustion. Regardless, Inez dashed over and threw her arms around me. Her limbs were painfully thin, but the hug was warm and crushing. Surprised, I froze before returning the gesture.

Death doesn't receive a lot of hugs. I felt awkward, but I had to admit that it was nice to see a friend, even if she smelled of sweat and fear.

Inez pulled back, clutched my shoulders, and smiled warmly at me. "You look better as a cloaked skeleton," she said. "It's more fitting of Death."

My jaw worked as I tried to find words. "How ... how are you here in the flesh?" I read her soul through those mismatched eyes to confirm the impossibility before me.

Inez Davidson, thirty-seven years old, still had no known date of death. Yet here she was. In Hell.

Inez's warm smile faded. "It was the Auditor. He returned for Sam, just as he'd promised. As retribution for

Sam's betrayal, he dragged us directly here. No Death, no Purgatory, just punishment."

"Sam? Where is he?"

Inez gestured toward the souls rolling their stones as they began to pass us. I looked past faces I recognized—I had reaped their souls, after all—but I didn't see Sam.

Wait. There he was. At the back of the crowd, leaning against a struggling woman's soul. He gave the appearance of helping without doing anything at all. He looked even worse than Inez, his face a mask of pain as he stumbled and hopped. His right foot was twisted outward, the ankle clearly broken.

And then I saw something that made my vision go red.

A little girl clutched Sam's hand. Beatrix, the Davidson's four-year-old daughter. She was here, in Hell. In the flesh.

"*What*?" I yelled. "The Auditor stole a *child*?"

I was going to kill him. Death does not judge, does not choose who dies, but so help me GOD I was going to find a way to *end* the Auditor. Permanently.

Despite his innumerable sins, the Auditor had always followed the Rules. He's the one who *enforced* the Rules! I'm sure he'd used some loophole to steal Sam and Inez before their time, but Beatrix was an innocent. Below the age of accountability.

The Rules were clear! Though children may suffer on Earth and die early, they were granted special status in the afterlife. Children had a special place reserved for them in Heaven.

"He's gone too far!" I screamed, stomping forward. "There's no excuse! Absolutely no reason in all the realms why—"

A warm hand on my shoulder pulled me back. I shook it off. Another hand stopped me. Two. A voice in my ear.

"Grim, stop. You're scaring her."

I stopped. Listened to the voice—Abigial's voice—even as my vision danced with dreams of inflicting such suffering upon the Auditor that even Lucifer would pale in fear.

Abigail and Inez stepped around me, hands on my shoulders, placing themselves between me and Beatrix, who hid behind her father. The condemned hadn't stopped rolling their stones, though they were now trying to angle away from me.

I shook myself. Reined in my anger.

Abigail leaned forward, fixing me with her gaze. "You good?" she asked. She looked worried. Even Conrad on her shoulder looked worried.

"Sorry," I said, then glanced at Inez. "Forgive me. I let my anger slip. Bad things happen when Death gets angry." Like the time I'd introduced mankind to murder.

Inez dipped her head. "No apology needed. I've been angry since I got here. For so many reasons." Her gaze drifted upward and away, and her voice dropped to a whisper. "He's so close. I wish—" her jaws snapped shut.

Close? Who was close?

Inez didn't finish her thought and shook away whatever she'd been about to say. Yet anger continued to burn behind her mismatched eyes.

Abigail said, "Never apologize for righteous anger, Grim. Especially when you're *right*. Change never came from being polite in the face of evil."

I nodded but realized I'd apologized to the wrong person. I stepped past Inez and Abigail and knelt near Sam. He stopped pretending to push the rock and stood with his weight fully on his left foot while the other spirits slowly moved on. Beatrix hid behind his leg. I rested my elbows on my knees.

"Beatrix, I'm sorry I frightened you. Do you remember me?"

I couldn't see her face behind Sam's leg, but her tangled

brown hair swished as she shook her head.

"Understandable. I wore a different face last we met. His face, in fact." I pointed toward Frank who was introducing himself to Inez. Beatrix glanced at the Taxman from behind her father. "I am the Grim Reaper," I said. "Death. You introduced me to that delightful story about cows who could type, and I told you a tale of my friend Evelyn and I almost getting eaten by a long-nosed crocodile."

Beatrix's gaze slipped to mine. Only one blue eye peered around Sam's knee. "You fell over the waterfall." She did remember me. Her voice was small. "I wanna go home."

"I want you to go home too." I kept my voice soft, but the heart I didn't have inside my skeletal chest shattered into a thousand pieces.

Sam patted Beatrix's shoulder and said, "Come on, Sweetie. We gotta keep moving." They turned and hobbled back to the crowd rolling stones. Inez and Abigail stepped past me to join them, chatting in the way people do when getting to know each other.

I let them walk away, the anger inside me no longer hot, but cold and sharp and full of purpose. Rocks clacked and clattered as I considered all the ways I could make the Auditor suffer. Frank joined me, stepping to my side, and we gazed after the others in silence. Abigail was walking beside Beatrix. The little girl looked up at Conrad with wide-eyed wonder. The dragon crawled down Abigail's cloak, sniffed Beatrix's hair, then licked her nose. She giggled.

"We'll fix this," Frank said.

"How?" I asked. "We're trapped and weaponless and without any allies."

"We watch for an opportunity. Then we strike."

I looked at my apprentice. "That's what you did, isn't it? Back when you swapped our places."

He nodded. "Death is the ultimate rigged game. I looked for an opportunity to win that game." Frank's goofy grin blossomed. "And it worked too. Just took patience and knowledge. Between us, we'll find a way to set things right." The grin faded, replaced by a determination that matched my own. For the first time in months, I was glad to have Frank by my side. Neither of us knew how to fix this travesty, but we wouldn't stop fighting until we had.

"If you see any opportunities," I said, "strike fast."

Frank nodded, but then a high whistle sounded dimly through the air, growing louder and closer. We both glanced up.

An arrow slammed into my shoulder from above.

Chapter 11

EDEN REBORN

I DROPPED TO MY knees with a yell as the arrow tore through my cloak. It ricocheted off my bones before skittering away. Red pain burned along the ribs where the arrow had scored me.

Another arrow hit Frank in the calf. He screamed and fell, scrambling as arrows clacked off the stone around us. Frank tore the arrow free with a stream of curses. There was no blood—we were spirits—but it clearly hurt.

"Come on," Inez called from the rolling stones. "You stop pushing for too long, and the centaurs start shooting." She pointed toward the rim of the Pit even as more arrows fell toward us.

Frank and I scrambled to join the rock pushers.

The arrows stopped, and I found myself pushing next to Sam. Or rather, I was pushing the boulder where he pretended to push. I recognized the soul he was leaning on for support. A former CEO of one of the Hell-based corporations. She'd died a decade or so previously. I don't judge, but I wasn't surprised that she'd ended up here.

Sam gave me a wry smile. "Welcome to Hell, Grim."

I gestured at his ankle. "What happened?"

He grimaced as our boulder caught on a small stone. It hesitated, popped to the left to clack against the stone Inez and Abigail were pushing with Beatrix, and then continued rolling. "The Auditor caught us unaware. I didn't have *Faith* on me"—Sam possessed a blessed letter opener, something he'd gotten from an angel who was feeling generous at the time—"and he dragged us down here. Apparently, we were kidnapped for a series of tests of the human body in Hell. The first test was throwing me into the Pit like they threw you." He waved at his ankle. "I failed the test. But a broken ankle is no reason not to push these *stupid* rocks."

"How long have you been down here?"

Inez answered, "Don't know. A couple of months? Not even sure why we're still alive. They haven't given us anything. No food, no water, no rest." Weariness shone in Inez's eyes, but there was determination too. And anger whenever she glanced at Beatrix, at her daughter trapped in Hell. I understood the feeling.

Our rocks hit another bump and clacked together.

"It's the nature of Hell, I suppose," I said. "This is a spiritual realm, so your body's incessant needs have taken a back seat to your soul's needs. Yet the body cannot be ignored forever."

Inez nodded. "I feel … stretched. I don't know how much longer we can do this."

We pushed in silence for a while. Silence, that is, aside from the *click-clack* of the rocks striking each other and the grunts of those pushing them.

"I'll get you home," I said eventually. "Somehow. All we need is patience, knowledge, and—" A section of cliff to our right opened to reveal a torchlit hallway. "—an opportunity," I finished quietly.

Xandu filled the doorway, positively beaming at our torments.

"Come to gloat?" I yelled.

"Nah," he said. "Well, maybe a little." Xandu's bear-like growl held a small chuckle. "But don't worry. You won't be pushing rocks for long, Reaper." Frank perked up at that, but then Xandu added, "You're all marked for the swamp of boiling blood once reconstruction is complete." The demon's grin revealed sharp teeth. Then the smile dropped, and he pointed at me. "Nigel wants to see you."

I stopped pushing and straightened. Frank also stopped, but Xandu shook his head.

"Just Grim and the dragon. Keep pushing, Taxman."

"Me?" Conrad squeaked from Abigail's shoulder, claw pointed at his own chest. Xandu nodded.

Frank scowled but I leaned close. "This is our opportunity. Watch and be ready." He nodded, glared at Xandu, but resumed pushing beside Sam.

Conrad joined me, landing on my shoulder with a *thump*. I stomped toward Xandu, cloak billowing around me. I wanted to see Nigel too. The Auditor would be with him, and they both had a lot to answer for.

***

Nigel's throne room was not what I expected. The first

thing that struck me as we stepped from the Musak-droning elevator was the smell. (It was, yet again, the same tune. I was starting to despise being rickrolled.) Instead of being slapped in the face with heady brimstone, a cool breeze lightly plucked at my cowl, gently laden with cherry blossom and hope.

Yes, hope has a scent as well. It is the scent of the forest after a gentle spring rain. The smell of the ocean at sunrise. Or that elusive whiff of jasmine in full bloom on a moonlit night. Hope is light and ethereal but unmistakable.

Not something I have *ever* associated with Hell or bureaucracies.

We strode down a winding dirt path under a gloriously beautiful spring day, complete with cloud-dappled skies and the choral melody of songbirds. Such peace surrounded us that Conrad's nervous tension faded away. He relaxed on my shoulder, closed his eyes, and drew a deep calming breath.

The last time I'd visited Level Three, when it had been Lucifer's throne room, I'd trekked through a grand series of stone chambers containing Hell's executive offices. Lucifer's seat of power had been all hellfire and brimstone backed by a lavafall. Soaring columns of fire had reflected his endless burning anger at Heaven for casting him out.

Nigel's throne room, if it could be called that, looked more like the Garden of Eden, complete with deer, squirrels, and yipping foxes. Cats napped on branches or sprawled in the warm sunshine. The sky above us gave no hints of the cavern roof that should have been there.

No, it didn't *look like* the Garden of Eden. This was an exact replica. Down to the Tree of the Knowledge of Good and Evil right ... there. Our grassy path wound through a rolling landscape too gentle to be called hills, but with ridges and curves that hinted at hidden meadows behind fruit trees. The Tree sat in one such meadow, golden-red fruit heavy on its branches.

A soaring cityscape backdropped the garden, growing steadily larger as corporate offices rose from Level Four below. Sunlight sparkled off glass-sided towers.

I glanced at Xandu as we walked, my sense of wonder overwhelming my anger at him. "How is this possible?"

Xandu spared me a smirk. "The Almighty isn't the only one who can create." He waved toward the surrounding splendor. "*This* is Nigel's vision for the future. A Hell to rival Heaven itself."

But it wasn't real. It was all an illusion. The cats gave

it away. Other cats in Hell were here in the flesh, full of vibrant life, and more real than their surroundings. These cats were spiritual constructs. Bits of imagination turned real-ish through Nigel's willpower. I could tell because they lacked that indefinable glow of mortal creatures in a spiritual realm.

Yet the strength of Nigel's illusory creation gave me pause. Everything was sharp. Perfect. Sight and sound and smell working seamlessly upon my senses to create an image of peace and harmony. If Nigel truly could create a realm to challenge Heaven, he would indeed fundamentally change soul management.

Had I misjudged him?

I glanced at Conrad, but the dragon was oblivious to anything in his beatific calm. We passed under a tree drooping low with pomegranate. Conrad plucked one free and inhaled deeply of the tangy sweet citrus.

"Mmmm..." he moaned then bit deeply into it.

The dragon jerked back, almost falling from my shoulder. "Gak!" He flung the red fruit.

It arced through the air and splattered beside a sleeping calico. The pretend cat went from dead sleep to hissing rage in a heartbeat, leaping up and away from the offending fruit. It landed with claws out, teeth bared, and back arched. The calico growled at the pomegranate with pure venom before stalking away.

Conrad smacked his lips with distaste. "Bitter as the tears of the damned."

Xandu gave the smallest of shrugs. "It's early days yet. We're still working out the kinks of creation."

We rounded a curve and entered Nigel's court. The curving landscape rose on both sides into low cliffs that formed a natural hollow. Flowering vines clung to the cliffs, the perfect backdrop to Nigel's ornate golden throne which sat upon a three-step dais. Fifty or so high-level demons gathered at the base of the dais, listening as Nigel gave orders.

Hell's new lord was tall, muscular, and clad in his impeccable Armani suit. Perfectly coifed black hair showed dashing hints of gray at the temples. Powerful hands stroked a sleeping white cat on his lap. A real cat. Nigel looked human, though nearly a giant, and exuded casual yet unquestioned power. This truly was the son of Lucifer.

But he did not belong on that throne.

The Auditor loomed behind the throne, impossibly tall and thin in his rumpled gray suit. His gaze met mine from behind his gold-rimmed glasses, and he smiled. Had he smiled with such malice when he'd stolen Beatrix? When he'd robbed the girl of her innocence and cast her into eternal torments as part of a bloody survivability experiment?

Rage surged through me. Rage I fought to contain. The Auditor would pay for his sins.

One hand clutched his clipboard. The other held my scythe, *Grace*. *Mercy*, the black blade of unmaking, hung casually from the arm of Nigel's throne. The katana-like blade was sheathed, but within easy reach. The implied threat was not lost on me.

Wait ... someone was missing.

"Conrad," I whispered. "If Nigel didn't kill Lucifer, who did he kill? Who's missing?"

The dragon inhaled sharply, then his head twitched from side to side like a chicken looking for a worm. "Uh ... there's Asmodeus. Mammon. Belphegor. Oh, and the Auditor. The Keeper of Records isn't here, but she was at the coup..." He blew an exasperated raspberry before abruptly freezing. "Beelzebub. I don't see the Lord of the Flies."

He was right. Beelzebub had always craved power. He wouldn't have missed this moment for anything.

Unless he was dead.

Nigel's sonorous voice cut off when he saw us at the back of the crowd. A broad smile creased his face, and he waved us forward. The demons parted, leaving a path to the throne.

"Ah, Grim!" Nigel greeted me like an old friend. His fingers never paused their slow stroke of the cat's long white fur, like a cinematic villain pretending at civility. "I've so wanted to meet you. Welcome! Welcome to my New Order." He spread his arms and stood, dumping the cat to the floor. The cat glared up at him before stalking down the dais steps in that affronted manner that only cats can achieve. Nigel didn't even notice, the full power of his dazzling smile focused on me.

No, Nigel wasn't a cinematic villain. He was worse. A politician. His smile was broad, warm, and benevolent.

I didn't trust it for a second. His eyes were cold, hard, and calculating.

I stopped before the dais and looked up at Nigel. I wanted to rage at him, to demand answers, but this situation required finesse. Patience. And that meant that I was right where I needed to be.

Death is always patient.

Chapter 12

CHAOS AND CATS

I GLANCED POINTEDLY AROUND Nigel's garden-clad throne room. "I'll admit," I said, "I do like what you've done with the place. It reminds me of the Garden of Eden but with a modern flare." I nodded toward the towering cityscape behind the throne.

Nigel's smile positively beamed. "Thank you, Grim. That means a lot, but this"—his gesture encompassed the throne room—"is only the beginning. I have big plans for Hell, Heaven, and Earth."

I would have blinked at that if I had eyes or eyelids, but the flame in my eye sockets flickered in confusion.

"Plans?" I said. "For all *three* realms?"

"Indeed. I had a lot of time to think in Abaddon. To prepare for this day. Why should Heaven and Hell's entire existence revolve around the fate of human souls? What makes *them* so special? Humans are weak, petty, and live for only the briefest of spans. *We* have been around since the beginning of time."

"We?" I said, my anger slipping a little. "Angels, demons, and the other spirits of the realms have always served the mortals as they have served us. But not you. You are nothing but a demigod who serves himself. A half-breed abomination who never should have been conceived. Of all Lucifer's mistakes, you were the worst."

Okay, perhaps my anger slipped more than a little.

Nigel's smile dropped. His eyes narrowed. "Watch your tongue, Reaper, lest I rip it out."

Good thing I didn't have a tongue. Though, perhaps I should have considered my words a trifle more carefully. Nigel continued.

"But I am a benevolent ruler. As was my father before me." He smirked and the gathered demons chuckled dutifully. Conrad, however, slithered into my cowl to hide. His claws tickled on my bones. Nigel spread his arms generously. "So, I'll let your taunts pass. This time. Evelyn told me about your history of ill-chosen words. How you whispered a lie into Cain's ear and introduced mankind to murder. How you promised Evelyn eternal happiness and then condemned her to Abaddon. Such delightful deceits. Yes, your love told me a lot of things in our time together." Nigel's smile bloomed again, but this time it bore a sharp edge. "And we had a lot of time together."

My jaw clenched so hard that my teeth hurt. Five thousand years Evelyn had been trapped in Abaddon with this monster after *I* had opened the realm of eternal darkness with my scythe. My failure had sent her there. I made a mistake, chose sides, and Evelyn paid the price. A price of blood, darkness, and unspeakable torture.

Yet they'd worked together to escape. She hadn't told me the full tale, but I knew enough.

The cat bumped my ankle, stealing my attention. I glanced down. Brilliant green eyes blinked upward. She gave a small "*Prrrow?*" and then bumped my ankle again.

Shock rolled through me. "Diana?" I muttered. "What are you doing here?" This was Frank's cat! At least, she had been before he died. Last I knew, she lived with the Davidsons.

But if the Davidsons were in Hell, why not Diana?

Being a cat, Diana wasn't overly forthcoming with answers, but wove through my ankles, purring loudly. She had a new collar: sky blue this time, but with a little bell that jingled lightly as she butted her head against me.

I folded my arms and turned my flaming stare on Nigel. "What do you want of me?"

Nigel dropped onto his throne and sat back, fingers steepled before his lips. He considered me, blue eyes thoughtful, then rocked forward and leaned on one knee. "I was surprised to find you in Hell, today of all days. You ruined some perfectly nasty plans I'd devised for tracking you down. Capturing Death himself and stealing *Grace*." He snorted. "Yet here you are, and you so thoughtfully delivered your scythe into my grasp. Now I have two of the great blades. Once I have *Justice*, nothing will stop my New Order."

Heaven help us all...

A shiver danced down my spine as the scope of Nigel's schemes opened before me. Three blades were created to balance power between Heaven and Hell. Heaven fashioned the flaming sword *Justice* and gave it to the Archangel Gabriel. Any struck by that blade were instantly judged and cast into the Lake of Fire. It was reserved for casting down Lucifer after Armageddon.

In response, Hell created *Mercy*, the black blade of unmaking. *Mercy* provided a true death, unraveling the immortal soul. Unwilling to leave such power in Lucifer's hands, the Almighty sent Evelyn to infiltrate Hell and steal the blade. Lucifer had raged afterward, but let the insult lie. He'd had bigger plans. Lucifer always had bigger plans.

Grace, my scythe, was something of a peace offering between realms. Forged in Hell and blessed by the Almighty, *Grace* provided balance, sending souls to where they were supposed to be. It was also the key to opening Abaddon, the realm of eternal darkness. The ultimate prison for Lucifer after the prophesied millennium when he is defeated once and for all.

Now, the balance of power was tipped in Hell's favor. With *Mercy*, the blade of unmaking, Nigel had taken Hell. With *Grace*, the blade of balance, he could take Earth, reaping souls with impunity. With *Justice*, the blade of judgment, Nigel could challenge the Almighty himself.

Diana tugged at my cloak, demanding attention with pitiful meows. I ignored her.

"You'll never get *Justice*," I said. "It would take an

army which you don't have. Angels outnumber demons two-to-one."

"But I do have an army," Nigel said, "one that numbers in the billions and grows daily. Now that I have the Reaper's scythe, that growth is about to become exponential."

I stumbled back in shock, almost tripping over Diana.

No. He wouldn't.

"The souls of the damned?" I said. "You would steal the human spirits entrusted to Hell's care? *That* is your army?"

Nigel perched on the edge of his throne and casually considered his fingernails. "Not *just* the damned souls."

And that's when it all fell together. "That's why you stole the Davidsons. To test how long the living could survive in Hell. With an army of both the living and the dead, Heaven's forces won't stand a chance. But why take the girl? The innocent have no place in your war!"

Nigel glanced back at the Auditor. "You're right. With enough crumbs, he *can* figure things out." Then to me, he sneered. "And yet you missed the point entirely."

Diana meowed piteously up at me and stretched up to claw at my elbow. Like a toddler begging to be picked up.

I shoved her down. "Why tell me? You know I'll move Heaven and Hell to stop you."

"Because I want you to know." Nigel leaned forward with a mad glimmer in his eyes. "To writhe with the knowledge of how I will corrupt the souls you've so carefully shepherded. That little girl down there? Raised in Hell, who knows what evils she might be capable of?" He snorted. "Hell's Bureaucracy was a joke. Lucifer went soft. In *my* Hell, souls will not suffer a single torment, but all the torments, cycling down and down through the levels until they beg to join my army of the damned." He leaned back and steepled his fingers again. "And I will start with your friends in the Pit."

"No!" I roared and lunged forward. Xandu's hand on my shoulder pulled me back. He shoved me to my knees.

Conrad's head snapped out of the neck of my cowl. His teeth snapped at Xandu, but the demon backhanded him. Conrad whimpered and crawled so deep into my cloak that he clung to my rib bones like a bat on a wall.

Nigel rose and drew *Mercy* with deliberate calm. He examined the curved black blade. "I considered using *Mercy* on you for the simple irony of killing Death himself. But that would end your suffering." He smiled again. I was really starting to hate that smile. "And I want you to suffer as I did! So, imagine my joy when Xandu presented me with *Grace,* the key to Abaddon." He flicked a finger, waving the Auditor forward.

My burning anger fled, consumed by sudden and unstoppable dread.

No.

"Enjoy your eternity in darkness, Grim," Nigel said.

No-no-no...

Diana leapt into my arms, headbutting my jaw in her demand for attention. I clutched her, unsure what else to do. I tried surging to my feet, but Xandu held me down. I couldn't run. Couldn't escape. Diana's purrs were small comfort as my doom stalked down the dais's steps.

The Auditor paused before me. His ash-dry voice filled with smug satisfaction. "I've been awaiting this day for a very long time," he said. "Goodbye, Grim."

The Auditor swung *Grace* like a pickaxe. The blade plunged into the dirt. A black tear, a rip in reality itself, rippled toward me from the blade.

The gathered demons scrambled back. The Gates of Abaddon split open like a hungry black maw, a grave waiting to swallow me whole. I stared into the empty darkness.

The void stared back, awaiting my soul.

"Wait!" I said, fumbling for something, anything to delay the inevitable. "You summoned both me and Conrad. Why? What do you want with the dragon?"

Conrad whimpered inside my cowl.

A flicker of annoyance crossed Nigel's expression. His jaw clenched, and he turned a fierce eye on the Auditor that seemed to say, 'Shut him up. Now!' The Auditor leaned forward and motioned to Xandu behind me. The brute dragged me forward beside the open Gates of Abaddon, not letting me stand, until I knelt at the Auditor's feet.

One of my feet slipped over the edge into Abaddon. I wrenched it back.

The Auditor bent nearly double until his face hovered inches from mine. His ash-dry voice was low and filled with scorn. "You thought we didn't recognize Lucifer's nightmare? I was one of the favored few in attendance when Lucifer tore Conrad from his very soul. That little wyrm is the only proof that the Dragon lives."

"Why keep Lucifer alive? Torture? Information?"

"Practicality. The Devil built Hell with his own willpower."

Of course. "And you have no idea what would happen if Nigel *actually* killed him with *Mercy*, Lucifer's own blade of unmaking. Hell itself might have unraveled without his power holding it together."

"It was the Keeper of Records who reminded us of Hell's origins," the Auditor said. "But don't worry. The Dragon *will* die once we've remade Hell in Nigel's image."

"But that will take centuries!" I yelled, abruptly realizing that I should have been shouting this entire conversation. No need for me to help Nigel keep secrets from his most trusted demons.

The Auditor cocked his head and smiled. Nothing good ever comes when an auditor smiles. "You're stalling, Grim. *I* am Death now." He flexed his long fingers around *Grace's* ebony handle, the scythe still half-buried in the dirt. "I am Judge and Executioner. For your sins, I banish you to Abaddon."

The Auditor swung his infernal clipboard into my skull. Stars flashed, the world spun, and then I was falling. Diana, Conrad, and I plunged into Abaddon.

The darkness swallowed us whole.

*****

I screamed into the void as my terror spiraled out of control. I'd lost. I *was* lost. Condemned to an eternity of darkness.

I gazed up at the lights of Hell, at the hole ripped into the very fabric of Abaddon itself with my scythe. A distant feather of hope that shrank to a pinprick as I plummeted ever downward.

I knew I would hit rock bottom eventually—Abaddon was riddled with caves that shifted in an endless maze of madness—but in this moment all I had were the screams echoing inside my skull. I tried to stop screaming, to rein in my terror, but I was no longer in control. It was like a tiny chaos creature had lodged itself in my head. It took complete control of my senses and was screaming itself hoarse while my thoughts skittered about seeking salvation. Something. Anything!

Salvation did not come.

Death is many things: sudden, relentless, inevitable. But I learned something in that moment.

Death is not always rational.

Sometimes the chaos takes over and there is no grand plan. I hadn't been cast into Abaddon as Judgment for my original sin. I was here because of an accident of timing. If

I'd entered Hell one day earlier, before Nigel's coup, things would have been vastly different. If I'd waited a day later, I would have known not to come.

Now Conrad, Diana, and I were condemned to an eternity of darkness because I ended up in the wrong place at the wrong time.

The last time I'd feared for my very soul, when the Auditor was ripping it from Frank's body, I'd cried out to the Almighty. He didn't save me. I doubted he even cared. Instead of Heaven intervening on my behalf, it had been Diana who came to my rescue. She had attacked the Auditor, pulled him off me, and dragged him to Hell. At least she was with me now, a small comfort in my time—

My screams cut off. Oh, God.

Diana could save me.

She'd stopped purring when the Auditor threw us into Abaddon. Her claws gouged through my cloak to my very bones as we clutched each other tightly. Her yowls of terror matched Conrad's high-pitched shriek from inside my cloak.

I had to hurry. If Abaddon's Gates closed, we were done. None could transit in or out of the Realm of Darkness. Not even a cat. I had to convince Diana to transport us out. Now.

I went for the direct approach.

"Diana, please. Save us!"

The cat's yowl warbled like a war cry, but nothing happened. She squirmed, looking for escape, and her little bell jangled.

"I promise you anything. Kibble, milk, fried chicken, you name it! You will live in the lap of luxury till the end of your days. A queen among cats. No, a goddess! Just, please, get us out of here!"

The pinprick of light was so small above us. Had it closed, or simply diminished with distance? I clutched the cat and screamed her name.

An abrupt squeezing sensation stole my voice. It stole my senses. It crushed me into an ever-compressing thread of nothingness until even that little chaos creature in my skull was silenced.

And then, everything was silence.

<u>Chapter 13</u>

CATASTROPHE

I'D ONCE WATCHED DIANA transition between realms, marveling as she spiraled down into Hell like water whirlpooling into a drain. This time, I felt it.

Traveling by cat was, perhaps, the most singular experience of my very long life.

I expected the sensation of having my soul sucked through a straw. The stretch and twist like I was a towel being wrung dry. What I didn't expect were the smells. Or were they tastes? Everything mixed together. A cacophony of cat hair, dragon shrieks, salami, baguette, pickle, and mustard that beat against my senses. It was like being assaulted by a sandwich in a dark alley.

The pressure on my soul tightened, squeezing and twisting until, with a pop that was more felt than heard, we materialized into the mortal realm.

I found myself lying on a plush carpet, squeezed between a couch and a wall. Which made sense once I thought about it. Cats travel between realms from the hidden places they love. A survival mechanism that kept humans from realizing that their darling kitty wasn't just sleeping under the couch but had popped out for a visit with their favorite demons.

Conrad was wrapped around my neck like a blue leather scarf. He groaned, "What the hell..."

The pressure on my soul had released, but the overwhelming smell of mustard and salami remained. I focused my gaze. An unfinished baguette sandwich lay under the couch, half-wrapped in wax paper, fallen and forgotten by whoever lived here.

Wherever 'here' was. I couldn't see much from my vantage beyond carpeting and the dim flicker of a television. Someone was watching the evening news in American English. That narrowed the possibilities. The couch groaned as they shifted.

Wait. That wasn't the couch groaning. That was a human sound. I listened more closely. Heavy breathing rose over the droning news anchor, and I heard another moan. Whoever was up there shifted again, causing the couch springs to squeak.

Oh, dear.

Diana squirmed out of my arms and shook herself. Her bell jangled. She sniffed at the sandwich.

"Diana," I said. "Wait—"

She didn't wait but snagged a piece of salami. It was gone in two bites. Her bell jangled again.

The groans and movement above us went silent.

"What was that?" a young man's voice said with a slow drawl.

A woman answered. "Sounded like a cat bell."

"When did we get a cat?"

"We didn't."

The springs shifted and suddenly a young woman's face peered upside down under the couch. Brown hair fell like a curtain around a flushed face, pooling on the floor. She spied Diana and grabbed at her.

Diana jerked away, and the woman's gaze fell on me.

I make it a point to remain invisible to mortals until

their final moments. Otherwise, there's entirely too much screaming. Yet, in the rush of escaping Abaddon, I'd come as I was: Death incarnate. A skeleton cloaked in black, visible to the world, and lying under this unsuspecting woman's couch.

And thus, the screaming began.

The woman tumbled off the couch and scrambled back, pointing with a shriek whose pitch climbed by octaves. She wore jeans and a baggy white sweatshirt embroidered with flowers around the words Pike's Peak State College. As our gazes locked, I read her soul. Paula Janke, twenty-three years old, death in fifty years.

It was too late to hide, so I snatched Diana and rose to my full height in the tight space between the couch and the wall. The young man lying on the couch gazed up at me wide-eyed. Alex Janke, twenty-four years old, death in seventy years. He too wore jeans and a sweatshirt, though his sweatshirt was green and emblazoned with a tractor. He leaned away from me, eyebrows arched, but at least he didn't scream.

The room wasn't spartan, but it wasn't well furnished either. A bicycle sat near the door by Paula, along with an open toolbox and an assortment of car parts. Paula was pressed against a wooden box that served as a television stand, pointing at me as she screamed. Her lung capacity was quite impressive. A metal folding chair beside the couch was the only other piece of actual furniture. A large upside-down cardboard box served as the coffee table, holding pizza, plastic cups, and a two-liter bottle of Diet Pepsi.

Yet, what the room lacked in furniture it made up in house plants. Green filled every nook and cranny. Grasses, vines, flowers, and small trees. It was a veritable indoor jungle.

Paula paused her screaming long enough to draw a breath. I raised a hand to forestall further screams. I may have even succeeded, Death can be quite commanding after all, but I'd forgotten one important detail.

Conrad uncoiled from around my neck.

The dragon's horns scraped my jaw as he poked his head out of my cowl. He blinked at his surroundings, squeaked in surprise, and then he crowed.

Yes, like a rooster.

"We're in the *real world!* Wahoo!" Conrad shot into the living room like a long-tailed blue bat. His wings snapped out, and he glided a tight circle around the room. Alex scrambled off the couch, turning to follow the dragon. Paula's screams reached a new pitch that spiked through my temple.

"Please!" I shouted. "Calm down!"

"Calm down?" she shrieked. "There's a walking talking skeleton in my living room holding a ridiculously fluffy cat, and now a *freaking dragon* is flapping around my living room! And you want me to *calm down?*" Her gaze shifted to her husband. "I told you this house was haunted!"

I shook my head. "We are not ghosts. Diana is a cat, with all the power that implies, Conrad is a nightmare"—he flapped past my face with more crowing—"and I am the Grim Reaper, terror of men's souls!"

Okay, perhaps I should have kept that last part to myself. It just slipped out.

Paula's face paled. "Oh, God. You're going to kill us." Her mouth worked wordlessly as she tried to find something to say. But at least she'd stopped screaming.

"I don't kill people," I said. "I merely reap their souls after they die, but that's not—"

Alex interrupted. "I thought Death had a scythe, not a cat." Unlike Paula's rapid-fire hysteria, Alex's voice was slow and thoughtful.

"I do ... did. Will again." I shook my head. "It's a long story." Conrad finally settled atop a potted tree near Paula and turned corporeal. The tree bent under his weight. He flapped his wings for balance before settling down. Though I use the word 'settle' quite loosely. Conrad practically quivered with excitement.

Diana squirmed in my arms, and I scratched behind her ears. Paula watched Conrad like a cornered mouse, but Alex remained focused on me.

"So," he said methodically, "instead of a scythe ... you're using a *cat* to reap our souls? That sounds messy." One corner of his lips quirked ever so slightly upward. "*Cat*-as-trophic, even. Or were you planning on *draggin'* us to the afterlife?" His gaze flicked to Conrad.

What? Oh. He was making a joke. I shook my head.

Paula groaned at her husband, "Really? Puns in the face of *Death*? Why did I marry you?"

"Because my jokes are purr-fectly *cat*-chy," he said with that amused non-expression. Paula groaned again and crossed her arms.

But she was calming down. I'd take the win.

I shifted the full power of Death's eyeless stare on Alex.

"I am *not* here to reap your souls."

I slid out from behind the couch and sat on the folding metal chair. It was cold and hard, but I didn't want to loom. I needed to diffuse the situation. Alex reclaimed his spot on the couch. Paula remained backed against the television, which had switched from news to advertisements for dental floss. I continued scratching under Diana's collar. She purred contentedly, eyes half-closed. I looked at Paula.

"Gallows humor is a common reaction to meeting Death," I said. "Almost as common as complaints and attempts to cheat me."

"So," Alex said, "you'd *cat*-egorize puns as—"

"Stop!" Paula rolled her eyes and stood. She glared at her husband and then considered me. "If you're not here to kill us, or to reap our souls, or whatever it is you do ... what do you want from us?"

"In truth," I said, "I'm not here for you at all. I'm not even sure where 'here' is." I glanced around, a sensation of the familiar warring with the certainty that I had never been in this room before...

Wait. Yes, I had. This was Frank's old living room, but with a new coat of white paint and much less—and much shabbier—furniture. We were back in Colorado Springs. "Diana is the one who brought us to your home."

"Really?" the young woman asked. She pointed an accusing finger at Diana. "Is she a Reaper cat—"

"—here to send mice to the next world," Alex interrupted.

Paula crossed her arms. "We don't have mice. I keep a clean house!"

I considered Diana's snack under the couch but refrained from comment. She closed her eyes and settled her head into the crook of my elbow. Her tail stilled. I continued my ministrations of her spine, her purrs reverberating my bones.

"No," I said. "Diana is a mortal cat, with all the wants and needs thereof." I remembered my promise to her, back in Abaddon. A queen among cats. A goddess for the rest of her days. "Which leads me to the sticky matter of asking a favor after so discourteously interrupting ... whatever you were doing on the couch."

Paula's cheeks flushed with embarrassment, and her hands flew to cover her mouth. "Oh, God, kill me now," she mumbled into her hands. Alex merely crossed his arms and eyed me, waiting.

Yes, I knew what they had been doing on the couch. I've spent enough time with humanity to be intimately aware of their habits and passions. I'm just glad we'd arrived when the kissing started, not five minutes later.

For the sake of courtesy, I ignored Paula's embarrassment and asked my favor of Alex. "Do you have any fried chicken?"

Chapter 14

A DRAGON BUFFET

THE JANKE'S DID NOT have any of that delightful fried chicken Diana and I had shared previously, but she seemed satisfied with the sliced ham Alex offered instead. She settled on the kitchen counter and nibbled.

Conrad went ballistic when Paula opened the fridge, literally bouncing off the walls when she offered him a snack. He wanted to try *everything*. Still unsure about the dragon, Paula satisfied his curiosity and set Conrad up with a buffet of meat, cheese, fruit, yogurt, and condiments. A collection of small glasses held milk, several fruit juices, and Diet Pepsi. He finally stopped flying loops around the kitchen, landed next to Diana, and dug right in.

Paula eyed the dragon nervously. "You said he was a nightmare..."

"Yes," I said, "drawn from a soul to exact eternal torments." I refrained from mentioning *whose* nightmare he was. Though I wondered why the Devil would create his own nightmare. It's not like Lucifer would torment himself. He preferred inflicting the suffering than receiving it.

I shook my head. Those weren't thoughts to put Paula at ease. Instead, I said, "Nightmares are very real, but they rarely reach the mortal realm. You have nothing to fear from Conrad."

She nodded, still focused on the dragon. He plucked a block of cheddar from the counter, sniffed it luxuriantly then ravaged it without any sense of table manners. Flecks of cheese flew everywhere. Diana shifted from her meal to scarf some up. Paula shivered and finally focused on me.

"Do you want anything? Can you even eat, you know, being a skeleton?"

I leaned against the kitchen counter and watched Conrad and Diana gorge themselves.

"I am a spirit and can turn corporeal if I choose. How do you think I was holding Diana?" I glanced down at myself.

"Though I supposed drinking coffee as a skeleton would be a bit messy." I focused my willpower and changed my form.

The shift wasn't immediate. Skin and muscle grew and expanded from my bones like an inflating balloon. My black cloak shrank and shifted to become a simple black suit. Within seconds, I was no longer a skeleton wrapped in Death's cowl and cloak, but the spitting image of Frank Totmann. A hefty balding man with a well-trimmed graying beard and brown eyes. It was the last physical form I'd had and the easiest for me to assume.

Regardless, a wave of exhaustion rolled over me. That had taken a lot of willpower, but not nearly as much as if I'd become someone else. I patted my belly. "Much better," I said. Paula's mouth worked like a gaping fish, but no sound came out. "Do you have coffee?" I asked. It had been months since I'd had a cup of coffee. I missed that bitter bite followed by suffusing warmth.

Paula shook herself. "Uh, no. Sorry, we don't drink coffee. Ghastly stuff. I have..." she waved vaguely at the line of glasses before Conrad. They were all empty. He was nose-deep in a yogurt cup making wet slurping noises. "...um."

"Water will be fine. Thank you," I said, trying to hide my disappointment. Didn't drink coffee? What kind of people didn't drink coffee?

No matter. I accepted a glass of tap water gratefully. I took a sip and Paula continued talking. It was a nervous patter about herself and Alex, jumping topics seemingly at random as she gave their life story. Alex threw in the occasional clarifying comment. I only half-listened, commenting when appropriate. As they talked at me, my thoughts turned inward.

I'd escaped Abaddon. Now what?

Nigel was still establishing his New Order. Soon he would send the Auditor to begin reaping souls and dragging them directly to Hell. Souls who would bypass Judgment to suffer eternal torments.

And not Torments the call center. They would suffer hellfire and brimstone. Whips and knives. Wailing and gnashing of teeth. And that was just the deceased. When would they begin stealing the living as they'd done to the Davidsons?

I briefly considered trying to warn Heaven but discarded the idea as soon as it came. Heaven wouldn't take this lying down. Once they learned that Nigel was about to violate every Rule there was about soul management, I had no doubt they'd kick off Armageddon early. Nigel had to be stopped before that happened. *I* had to stop him by rescuing Lucifer, a dauntless task that now bordered on impossible.

Yet, despite the gravity of the situation, my thoughts continually bounced back to my friends trapped in the Pit. Frank, Abigail, and the Davidsons. None of them deserved the torments Nigel had planned. None had been Judged. They'd all stood by me, helped me when I desperately needed it, and I'd left them trapped in Hell with only a vague promise and instructions to 'be ready.'

Ready for what? I wasn't even in the same realm anymore.

I had to return to Hell. But how? I took another sip of my water, grimacing at my thoughts.

Paula blanched at my expression, but she didn't stop talking. Her tone merely rose in pitch. I replaced the grimace with a smile. It didn't seem to help.

Simply returning to Hell wouldn't improve my odds of success. I'd lost my scythe with all its powers. I couldn't travel instantly, parse souls, or stop time. While I could reach Purgatory the old-fashioned way—passing through the ether like a deceased soul—the Hellmouth was still closed. And I'd wrecked Charon's gondola.

Perhaps if I had a weapon, I could force my way in. Unfortunately, I doubted Alex and Paula had blessed blades just lying around. From our one-sided conversation, I'd learned that they were newly married college students. Paula was studying horticulture, and Alex was some sort of engineer. Or perhaps a mechanic. Both? I wasn't sure, and Paula's story grew more jumbled the longer she talked.

Perhaps my silence, the silence of Death, was unnerving her.

I drained the water glass and set it on the counter. "Thank you for your hospitality," I said, breaking into the conversation when Paula paused for a breath, "but I really must be going."

Alex cocked an eyebrow. "Heading out to *cat*-ch more souls?" He nodded at Diana, who was licking up cheese crumbs from Conrad's ravaging.

I cocked a matching eyebrow. "You already used catch."

Alex shrugged. "Couldn't think of any better words that started with C-A-T."

I chuckled. "No, I'm not out to *cat*-ch souls, and I'm not *draggin'* them to Hell," I said with a nod toward

Conrad. He'd finished his buffet and lay belly-up amid the wreckage in pure draconic bliss. I smiled. "I need to visit a friend." The only friend I knew who trucked in the magical, blessed, cursed, and other esoterica.

A friend who I wasn't sure wanted to see me.

It was time to visit Cordelia's Apothecary Supply.

Chapter 15

A GRIM RIDE

WERE I ALONE—OR EVEN with just Conrad—I could have flown at the speed of thought to Cordelia's house. Spirit travel wasn't as fast as simply using *Grace*'s power to transport instantly from place to place, but I would have arrived within seconds. Yet I couldn't leave Diana behind. I'd made her a promise that I fully intended to keep. She would be a goddess among cats to put even Bastet to shame.

Unfortunately, my hosts couldn't drive me to Cora's house. The car parts in the living room were from Alex's pickup. He swore it was almost fixed, but from Paula's long-suffering sigh, I assumed this was a frequent and in-accurate assertion. Their only other mode of transportation was Paula's bicycle.

Death does *not* ride a bicycle. I've always wanted to try a motorcycle, something big and loud with my cloak flapping in the wind behind me. But peddling myself across town like a school kid headed to the park? No. Out of the question.

Instead, I asked them to call me a cab. I still had Louis's number memorized.

Louis arrived with a screech of tires and a honking horn. In the living room, I bid my hosts goodbye, scooped Diana into my arms, and ... eyed Conrad. He waddled into the living room and paused to burp loudly.

"Conrad," I said, "you can't be seen like that."

"Like what?" His gaze wandered over himself. Searching for anything worthy of disdain, he arched his neck toward his tail and overbalanced, collapsing against the couch. A wing waved toward me like he wanted to make a point. It hung in the air briefly before dropping to the floor. Conrad rolled onto his back, distended belly skyward. "Oh, man. I'm never leaving Earth. Food is amaaaaazing!"

"Yes, it is," I said heartily. "But that's not my point. You saw how Paula and Alex reacted to you. Little blue dragons aren't exactly common in the mortal realm."

Conrad's head shot up. "What?" He looked to our young hosts. They shook their heads. "Well, they should be! I thought humans liked dragons?"

"Like or dislike is not the point," I said. "Dragons haven't existed since the age of the dinosaurs. You need a disguise. Can you change your appearance like I did?" Most nightmares were limited to their assigned form, a mere shadow of their host's soul. But Conrad wasn't like most nightmares. He was a piece of Lucifer's soul. That implied power that perhaps even he didn't realize.

Conrad regarded me upside down for a moment then groaned dramatically and rolled to his feet. He compressed into himself as though tightening every spiritual muscle in his body. At first, nothing happened. The dragon quivered, grunted loudly, and then—with a *pop*—he turned into a small, wire-haired terrier.

Who was blue.

With wings.

Conrad's silver eyes popped open. His tongue lolled, and he spun around examining himself. Satisfied, he grinned up at me and wagged his blue tail. "Woof!" he said.

Not barked. Said. Like an actor reading a script poorly.

I sighed. He'd changed, which was more than other nightmares could have done. It would have to do. "Stay close," I said, "keep your wings furled, and for Hell's sake, don't bark like that."

"Woof!" Conrad said, wagging his tail so enthusiastically that his entire body quivered. I shook my head, opened the door, and stepped outside.

Cold slammed into me like a wall of ice. Late winter had Colorado Springs firmly in its grasp. And it wasn't the charming kind of winter with snowmen and Christmas lights. It was the other kind. The kind of winter when snow and rain mixed and mingled to create a frozen, muddy, miserable wasteland. Sharp pellets of death blew sideways, and the wind cut through my thin suit. Darkness lay heavily across the city. Streetlights made orange cones of brightness in the gloom that did little more than show the sideways motion of the snow.

At least the weather would keep anyone from looking too closely at Conrad.

Diana yowled her displeasure and tried to leap for the closing door. I held her tight and focused on my attire. The thin suit expanded once again into a black snow jacket with puffy sleeves. A wave of dizziness washed over me, and I paused to draw several deep breaths. My willpower was strong, and this was but a small change of my physical appearance, but it was my second change that night. Yes, Death has more power in the mortal realm, but even I have limits. Once the dizziness passed, I half-unzipped the jacket and let Diana crawl inside with me.

Despite the exhaustion creeping into my bones, it was nice to be merely corporeal, and not actually mortal. Such a transformation would have been impossible while I was trapped in Frank's body. The Rules forbade spirits from physically changing the real world but allowed us to change our corporeal forms to *interact* with the world.

That thought gave me pause. Had Nigel wiped that Rule away with the others? Or was it one of the Rules maintained in Heaven's half of the Rulebook?

I stretched my will and one hand toward the sleet pelting me and tried turning it into flaming embers.

Tingles ran up my arm, like the warning of a muscle cramp, but nothing happened. I nodded to myself, pleased to find *something* that Nigel hadn't corrupted. Hell's influence in the mortal realm was still limited. They could steal souls, but they couldn't remake Earth in their own image.

Yet.

Louis honked again. Feeling rather good after failing to change the world, I strode down the snowy walk with a spring in my step. Conrad pattered beside me, gazing happily at the snow-swept misery around us. He snapped at the sleet and waggled his tail ceaselessly.

I slid into Louis's cab, let Conrad jump onto the floorboard, and slammed the door against the cold. Cracked leather seats crunched when I sat. The familiar smell of antiseptic and artificial lemon wafted over me on a wave of warm air.

Louis wore his typical half-grin as he leaned an arm over the bench seat. "Where to pal"—his eyes bulged—"*holy shit*!" Louis lurched away from me like he'd seen a ghost. His mouth opened and closed a couple of times before he said, "Grim? I thought you were dead!"

Oh. Right.

The last time Louis saw me, he'd driven me in Frank's body to the hospital after my fatal heart attack. He'd watched me die. Perhaps I'd chosen the wrong corporeal form.

Well, in for a penny, in for a pound.

I smiled broadly. "You know what they say, you can't keep a good man down."

"Yeah?" Louis's gray eyes narrowed. "So how do you explain the ER nurse who very solemnly told me that my friend was dead." I blinked at him, surprised at the sudden tightness in my throat. He had considered me a friend? I ... hadn't expected that.

Louis drew a deep breath. "So, what, you faked your death? Are you in the CIA or something? Because as a cabbie I read people for a living, and that nurse was telling the truth. You were dead."

Well, this was awkward. However, it wasn't the first time somebody had asked if I was in the CIA. Did I *look* like a secret agent? The mere idea!

And yet ... I *could* lie.

Agent Grim, reporting for duty. I opened my mouth to spin a yarn worthy of an international spy and—

Diana yowled from inside my jacket like she was dying. She squirmed, claws digging painfully into my chest until her head popped out of the jacket's neck just below my chin. She yowled again, a piercing, angry sound.

Louis blinked. "Why do you have a cat inside your jacket?"

"How else would you transport a cat in a snowstorm? It's not like I have a cat-sized snowsuit to give her." I buckled my seatbelt—I vividly remembered Louis's erratic driving habits—then gestured toward the road, hoping to sidestep awkward questions. Agent Grim, playing it cool. "Shall we? I am in a bit of a hurry." The fate of Hell itself rested on my shoulders.

He nodded slowly, gaze flicking from Diana to me. "Okay, no problem. Got an address?"

I gave him Cora's address. He nodded. Questions still burned in his eyes, but Louis threw the cab into gear. His tires spun briefly before catching traction and shooting us into suburbia's icy wasteland.

I quickly learned three very important facts.

First, Louis's driving habits were not tempered in the slightest by the slick roads. If anything, he took wicked pleasure in sliding around corners and then slamming on the gas when traction again took hold. There wasn't much traffic out, but that was small comfort as Louis took up most of the road. I clutched the door and held on for dear life.

Second, dragons love riding in cars. Conrad leapt onto my lap and pressed his snout to the window. His blue tail wagged incessantly. When Louis slid around the first corner, Conrad actually said, "Wheee..." loudly enough that I had to clamp a hand over his snout.

Third, unlike dragons, cats *despise* riding in cars.

Within less than fifteen seconds, Diana exploded out of my jacket like a white-furred tornado. Claws dug into my chest, and Diana launched herself at the front seat. She landed on the seatback with the sound of tearing leather. Her back foot missed, and she scrambled for purchase. Diana's green eyes widened into black saucers of terror. Chest-deep yowls reverberated inside the small cab like a berserker's war cry.

Conrad howled in harmony.

"Hey, whoa!" Louis yelled, glancing at Diana as we slid left around a corner. Diana rode the seatback like a surfer, knees bending with the car's motion. She yowled again, her tone warbling like a banshee about to vomit. The cab swerved back to the right as Louis finished his turn and Diana used the momentum to scramble onto the headrest behind him.

She yowled into his ear. Louis swore, clutched the steering wheel, and leaned away from the enraged goddess towering over him.

I lunged for Diana, but my seatbelt jerked me to a stop. My fingers brushed her silky fur. Diana swiped at me, fear shifting into anger, and scratched my hand. I snatched it back. I didn't bleed, an advantage to being a spirit, but it still hurt.

Diana scrambled onto Louis's lap. He screamed, and the car jerked to the right.

"Hey, whoa!" he yelled again, looking down. "Not under the brake! Git. Out. Of. There!" I heard stomps and yowls, and Louis began a rising-tone monologue of curses that would have made Lucifer himself raise an eyebrow.

Diana's yowls trebled in volume. She did not appreciate Louis's attention.

The engine revved. We went into a sideways slide that felt slow despite our velocity. The road was clear but slick, and we flew toward the curb. An imposing line of barren trees slid out of the darkness to greet us.

"No. No. No!" Louis shrieked. "Get off the gas you stu—"

I didn't hear the rest of Louis's imprecations. The trees loomed outside the window, and I reacted out of instinct.

Millennia ago, before I'd become the Grim Reaper, I'd been a guardian angel. My entire purpose had been to protect my charge. True, I'd failed at my duties by whispering a lie into Cain's ear and inciting him to commit humanity's first murder, but those protective instincts had never left me. They guided me as I watched over humanity's souls and shepherded them to their final rest.

I shifted into a spirit and flew through the cab toward the trees. I materialized and slammed my palms onto the fender. The metal was cold and slick. I yelled and pushed, willing the cab to *stop.*

It did not stop.

The laws of physics are—generally—as immutable as the Rules which govern the spiritual realm. One does not simply ignore gravity and inertia. Yet, the Rules do allow for spiritual intervention in the mortal world. We cannot change the laws of physics any more than we can inter- fere with human free will. However, we can redirect those forces.

In my haste to act, I forgot that minor distinction as I tried to force Louis's cab to stop.

The cab slammed into me. My yell cut off when my face bounced off the hood. Stars flashed, and I shook my head.

Through the windshield, I saw Louis's head snap up. His gaze locked with mine. His eyes bulged. He knew then that I was *not* of the mortal realm.

I cursed myself as a fool. In the millennia since I'd been a guardian angel, I'd forgotten the finesse required to act upon the world without being seen. But now was not the time to relearn such skills.

We bounced over the curb. I went briefly airborne then slammed back onto the hood. Stars flashed again, and I drew a wheezing breath.

Why the hell was I still corporeal? I wasn't some weak human. I was Death! And Death does not get thrown around like a ragdoll.

I flashed back into my spiritual form, shed Frank's skin in an explosion of flaming embers, and once again became the cowled Reaper. In the split second before Louis t-boned an oak tree, I grabbed his fender and *pulled,* using all my willpower to redirect mass and inertia into a spin.

It worked.

The driver's door hit the tree and buckled. Glass shattered, and the cab spun around the tree with a shriek of tortured metal. Sod and snow flew through the air. The engine revved. Then, with an abrupt jerk, Louis's cab rocked to a stop. It came to rest straddling a sidewalk beyond the trees.

The cab's engine died, and the night became abruptly quiet. The sleet continued unabated, muting both sight and sound. Louis's headlights bored a tunnel through the snow-lit night, fixed firmly on me: Death incarnate.

Exhaustion slammed into me harder than Louis's fender had. Three changes in one night. I almost fell forward but caught myself with a step. My willpower wavered, and I felt an overwhelming desire to just sit down and do nothing. My vision blurred. I shook my head and gazed past the cab's headlights to Louis.

His eyes were wide. His hands clutched his steering wheel. His gaze ran over my cloak and cowl and the full import of what I'd just done slammed into me.

Damn. I was seriously off my game today. I'd revealed myself to not one, not two, but *three* humans in a matter of hours. And not the humans who were *supposed* to see me as I reaped their souls.

What was worse, Louis knew me. We'd met. Bonded over shared relational woes. Our next conversation was going to be very awkward.

I put all my strength into expanding back into Frank's corporeal form, and then it took everything I had just to remain standing. I drew deep breaths of cold air until my lungs ached. Icy crystals of death sleeted sideways into me until I was certain that I could walk back to the cab without falling.

Louis watched silently, fingers white-knuckled on the steering wheel. I pulled open the back passenger door, pushed Conrad off my seat, and slid inside. It was only marginally warmer. Wind whipped through Louis's shattered side window. Snow formed a mini tornado through the cab until I closed the door.

Diana mewled from beneath the seat. I reached down and retrieved her as gently as possible. She clung to me like a lifeline. When I half-unzipped my jacket, she crawled inside and curled against my chest.

Louis's jaw worked a few times before he said, "Who ... no. *What* the hell are you?"

I zipped the jacket up around Diana and met his gaze. "I never lied to you, Louis. You know my name and have now seen my true form."

"Mary, mother of God..." Louis's whisper came with that look of understanding I knew all too well. That moment of dawning comprehension when a mortal soul fully understood who and what I was. Louis ran his fingers through his sandy hair. "You really *are* the Grim Reaper?

I thought maybe, you know, I was going crazy. Seeing things. Hearing things. I swear your dog was cussing you out right before we crashed."

I glared at Conrad, who smiled sheepishly from the seat beside me. Louis also glanced at the dragon-turned-half-dog. At first, his gaze slid past Conrad, his mind only seeing what it expected to see, not the blue fur and obvious wings. But then his gaze snapped back, and his eyes widened once again.

Conrad waved a paw. "Heya. How's it going?"

Louis made a strangled sound in the back of his throat.

I sighed. "Louis, meet Conrad. He's a nightmare, and I mean that in the literal sense."

"He sure looks like one. Are those wings?"

Conrad fluttered his wings, then spun to pose like a diva with a sultry glance over one shoulder, blue wings draping him like a cape. Louis swallowed, blinked a couple of times, then forced his gaze back to me. "Well, uh, thanks for not killing me, Grim. I thought I was a goner for sure!"

My lips pursed. "Why does everyone assume that I kill people? I just reap their souls. It's in the name."

"Huh, I guess it is. 'Grim Reaper.'" Louis chuckled, his normal cheerfulness reasserting itself. "Man, I can't wait to tell Nichole that I had old rattle bones himself in my cab!"

"Rattle bones?" I cocked an eyebrow. Louis grinned, and I shook my head. "I would prefer if you kept this between us. I'm on something of a, well, a secret mission. I've recently escaped eternal imprisonment, and my mission could be imperiled if the wrong spirit learned that I was free."

Louis cocked an eyebrow. "Who's powerful enough to cage *Death*?" He raised both palms. "Nope, never mind. I don't want to know. One nightmare is enough for today. My lips are sealed." He motioned as though zippering his lips.

Two cars had stopped as Louis and I talked. Their drivers, both men, walked toward us in the headlight glow, hunched against the sleet.

"You okay?" one called out, hand raised to block the headlights. Louis waved cheerily through his shattered window.

"We're good! But I'm gonna have a doozy of a time explaining this to my boss! Guess I was driving a *bit* too fast."

About time he realized that.

"Need me to call a tow?" the man asked.

"Nope!" Louis said. He cranked the ignition. The lights dimmed, and then the cab roared to life. It rattled a bit like something under the hood had come loose, but Louis slipped it into gear. The tires spun. We didn't go anywhere. The men jogged to the rear of the cab. With them pushing, and Louis feathering the gas, traction finally took hold, and we pulled slowly back onto the road.

Our rescuers watched as we turned onto the snow-covered lane. Louis threw them a wave and, for the first time since I'd met the cabbie, he drove calmly into the night.

I sat back, petted Diana under my jacket, and let my tired thoughts turn muzzy. They drifted toward my coming meeting with Cora, Abigail's mother. She'd supplied Frank with the supplies to swap our souls. She'd also been my first kiss.

Yes, Evelyn was my first and only love, but spirits do not connect physically the same way humans do. Cora gave me my first kiss soon after I'd been trapped in Frank's body, a warm and fleeting moment that I would cherish forever. It's a good thing that 'the Kiss of Death' is merely a metaphor. I liked Cora and wished her a very long and full life. She hadn't known my true identity at the time.

She did now. She hated me for taking Abigail's soul. Hated that her daughter had died too soon. And here I was, the Grim Reaper, coming to ask a favor. Something told me that this wouldn't end well.

Chapter 16

DOPPELGANGER

ICY SLEET COATED THE left side of my face as I tromped up Cora's walk. Conrad trotted alongside, tail still wagging so hard his whole body quivered. At least somebody was enjoying themselves.

Lights were on behind the curtains, so I knew Cora was home, but the porch was dark. At least the wind calmed slightly once we'd climbed the steps, blocked by the snow-plastered overhang and an evergreen bush with aspirations of being a tree. I raised my hand to knock on the teal-blue door, then paused.

I was still wearing Frank's face. Considering Louis's reaction, perhaps that wasn't the wisest idea. I wanted to avoid dramatics, and this conversation was going to be difficult enough as it was. I had to convince Cora to help me without spilling the beans that her daughter Abigail was trapped in Hell. That I'd not only failed to rescue her but gotten her condemned to the Pit. Knowing Cora, that little tidbit of information wouldn't go over well.

I couldn't assume my cloaked Reaper's form. A nosy neighbor had eyed us suspiciously through their window when Louis's cab rattled up. It wouldn't do for them to see Death literally knocking on Cora's door. But what form could I take?

What form did I retain the strength to take? My willpower was strained to its limits after four changes in one night.

The answer came as soon as I asked the question. My jaw worked as I hunted for a different solution, a different face I knew well enough to assume with ease, but nothing came to mind. I hadn't looked like anything other than a cloaked skeleton for over five millennia.

So, I assumed the first face I'd ever known. The face of the guardian angel I'd been before my original sin.

Frank's face and form shifted. I grew taller, thinner,

and sprouted shoulder-length black hair. The hand that remained poised to knock lost its age spots and darkened to a Mediterranean tone.

For the first time since Cain murdered Abel, I wore my true face. It felt ... freeing. Terrifying.

Exhausting.

My knees buckled, and I dropped. I caught myself with a hand on one knee, the other knee slamming hard onto the snowy porch. I blinked, vision wavering, and focused on breathing. Five changes in one night.

Conrad cleared his throat, and I realized that I'd been motionless for several seconds. Like my brain had gone on a brief holiday. "Are you gonna knock, Bones? My tail's about half numb." Diana mewled in agreement from under my jacket.

Steeling myself, I rose and knocked.

An eternity of icy darkness passed before I heard footsteps inside. The peephole darkened and there was a sharp indrawn breath from beyond the door. Then the door abruptly flew open, releasing a wave of warm air that made the thin snow swirl on the porch.

Cora glared at me, then shivered as the cold air hit her. She grabbed a green shawl from an unseen rack and slung it around her shoulders, hitching it tight as she crossed her arms. Her graying hair was loose and pulled behind one ear. Though she wore a flowered white dress I recognized, she didn't have her normal clatter of jewelry. Only a heavy Celtic cross on a long chain graced her neck. A holy relic that had once belonged to Abigail.

Cora's voice, normally warm like honey, was cold and sharp as a dagger.

"Really, Earnest? You disappear for two and half years, and then show up at midnight, unannounced, in the middle of a snowstorm? You're a piece of work, you know that?"

Earnest? Who was Earnest? My jaws flapped. "I ... uh..."

Cora's eyes narrowed, and she leaned forward to examine me more closely. Suddenly, her eyes widened, and her hand shot to her mouth.

"Oh, God. I'm so sorry. You look just like my ex. Showing up in the middle of the night with some personal crisis that only I can solve is exactly the kind of thing he'd do. I just assumed—" Cora stopped, visibly took hold of herself, and extended a hand.

"Hi, I'm Cora. What brings you to my door on such a lovely and *late* evening?"

I shook her hand firmly. "I'm here with a personal crisis that only you can solve."

She snorted. "Okay, I deserved that. And you are…?"

I drew a deep breath. Here goes. "It is I, the Grim Reaper, terror of men's souls"—Cora inhaled sharply and released my hand—"and apparently the doppelganger of deadbeat ex-husbands."

"Grim? What are you doing here?"

"I know you're angry with me about Abigail, but when last we spoke, you said you were my ally. I am in desperate need of an ally right now."

She considered this briefly before grabbing my elbow and pulling me into the house. Conrad leapt inside, and the door slammed shut on our heels. Warmth flowed over me. Diana squirmed, and I half-unzipped my jacket. She poked her head out with a plaintive mewl.

Cora's living room was small but comfortable. A flower-patterned couch lay against the righthand wall with a dark blue recliner opposite a small television. Floor lamps provided light while assorted photographs and knick-knacks told the tale of a life well-lived. Cora had two grown children in addition to Abigail, a son and a daughter, and if I remembered right, a grandchild or two. The pictures certainly indicated a happy extended family.

An ache formed deep in my soul, surprising me. I'd never had a home or even a place to put up my feet. Death does not rest. I am constantly on the move. Stop time, reap souls, rinse and repeat for eternity. What would it be like to have a place to relax? To stop moving and just ... be.

Diana mewled again, and a smile blossomed on Cora's face. "Diana! Come here, you gorgeous little lady." She pulled the cat from my jacket and cradled her, making those silly googly sounds people make around babies and cats.

Diana took the attention as her due. She sniffed Cora, allowed herself a few scratches behind the ears, then squirmed free and jumped to the arm of the couch. The cat shook herself, flinging tufts of long white hair. Satisfied that she was the goddess of her new domain, Diana went exploring.

Cora smiled, then knelt before Conrad. "And who are..." Her cooing tone died in a strangled gasp. Apparently, the sight of a blue terrier with wings was just too much.

"Hiya, Gorgeous! I'm Conrad!" the dragon said.

Once again, I sighed at him. "Conrad. Dogs don't talk. What's the point of a disguise if you're going to open your mouth and ruin it?"

"Disguise?" Cora said, rising with a cautious step back. "Are you a demon?"

"Nope!" Conrad shook himself, tensed his entire body until I thought his silver eyes would burst, and then with a *pop* more felt than heard, he was once again in his draconic form. *He* didn't look tired after changing. Blue scales shimmered as he took a bow. "I'm Lucifer's nightmare! That's right, Beautiful. You're looking at the spitting image of the Devil himself."

Cora blinked several times at this pronouncement. I could see her mind working, trying to reconcile her worldview with Conrad's presence. Finally, she said, "I expected the Devil to be taller. And less blue." Her gaze swiveled to me. "So, what's your personal crisis that only I can help with? I assume it has something to do with *him*." She pointed at Conrad. He wandered toward the coffee table where Diana was sniffing at a small charcuterie plate: meat, cheese, crackers, and a small bunch of grapes.

Cora had proven herself capable of hearing hard truths, so I didn't beat around the bush. "Indeed. I need weapons to face down the darkest threat Hell has ever known."

"What about your scythe? What's it called?"

"*Grace.* It was … stolen."

"Again?" Cora rolled her eyes. "Who got it this time? Some old granny not ready for the great beyond who was more than she seemed?" She waved mockingly with her fingers as though spreading magic through the room.

"No," I said firmly. I *had* run afoul of such an old granny a few years back. She'd been a priestess of an ancient Mayan fertility goddess. Fortunately, Analisa Agonos was not today's problem. "I was in Hell researching an … issue"—I carefully sidestepped mentioning Abigail—"when I stumbled into a coup. Remember Damien Nigel?"

"Yeah, everyone does. He's been running for president for almost a year. Nine months until Election Day, and I'm sick of the ads already." Her eyes narrowed. "Didn't you say he was some kind of half-human demigod?"

"Not just a demigod. The King of the Demigods. The last of them, and the son of Lucifer. And now he's dethroned his father and is threatening to radically alter the very nature of what it means to die. I intend to stop him, rescue Lucifer, and restore order to Hell. But I need your help."

Cora's eyebrows climbed as I spoke. Then her shoulders sagged, and a deep sigh escaped her. "And here I was looking forward to a nice quiet evening with a mindless romance novel and a glass of Pinot Noir." She glanced at the coffee table and then squawked. "Hey!"

Diana sat on a tattered paperback, her happily flipping tail threatening a glass of red wine. From the bit of the cover I saw, it looked like the same shirtless hero from the book Charon had been reading in his camp chair. Conrad sat opposite Diana, the two of them scarfing up Cora's late-night snack.

Cora stomped toward the table, but both the cat and dragon growled around their feast in a rumbling, snarfing way. Cora paused. Her lips thinned. She reached carefully past Diana to rescue her wine glass. The food was a lost cause.

Cora downed the wine with a single gulp then examined the empty glass, brows furrowed. "Dragons, demigods, and the Devil himself. Good Lord, I need something stronger than wine." She spun for the kitchen.

"Like what?" I asked.

"Coffee and whiskey."

Chapter 17

CORDELIA'S APOTHECARY SUPPLY

WE SAT AT CORA'S small kitchen table sipping something she called Irish coffee. It had a hearty kick, but after the first few sips, I could see why she enjoyed it. The harsh winter storm howled outside the windows, but the Irish coffee was warm and comforting. Like Cora's presence.

Anxiety urged me to get to the point as we chatted, to ask Cora for weaponry so I could return to Hell, but I reined it in. She clearly wasn't going to help me until she understood what had brought me to her door. Plus, I was exhausted. Sitting felt good.

I took a sip of my Irish coffee, realizing how much I'd missed Cora. I'd missed her warm soul and fiery wit. She was a fantastic conversationalist, asking clarifying questions at the right moments and refilling my mug when it emptied.

I was halfway through my tale—we'd just entered Alvin's waiting room—when Cora stopped me with a raised hand.

"This friend you're helping, the one who you're obviously avoiding naming? Is she someone I know?"

A lie sprang to my tongue and pushed against the back of my teeth, but I swallowed it. Lying in Hell had brought me no end of trouble. It landed Abigail in the Pit and me in Abaddon. I couldn't lie to Cora. She was more to me than an ally. She was a friend who deserved better.

But how do you tell a mother that her daughter was dragged into Hell and was suffering unthinkable torments?

Very, very carefully.

"Yes," I said, fingering my coffee cup, "you know her." I drew a deep breath. I really didn't want to say this, but bad news doesn't improve over time. Just get on with it, Grim.

"It's Abigail. She—along with countless other souls—was pulled from Purgatory into Hell without Judgment as part of Nigel's power grab—"

"*What?!*" Cora shot to her feet. "Abigail? *My* Abigail is in Hell, right now, and you're *just ... now ... telling me?*" She slammed her Irish coffee to the table. Black ambrosia splashed onto her hand, but she didn't notice.

Okay, perhaps that wasn't as careful an explanation as I'd hoped. I rose. "Abigail is why I went to Hell in the first place," I said. "To find out what went wrong and, hopefully, to rescue her."

"Oh, you're doing a bang-up job of that, sitting here calmly sipping your Irish coffee!"

"Hey, coffee and whiskey was your idea! And things got ... complicated in Hell. If it weren't for Nigel's coup—"

"That's just an excuse." Cora's finger jabbed into my chest. Her other hand clasped Abigail's cross around her neck. "*Nothing* is more important than rescuing Abigail."

"There's more at stake than—"

"Not for me!" Cora noticed the coffee on her hand and spun toward the sink for a towel. She wiped her hands and flung the towel onto the counter. "Where is Abigail, exactly?"

"Last time I saw her, she was condemned to Hell's fourth level pushing stones. Xandu wanted to drop all of us into the swamp of boiling blood, but it was still under construction."

Cora paled. Hmmm... Maybe I shouldn't have added that last bit. She drew a shuddering breath and then stomped out of the kitchen.

"Where are you going?" I asked. Her footsteps receded upstairs.

"To change! I'm not rescuing my daughter from Hell in a flowered dress!"

I stepped from the kitchen in time to see Cora disappear into a doorway at the top of the stairwell. "You can't go to Hell!" I yelled. "You're mortal. It's too dangerous!"

Her only answer was a slammed door.

***

Barely two minutes later, Cora flew down the stairs while pulling her graying hair back into a severe bun. She'd changed into camouflage cargo pants, hiking boots, and a denim vest with entirely too many pockets.

I stared, trying to adjust my mental image of Cora. She

normally wore matronly dresses, a gentle smile, and entire-ly too much jewelry. A charming middle-aged tax auditor whom I'd come to know and cherish.

This new Cora was frightening. Formidable. Like a free-dom fighter prepared to burn the world if anyone got in her way.

Now I saw where Abigail got her fire.

I carefully stepped aside as Cora hooked a left at the bottom of the stairs and dashed down the main floor's short hallway. I followed her into a small office on the right. It had a computer desk, bookshelves, and a conspic-uously delightful table in the corner decorated with arcane baubles. A camera sat before a cloth backdrop that read CORDELIA'S APOTHECARY SUPPLY.

Cora flung open a closet door and stepped into the darkness. Surprised at the size of the closet, I followed. Cora yanked a small chain, and a bare bulb flashed on.

Full shelves surrounded us, the entire product line for Cordelia's Apothecary Supply. Herbs, potions, trinkets, and more. Glass bottles and plastic baggies. Artifacts that looked ancient and others that were clearly knockoffs. Everything was carefully labeled, but I had no idea which items would help us on our quest.

I considered arguing once more against Cora joining me, but I didn't think she'd take 'no' for an answer. Besides, I needed the help. It wasn't like I could ask Heaven. I was trying to avoid Armageddon, not kick it off.

I glanced around. "So, what do we need?"

"Salt, amulets, rings, a few candles..." Cora's voice drifted, and she plucked items from the shelves. Several pounds of salt split into two plastic bags went into her cargo pants. Rings slid onto her fingers, and amulets joined the Celtic cross around her neck. Everything else went into pockets seemingly at random.

"Is everything in here magical?" I asked in wonder. Cora carefully tucked a bundle of finger-sized candles into the upper pocket of her denim vest. A baggie holding two crow feathers stuck out of the opposite pocket.

"Hardly. Most of these"—she waved a dismissive hand—"are just ingredients. Bits and bobs for various spells."

I pointed to one shelf. "Are those wooden stakes?"

"Yup. They're my best-sellers. People keep begging for silver bullets too, but it's a nightmare getting a license to sell ammunition."

I eyed her sideways. "You know that vampires and werewolves aren't actually real, right? I mean, there are night-mare versions, sure, but nightmares rarely escape Hell's Basement."

She paused. "Why not?"

"They're still part of the souls they were torn from. Human souls only travel in one direction. To return to the mortal realm, they'd need help."

"What about Conrad?"

"Case in point. Diana brought us both here."

"But he said he's the Devil's nightmare, and I somehow doubt that anybody tells Lucifer where he can and can't go. Why would a piece of his soul be restricted to Hell?"

I raised a finger to protest, but the words died unspoken. She was right. How had I overlooked such a simple fact? When I first met Conrad, he was helping Abigail escape. But he should have been able to go anywhere he want-ed—just like Lucifer did. Why hadn't he taken Abigail straight to the mortal realm? What game was he playing at?

Dragons are tricksome creatures. I'd been accepting en-tirely too much at face value.

"Well, my point remains. Vampires and werewolves aren't real." I retrieved a stake to examine it.

"Don't tell my regulars that. Most of my money comes from people who believe all sorts of crazy things. Selling to the weirdos and the cosplayers keeps Cordelia's Apothecary Supply afloat. But I get enough genuine practitioners on my website to keep things interesting. Take these for example." She started slipping bracelets onto her wrists, each clattering against the other as they settled. "They're supposed to provide strength, endurance, and wards against evil, but I'm not entirely convinced they're truly magical. Yet the genuine practitioners buy *all* my jewelry. So … maybe they work? They can't hurt. And I feel better having them on." Bracelets clinked as she rotated her writs to show them off.

Yes, Cora always had clattering jewelry. It was her armor.

I fingered the stake in my hands. I wasn't sure how to ask my next question. It was a question that historically led to torture, fire, and a visit by Yours Truly, but I plowed on anyway. "Are you a practicing witch?"

"Heavens, no!" Cora chuckled despite the tension radiating from her. "That takes a lifetime of study! And you don't have to ask with such dread. Genuine witchcraft is only frowned upon these days. Nobody burns witches at the stake anymore. I am, at best, a dabbler in the dark arts.

That's how I met Frank. He was researching demon summoning circles and found my site." She turned and gently pushed me into the doorway with a ring-laden hand. Once I'd moved, she knelt beside a knee-high safe by the door that I hadn't noticed. The safe's metal dial whirred and clicked as she spun it.

"Have you dealt with many demons?" I asked.

"A few," she said with an enigmatic half-smile. But then the smile dropped, replaced with worry. "The worst was that incident at the Davidson's last fall." When the Auditor and Xandu had come to reap my soul. The dial stopped with a click, and she swung the door open. "Here we go! These, my dear Grim, are my truly magical items."

I knelt beside Cora. My dark hair fell across my eyes, and I tried to brush it aside. It flopped back in front of my face. I scowled and hooked it behind one ear. Only half of it stayed. I'd forgotten how unruly hair could be.

The safe's three small shelves were almost bare. Just a few items per shelf, which wasn't surprising. Imbuing a physical object with magic requires either a powerful spirit's intervention—as needed for blessed and cursed blades—or a tremendous deal of faith and willpower by the human practitioner. Human-created items with genuine magic are rarer than people realize. Cora's Celtic cross is one such item; a holy relic blessed by Saint Patrick himself.

Cora carefully withdrew a narrow dagger with a gold and sapphire cross guard. Silver and gold cobras twined up the handle. Their hoods spread at the pommel as though prepared to bite whatever hand clutched the blade. Cora glanced at me. "Will a cursed dagger affect demons?"

That's how Xandu lost his forearm. To his own scimitar. I smiled at the memory. "Yes. It won't banish or kill them, but it'll hurt."

"Good enough." She pulled a simple leather sheath from a nearby shelf, secured the dagger, and then clipped it to her belt. She withdrew another blade from the safe, and I gasped. It was a cheap and dull letter opener shaped like a miniature longsword.

"That's *Faith*!" The blessed letter opener had belonged to Sam Davidson. He'd once used it to banish a demon right in front of me. "How'd you get it?"

A worried shadow crossed Cora's face. "I asked Sam if I could borrow it, just for a day. I wanted to test whether blessed and cursed blades would interact with proximity."

"And?"

She shrugged. "No interaction at all. But when I called Sam to tell him, he never answered. The whole family just disappeared overnight. Haven't seen or heard from them in months."

My jaw clenched. "I hadn't gotten to that part of my story yet. Sam, Inez, and their daughter Beatrix are in Hell ... in the flesh. I *still* don't know what happened between Sam and the Auditor, but Hell's final arbiter of the Rules returned for his vengeance."

Cora's hand flew to her mouth. "Oh, God. I left Sam defenseless. If I hadn't taken *Faith*—"

I stopped her with a raised hand. "It was pure coincidence. You couldn't have known."

Tears brimmed Cora's eyes, and she wiped them away. Anger and determination washed over her. She pressed *Faith* into my hands.

"You take this for Sam. I've had it long enough."

I nodded and tucked the letter opener inside my jacket. "Any other surprises for us?" I asked, eyeing the safe.

"Just one. Here, hold these," Cora retrieved two neon green plastic pistols and shoved them into my hands. "They're my *second*-best sellers."

I examined the cheap plastic guns. They looked like

futuristic laser pistols from a low-budget movie. "I don't understand." I'd expected something ancient and powerful. A spell or artifact that would drive Nigel to his knees. Not ... toys.

Cora reached into the safe's bottom back corner. "I hate disappointing the customers who want silver bullets, so instead"—she rose and presented a quart jar full of clear liquid—"I offer them my Holy Water Squirt Guns."

I blinked. "I'm sorry. What? Did you just say, 'Holy Water Squirt Guns?'"

Cora grinned, grabbed a funnel, and slid past me out of the closet. "Patent pending. You should see my reviews. According to one customer who, in his own words, 'has seen some shit,' they actually work against the minions of Hell. Come on, let's fill those and get going!" Her voice trailed into the hallway.

I stared at the plastic pistols in my hands and felt a twinge of hope. With Cora's infectious confidence, how could I not?

Nigel thought he had everything figured out. He'd deposed Lucifer, banished me to Abaddon, and was remaking Hell in his own image. In time he'd pull all of humanity into his unstoppable army of damned souls and challenge

Heaven itself. He had the full power of Hell at his back.

But I had Cora. Hell wouldn't know what hit them.

Chapter 18

THE POWER OF COFFEE

MY PLAN FOR RETURNING to Hell was simple: travel by cat. Assuming I could convince Diana to help.

I found her in a food coma on the back of Cora's couch. Conrad was nowhere to be seen, though I heard rattling in the kitchen. I glanced toward the doorway and almost headed in that direction but stopped myself. Questioning Conrad about his potential duplicity with Abigail could wait. I needed to convince Diana to take us back to Hell first.

Crushed crackers and bits of cheese from Cora's late-night snack were scattered over the couch, coffee table, and carpet. Cora's lips pursed at the mess, but she said nothing. Instead, she went to the front closet and rummaged around.

"Diana," I said with a gentle scratch behind the cat's ears, "it's time to return to Hell."

She ignored me. I tried raising her chin with my forefinger, but she shifted away. Her eyes didn't open. I tried again and a low half-growl, half-sigh rumbled from her chest. It was definitely not a purr.

Cora returned, buttoning up a thigh-length black leather jacket that hid her pocketed vest and assorted weaponry. The heavy sleeves mostly quieted her rattling bracelets, but not entirely. I scratched the back of my neck, still trying to reconcile this fierce warrior with the charming tax auditor I knew.

"I don't think Diana's taking us anywhere," Cora said, eyeing the sleeping cat.

I scowled. "She just needs convincing, and I'm not below bribery. Do you have more sausage?"

Cora turned me to face her and zipped my puffy black jacket. After a few tugs to pull the waist down over my water pistol, she stepped back to examine her work.

"Diana won't wake up for hours," she said, looking me

up and down.

"We don't have hours! I've delayed too long already. Who knows what torments Abigail and the others are facing in my absence?"

Cora's mouth thinned, but her gaze met mine. "How do you normally travel to Hell?"

"With *Grace*, but the Auditor has my scythe. I could get us to Purgatory, but no further. Nigel has somehow violated the Rules and the Hellmouth is closed." No point even mentioning Charon's back door. Cora wouldn't survive a swim in the river Acheron.

Cora's hands fell to her hips, and her gaze drifted as she thought. "What about a denizen of Hell? Could a demon get us in?"

"Perhaps. But who would we ask? We could call an IT help desk and talk our way up to a demonic supervisor, but I doubt that would help." Not after my capture outside Alvin's office. "I'm a known enemy of Nigel."

Cora's head tilted, her brows furrowing. "IT help desks ... connect to Hell?"

"IT support is the most common modern link between Hell and the mortal realm. That's how I first connected to Abigail."

"That *does* make a horrible kind of sense. Fortunately, calling IT isn't our only option." She took my hand and pulled me toward the kitchen where Conrad's rattling about had gone suspiciously silent. Her hand was warm, her grip firm.

"How else would you contact Hell?" I asked.

"The old-fashioned way," Cora said. "We're going to summon a demon."

***

My second demon summoning was similar, yet vastly different from my first. When I'd summoned Alvin six months ago, the spell had required an intricately chalked circle of Sumerian design, the bone dust of a Sumerian priest, cinnamon, candles, and blood. After the incantation, Alvin had arrived in a firestorm of red electricity, threatening my eternal soul for daring to summon him.

In structure, the circle in Cora's kitchen was much the same, though of chalked Celtic design and overlain with blessed salt from the Irish Sea. No bone dust required. There was a six-pointed star inside the circle with heavy candles set at intersection points. A simple kitchen stool sat in the middle of it all. Cora's blessed Celtic cross lay under the stool, wrapped in its heavy chain. A steaming pot of black coffee sat atop the stool.

I eyed the spell book lying open on Cora's counter. Conrad lay sprawled beside the book, belly once again distended. The shredded remains of a loaf of bread, two empty pickle jars, a ravaged jar of peanut butter, and a half-eaten onion littered the counter around him.

I'd tried questioning him about his Lucifer-level access throughout Hell while Cora set her circle up, but Conrad had just mumbled sleepily about peanut butter and pickles being the perfect combination, food was amazing, he loved it here, blah blah blah ... snore.

Conrad smacked his lips in his sleep, and I wrinkled my nose at the dragon's breath. "Cora," I said, flipping pages in her spell book, "I don't see anything in this spell about coffee. Are you sure you know what you're doing?" I glanced toward the pot on the stool.

"Yes, I know what I'm doing." Cora lit incense sticks that smelled of apple and cinnamon. "I've summoned a demon every morning for the last two and a half years."

"You ... *what*? Why?"

"Because sometimes you have to make a deal with the

devil to get what you want," she snapped. "After Abigail died, I *had* to talk to her one last time. No, coffee isn't part of the spell, but it *is* part of the bargain I struck," she said, drawing the cursed blade from her belt sheath. She began chanting in Latin.

"Hold on," I interrupted. "*Every* morning? When I stayed up in your guest room six months ago, I think I would have noticed if you'd had a demon in your kitchen."

Cora stopped chanting and sighed. "You're a heavy sleeper. Everything was done and cleaned up before you even cracked an eyelid. Shush now."

Cora resumed her chant and pricked her finger with the cursed blade. She flicked the blood into the circle. It hit the floor, and a wall of translucent white shot up from the perimeter of blessed salt. Cora continued chanting, and the hexagon at the star's center glowed white. The heady scent of brimstone filled the kitchen.

A demon's hideous form rose without fanfare through the glowing portal. He wore the ubiquitous rumpled gray suit, was about Cora's height, and had his arms crossed. I blinked in surprise when I recognized his prune-like face and oversized tusks.

Brutus Bureaucracy, Alvin's cranky receptionist.

"You're early," he said in that gravelly voice. "But considering the day I've had…" Brutus swept up the coffee in a meaty fist, flipped the lid open with a clawed thumb, and half-drained the pot in a single draught. A shiver of pure delight wracked the demon. He moaned, "Hell's bells, I needed that!"

Brutus hooked his hip onto the stool and sat, coffee pot cradled in his hands like an oversized mug. He eyed Cora for a long moment as though gathering his thoughts before his gaze finally found mine. The eyes are the windows to the soul, and he read me like a book. The demon froze.

"Grim? How…?" He shook his head and started again. "Nigel just announced your banishment to Abaddon."

I smiled what I hoped was an enigmatic smile and hooked my hair behind an ear. It flopped forward again. "I have powers that Nigel can't begin to comprehend." Namely, a fluffy white cat with a penchant for cross-realm travel. "Escaping Abaddon was a snap." I snapped my fingers for punctuation.

Brutus's wrinkled face curled inward as his lips pursed. His red-eyed gaze flicked between Cora and me from under heavy brows. "And now you've summoned me. Why?"

"Hell is still closed to visitors," I said. "I need your

help—"

"*We* need your help," Cora interrupted. "Can you get us in?"

Brutus snorted. "Yeah, I can get you in, that's easy. But again ... why? Why should I help Nigel's enemies infiltrate Hell?"

I crossed my arms, doing my best to exude supreme confidence. "I'm going to stop him. With your help, we'll return Hell to its former glory."

"Yeah, right," Brutus growled. "Even if you managed to dethrone Nigel—which isn't likely—who would take his place? You?"

"No. Lucifer is the rightful Lord of Darkness. Hell's throne is his, not mine."

"But the Dragon is dead." Brutus raised the coffee pot as if in salute to the fallen and then took another swig.

"Lucifer lives, and I can prove it." I grabbed Conrad from the counter and thrust the dragon toward Brutus. Conrad protested weakly, but he was too engorged to put up much of a fight. "Conrad is Lucifer's nightmare."

Brutus nearly choked. "Lucifer's ... *what?*"

"See for yourself." I lifted Conrad's chin with a finger so Brutus could read his soul through the dragon's drooping eyelids. Surprise lit the demon's red eyes.

I smiled. "Lucifer is imprisoned somewhere in Hell's lower levels," I said. "Get us into Hell, and we will free Lucifer and put an end to Nigel's madness." Conrad wriggled in my grip, so I cradled him in my arms. He stopped struggling and snuggled in for a nap.

Brutus's eyes narrowed until I could barely see them under his wrinkles. His claw tapped the nearly empty coffee pot. "The Bureaucracy family has no love for Nigel. Alvin's making deals to cling to power, but our days are numbered. Hell's Bureaucracy has no place in Nigel's New Order." He grunted again then asked, "What payment do you offer for passage?"

"Payment? I'm trying to save Hell—to save *your* job—and you're quibbling about a transit fee?"

He just grinned. Damned bureaucrat.

I glowered. "You're not getting my soul."

"Don't want it." Brutus took a deliberate sip of his coffee and glanced at Cora over the rim. "You know what I want."

Cora rolled her eyes. "You're as subtle as a freight train, Brutus. I'm not extending my bargain with you. I still owe you six months of morning coffee from our last deal." An expression that looked surprisingly like a pout crossed the demon's face. "But I have something better," Cora said.

"Oh?" Brutus perked up, pout vanishing.

Cora smiled. "Keeping you in coffee is expensive, so I've been buying in bulk. For our passage to Hell, I'll provide one year's supply of coffee as our transit fee."

Brutus's claws drummed on the pot. "But coffee's not allowed in Hell."

I chimed in, "That's not in the Rules."

"No," Brutus said, "but it's been a standing policy for centuries. Ever since humanity got addicted to the stuff. Nothing that might alleviate a soul's torments is allowed. No chocolate, no candy, no coffee."

"But what about cats?" I asked with a surge of pique, "Cats bring joy wherever they go, and you haven't banned *them*." Heavens, more sarcasm. I really needed to work on that.

Brutus gave me a look. "Nobody controls cats. You know that. Banning them would be like banning phoenixes from Heaven. Simply can't be done."

"Seems to me," Cora said slowly, "that thumbing your nose at such a stupid rule would be a properly demonic thing to do."

"True..." Brutus looked thoughtful. "But I'd need a coffee maker."

"Drip or French press?"

"French press. Biggest one you can find."

"Done," Cora said, smiling broadly. "You can take delivery on our last scheduled summoning in six months."

A chuckle rumbled from Brutus's chest. "Agreed. But transit only. I can't be seen siding with the Grim Reaper. The Department of Bureaucratic Torments is on thin ice as it is with Nigel's New Order."

A slow smile lifted my cheeks. We'd done it. And for a smaller price than I'd expected.

Brutus glanced between us. "Well, come on. Torments await."

HELL'S ELEVATOR

OUR DESCENT INTO HELL was not quite what I anticipated. I expected to transition instantly from Cora's kitchen to Brutus's office. Instead, an actual elevator wrapped itself around us when we passed through Cora's floor. It had faux-wood paneled walls, scuffed linoleum, and reflective steel doors.

And Musak. Tinny piano played off-key just above audibility. I sighed with annoyance as soft strings joined the chorus. I didn't recognize the song, but at least it was something different. I was, for once, not being rickrolled. After a few moments, Cora began humming along.

She abruptly glanced toward the ceiling. "Is that 'The Sound of Silence?'"

"I wish it was silence," I said.

Brutus shrugged. "I like Musak. Calms the nerves before a summoning. Especially that one tune. What's it called? Something about never giving you up?"

I shook my head. No accounting for taste. That song would be stuck in my head for hours!

We'd left Diana behind. She deserved her rest after saving me from Abaddon. In my arms, Conrad's engorged belly deflated until he returned to normal Conrad size. We'd departed the mortal realm, so he was returning to his proper spiritual form. He licked his chops and crawled up to sit on my shoulder. The little dragon rubbed his empty belly and sighed a very depressed sigh. His breath still smelled of onion. I turned to Cora. My breath caught at the indefinable yet unmistakable solidity of her.

Right, she was a mortal in a spiritual realm. Like the cats we'd seen backstage, she was more solid, more real than the spiritual constructs around her. There would be no hiding Cora's mortality.

"So," I said, asking Cora a question that had been nagging me, "did Frank ever know about you summoning demons?"

"Heavens, no!"

"Why not? He too wanted to summon a demon." To ask it for a soul-swapping spell to cheat Death. "Seems a natural point of conversation."

Cora's lips pursed. "Dating is hard in middle age. Sure, Frank and I met through Cordelia's Apothecary Supply, and I was happy to talk shop, but"—she bit her lip—"daily conversations with a demon isn't exactly something you bring up on a first date. I didn't want to scare him off."

"I see," I said, though I wasn't entirely sure I did. I had no experience with dating. Only one love had ever captured my heart. Evelyn. I still yearned for her, despite our millennia of separation. What was she doing now? Menial busywork in Heaven, I supposed. Punishment for failing as a guardian angel. Elizabeth had escaped on that fateful night at the Davidsons, but—

A realization rolled over me. Elizabeth. I hadn't checked on Evelyn's charge in over a month. Fool. The girl was important enough to Heaven that they assigned Evelyn as her guardian angel, but they *still* hadn't sent Liz a replacement the last time I checked. Had Hell learned of Liz's importance yet? I'd intended to keep a steadier eye on the girl but, with one thing and another, I'd only popped in to see her twice since Evelyn got banished to Heaven.

My lips pursed. I silently swore to check on Liz once this crisis was over. Once everything was back to rights in Hell.

Assuming I saved Lucifer, which was a big assumption.

"Brutus," I asked. "Where in Hell will we arrive?"

"IT, Level Two," he said.

"Hmmm..." I supposed made sense. "We need to reach the Pit on Level Four."

Brutus nodded. "Easy enough. IT is always busy. You should be able to slip out unnoticed."

Fast breathing from Cora caught my ear. I glanced over. Her face was pale, and her pupils were dilated.

"Are you okay?" I asked.

She nodded, paused, then shook her head. "Not really. It just hit me. I'm going to *Hell*. By choice."

Brutus growled. "You can't go back now. We struck a deal."

"I know," Cora snapped then drew a shuddering breath. "And I'm not backing out. My Abigail is trapped in Hell, and I'm not leaving without her." Her cheeks flushed, and Cora glanced up at me. "I'll be fine."

The elevator stopped. The door slid open with a cheerful *ding*. A smoked glass door blocked our way, and Brutus said, "Welcome to Information Technology, the hub of Hell's Bureaucracy." He pushed the glass door open.

It stopped partway, bumping into a large sleeping black tomcat. He leapt up with a hiss and glared sleepily at Brutus, who inhaled sharply. I blinked in surprise. That was the same battle-scarred tom who'd jumped onto Teri the minotaur's shoulders when we were backstage.

With a flick of its tail, the cat turned and strolled into IT like he owned the place. Brutus sighed in relief and pushed the smoked door the rest of the way open.

Unlike the cavernous cubicle farm of Customer Annoyance, IT was a brightly lit mix of server farm and open-plan office. Though most mortal offices didn't feature broad flagstone floors, a throwback to Hell's bad old days, I'm sure.

IT spread as far as the eye could see. Desk clusters sat between massive server stacks which pierced the low drop ceiling. Each server stack featured a glass door like the one Brutus held open. Signs above the doors indicated the elevator's destination. The one nearest us said, IRS BUILDING, COLORADO SPRINGS.

Demons and nightmare messengers scurried through

IT like it was Grand Central Station. And, I suppose, for them it was. Yet, despite the frantic activity, the demons were careful to step around the cats napping on the floor.

Cats lay *everywhere,* little puddles of fur practically pulsing with life. The black tomcat stalking away from us was given a wide berth. Fear shone in the demonic faces rushing past. What had happened in my brief absence? Had Nigel committed some further atrocity, or was this residual fear from the coup?

Good heavens, had he done something to my friends in the Pit?

A cluster of eight desks sat before us, only half-filled with damned souls murmuring into their headsets. Three were focused on their screens while the fourth thumbed a heavy tome that was thicker than a first-edition Bible. Black computer towers sat between each monitor, two of them with slumbering cats pooled on top.

"Finally, more souls!" a sharp female voice said as we stepped from the elevator. "And you brought me a live one! Good."

Conrad squeaked in my ear, a scared sound that made me jerk away. He scrambled down my back, claws gouging into my skin, before disappearing into the crowd with a scrabble of claws on flagstone. Where was he going? I didn't want to call after him, to draw attention, so I turned toward the voice.

A short, mousy-looking demon with a ruddy complexion stormed toward us. She wore the ubiquitous rumpled gray suit and, oddly, only had a small left horn poking out of her shoulder-length brown hair. The right horn was broken off at her hairline. Severely straight bangs framed a face that looked like it hadn't smiled in centuries.

"Sorry, Linda," Brutus began, "but these two aren't—"

Linda waved a dismissive clawed hand. "Don't care, Brutus. They're here, they're mine. Those idiots in Customer Annoyance suck up all the new arrivals while IT is eternally understaffed. Information Technology is our fastest-growing industry! But who gets all the souls? *Customer Annoyance.*"

"Take it up with HR," Brutus said firmly. He tried to steer us away from Linda, but she grabbed Cora's arm. Claws pressed into Cora's bicep, and she gasped.

"Hell's Resources can kiss my bright red ass," Linda said. She whirled away, dragging Cora toward the nearest desk cluster. "Keep up, stretch," she yelled at me over her shoulder, "or find yourself on my bad side."

This was Linda's good side? I opened my mouth to protest, but the words died unspoken. We were infiltrating Hell. It wasn't like I could demand she release us on my authority as the Reaper. I glanced at Brutus. His lips pursed, and then he shook his head.

"Transit only," he muttered then nodded to the right. "Internal elevators are that way. Good luck." Brutus lumbered away. In seconds, he was gone behind the server stacks.

I stared after him. Good luck? That's it? Brutus delivered us into captivity and then had the gall to say *good luck?*

"Hey!" Linda snapped, stealing my attention. Cora was slumped in a swivel chair before a computer screen, her arm still clutched in Linda's claws. The demon pointed at the chair next to her and arched an imperious eyebrow. Lacking any brilliant ideas for escape, I cast my eyes downward so she couldn't read my soul. Long black hair fell across my face, and I slouched toward the desks trying to mimic Cora's defeated posture.

It wasn't hard.

"Sit." Linda shoved me into the chair. She was surprisingly strong for such a small thing. I sat. Our cluster-mates didn't even glance at us. They just slumped deeper into their chairs as though hiding from enemy fire behind their computer monitor's defilade.

Linda gestured to our blank screens. "Answer calls after the fifteenth ring, not before. Be courteous no matter what. Hell gives service with a smile."

My teeth ground. We didn't have time for this. Besides, I knew less than nothing about computers. People used them to store and search for information, but the hows and whys were beyond me. I raised my hand. "Look, Linda, I think there's been a misunderstanding. Cora and I are not computer techs—"

Linda slapped the back of my head. "Don't interrupt."

My head rocked forward, and my jaw dropped. I'd never been so casually disrespected in my life. Righteous anger burned inside me. My vision went red.

How dare she? I would tear her apart!

No, I wouldn't tear her apart. I would do much worse. Cora had gifted me powerful arcane weapons. I had the blessed letter opener *Faith* and a pistol full of holy water nestled under my jacket. Linda would *rue* the day—

Cora's warm hand on my wrist pulled me back from impassioned calamity. I glanced over, jaw clenched. Cora was still slumped as though defeated and broken, but her eyes burned with purpose. She shook her head ever so slightly.

Right. Calm down, Grim. I drew a deep breath. Don't blow your cover in the first five minutes. I kept my eyes on the keyboard, and Linda droned on as though I'd never interrupted.

"Once you've answered, follow the generative text cues on your screen. IT's goal is confusion and obfuscation, but occasionally the system spits out gibberish. If that happens, you'll find the correct responses in here." She tapped the heavy hardbound volume sitting between our keyboards. "Now, headsets on. Welcome to Hell." Linda stepped back and crossed her arms.

Cora and I shared a glance. We were trapped so long as Linda hovered over us. We couldn't afford to cause a scene. My shoulders hunched against the weight of her regard.

I slipped the headset on. Cora did the same, a couple of loose bracelets clinking sadly. I glanced at the tome between us. It was old and battered. Inscribed on the cloth binding was a title that wrapped up our entire problem with a pretty little bow.

The Unhelpful Helpdesk: Hell's Guide to Service with a Smile.

Chapter 20

THE UNHELPFUL HELPDESK

A POWERFUL RINGING IN my ears nearly jolted me out of my chair. It was like Notre Dame's bells had taken up residence inside my skull. I glanced around, but my desk-mates were unmoved. Linda's reflection in my screen loomed over my shoulder, arms crossed like a disapproving teacher. Cora was surreptitiously scanning our surroundings, looking for an escape. As I should be.

Ring. Ring.

I jumped again, then pursed my lips at my own stupidity. It was coming from my headset. I glared at my computer screen. It was black except for a pulsing lime-green button that said, answer call.

Ring. Ring.

I reached toward the screen.

Wait, Linda said fifteen rings. How many was that? Seven? Ten? I could barely count through the literal ringing in my ears that seemed to echo in the silence in between. My finger hovered above the button.

Ring. Ring.

Was that fifteen or fourteen? Close enough. I tapped the screen.

Nothing happened.

I tapped harder.

Ring. Ring.

My teeth ground. I wondered how this infernal computer would react to a muzzle load of holy water.

Again, Cora saved me from impassioned calamity. She reached across me and grabbed a small device to the right of my keyboard.

"Move the mouse, follow the curser, click the left button," she said, then twitched. A matching pulsing green button appeared on her screen as well. She returned to her desk space and rested a hand on her mouse. Her lips moved as she counted rings.

Ring. Ring.

I wiggled my mouse, my whole body tensing. What cursor? I didn't see—ah ha! I moved the little arrow to the pulsing button and clicked.

A line of white text appeared on my black screen. I read it aloud.

"You've reached Bridewell Incorporated Tech Support. My name is—" A blank line of text greeted me, and I stopped. I couldn't admit to being the Grim Reaper. Linda was watching us. Listening and looming. So how could I...

Wait, Nigel had burned Hell's Rulebook. I'd nearly forgotten!

I could lie. Be anybody I wanted to be.

Faced with sudden opportunity, my brain ricocheted across history, searching for the perfect nom de plume. A million possibilities crowded my mind. It seized up. Panic slammed into the logjam, kicking and screaming before breaking through. A flood of names spilled forth. Victor Hugo. Vincent Van Gogh. Vasco de Gama.

Why was I stuck on V?

I must have paused too long. Linda's palm smacked the back of my head again. I rocked forward and blurted out, "Vasco! My name is Vasco de Gama!"

"Hello?" a timorous woman's voice said. "Is anybody there?"

"Yes. This is Vasco de Gama of Bridewell Incorporated Tech Support."

The voice dimmed as though the receiver had been pulled away. "I hate these stupid machines. I can never understand them." A long and loud *beeeeeeep* filled my ear.

"Gak!" I yelled, bouncing in my seat like a man electrified.

The prolonged beep ended, and the old woman came back on. "Hello? Operator? There's supposed to be an operator when I push zero. Anybody there?"

"Yes! Hello," I yelled into my headset. "Can you hear me?"

The caller muttered a few choice words about stupid machines and then silence filled my ears. Lines of script disappeared from my screen. I hadn't noticed them appear.

Linda slapped the back of my head again.

A growl rumbled deep in my chest. If she touched me one more time...

"I've seen worse on a first call," Linda said. "Barely. This time, stay on script."

Ringing once again filled my ears. The pulsing green button reappeared.

We didn't have time for this! We needed to reach the Pit and get on with rescuing Lucifer. But we couldn't do anything with Linda looming over us.

I glanced at Cora. She was reading her script with a smile in her voice. If it weren't for the white-knuckled grip on her headset cord, I might have thought she was enjoying herself. Her other hand was caressing the bulge of that cursed dagger under her leather jacket.

"No, I can't see what you're seeing," Cora said, rolling her eyes. "Describe it." There was a pause. "Wait, back up. Is your computer on?" Pause. "No, not 'is it on your desk.' Does it have *power*?"

I noticed Linda's scowling reflection nodding in approval. My fingers drummed on the desk. Hopefully, she'd go away if we proved ourselves competent.

I counted to fifteen rings and clicked the button on my screen. "You've reached Bridewell Incorporated Tech Support. My name is Victor Hugo," I said, rushing through my speech. More generative text appeared. "What can I help you with today?"

"My system access never went through," a man said.

Text appeared. "To request access, please complete a Form-5 online and hand deliver it to our office." Wait, wasn't that the same form I filled out in Purgatory?

"I can't *get* online. That's why I need system access."

My script didn't change, so I read it again. "To request access, please complete a—"

"Look, *Victor*," he growled, "you guys are in the basement, right?"

No, we were far *far* below Bridewell's basement. A single word appeared on my screen, and my shoulders sagged. "Yes."

Something nudged my leg. Conrad, I hoped. I ignored him.

"Me too," my caller said. "Figured I'd fill out the form in person. So how 'bout you open the door I've been banging on for five minutes?" Several dull thuds echoed through the headset. The presence at my ankles pushed hard against my leg. I glanced down. Haggard yellow eyes gazed up at me. It was that black tomcat.

A new line of script appeared. "We cannot process manual forms at this time."

"Wait, you just said—"

I continued reading. "The supervisor in charge of manual system processing is out of the office for the remainder of the week. However, our online process is simple and easy to—"

"I can't get online!"

"—access. Just fill out the Form-5, print it, and deliver it to Tech Support during normal office hours." Seriously? No wonder people hated calling tech support. But I didn't dare deviate from my script with Linda right behind me.

"'Normal office hours?' What do you call nine o'clock in the morning? A coffee break?"

The cat at my feet launched himself onto the desk. He danced across my keyboard, tail up.

"Gak!" I said. I did not need to see a cat's butt right now! I tried and failed to shove him aside. He nipped my hand but started purring.

His butt swayed right in front of my face. I craned my head past him.

A line of gibberish flowed across my screen.

"I, uh … One moment, please." I forced a smile into my

voice.

More gibberish appeared.

Linda leaned past me and tapped a series of four letters at the front of the sequence. "Look this code up"—she flipped open *The Unhelpful Helpdesk*—"in here."

I scanned tightly packed text on the page. My eyes swam before I figured out the indexing pattern and started flipping pages.

In the long silence, my caller asked, "You still there?"

"Yes, I'm here. Just looking up—"

The cat flopped onto the book, pinning my hand. Those haggard golden eyes stared up at me, demanding obeisance. His purrs vibrated my entire arm.

I pride myself on my eloquence, but in that moment my mind blanked.

"...uh..."

What was I supposed to do?

The cat purred. Linda loomed. My caller swore.

"This is ridiculous!" he said. "I want to talk to your supervisor."

That popped up another set of generated gibberish with a different index code. I grabbed the cat with both hands and dropped him into my lap. He struggled, claws gouging my legs, and tried to climb back onto the desk. I held him down with one hand and frantically flipped pages with the other.

Where was that code? I improvised, "As previously stated, my supervisor is not available. If you'd like to speak with them, call again next week."

Flip, flip.

Ah ha! I squinted at the page. "(Corporation Name) is sorry for—"

"'Corporation name?' I knew it! You aren't in Bridewell's basement at all, are you? This is some scammy call center."

I cleared my throat, flinched in anticipation of Linda's slap, and re-read my line in a rush, "Bridewell Incorporated is sorry for your inconvenience. If you'd like to file a formal complaint, please visit our website at—"

"I! Can't! Get! Online!" my caller screamed before the call abruptly went dead.

I drew a shuddering breath and glanced back at Linda. She hadn't slapped me. Instead, she nodded. "Confusion and obfuscation delivered with courtesy. That'll do. But smile more next time. Like your friend here." She nodded toward Cora.

Cora wore a broad smile that didn't touch her eyes. "I don't care if you're a master gunnery sergeant in the Marines who's three sheets to the wind. Bridewell Incorporated has a clear no-swearing policy." She paused, her smile still fixed as she read her screen. "Uh, huh." Pause. "Try using guacamole."

Guacamole? To fix a computer? I glanced at her screen, but it said nothing about condiments.

"Yes, guacamole. So, your guacamole computer guacamoled the bed and won't guac-ing turn on. Right?"

Pause. Sigh.

"Is it plugged in?" Pause. "You meant the *guacamole* cord? Uh, huh. Yes. Now push the power button. The circle broken by a little line." Cora's smile turned genuine. "Thank you for choosing Bridewell Incorporated. May you also have a wonderful guac-ing day." The call ended, and Cora's screen went dark.

Linda absolutely beamed at her. "Oh, I'm keeping you. You're positively wicked!" To me, Linda said, "Now reboot your system to fix the gibberish text and keep answering calls. We have a quota to maintain."

Someone shrieked from the cubicle cluster to our left. Thick black smoke roiled from one of the computer towers.

Linda stomped over, voice rising with every word. "What in Lucifer's name did ... you ... *do*?" Silence spread like a virus through IT as all heads turned toward the focus of Linda's wrath.

Something new bumped my leg. Now what? I'd finally gotten the first cat settled into a purring lump on my lap.

Whatever it was must have bumped Cora too. She flinched and leaned back to look under her desk. Tension drained from her shoulders. "Thank God!"

"God had nothing to do with it!" Conrad protested, his head popping up between us. "That fire was all me."

While I appreciated Cora's gratitude, it was misplaced. One of Hell's fundamental aspects was permanent separation from the Almighty. He wasn't rescuing anybody from Hell's depths, especially not me. We were on our own.

I was used to that.

The dragon's silver eyes turned my way. "So, Bones, ya want to blow this joint?"

"Sky high," I said. An eternity of customer service was cruel punishment indeed. Only five minutes in that chair made me itch down to my bones.

Cora and I slid from our chairs. I tried to dump the cat,

but he dug his claws in. His purrs vibrated through me. I swear he gained ten pounds.

Conrad bounded away across the flagstone floor. Cora and I ran after him, watched by our desk mates from behind their computer monitor defilade. Linda's tirade reverberated through IT as we fled.

Chapter 21

SECRET AGENT GRIM

CONRAD SLOWED TWO AISLES away into a fast trot. He turned left and slid into the flow of demonic and nightmare foot traffic. Cora and I scrambled to keep up. The black tomcat in my arms shifted. He half-climbed up my chest to my left shoulder where he lay with his hips still in my arms. His rumbling purrs in my ear drowned out everything else. A back foot slipped under my elbow and landed on my holstered water pistol. He pushed off it and squirmed back into a comfortable position.

I'd taken three steps before I realized that my left hip was now warm and wet. My gaze snapped to the cat. Did he just … no, wait. That was the holy water.

"Cora," I hissed. "*Cora*! My squirt gun is leaking."

She grimaced, throwing me an abashed look as she jogged after Conrad. "Sorry. They do that sometimes."

Great.

The busy aisleway was broad and low. We passed server towers every dozen yards, each with a destination sign above the smoked glass door. Chicago, Shanghai, Dubai. All leading upward into corporate buildings around the world, not downward as we needed.

Conrad wove through the foot traffic like a water moccasin stalking its prey. I was surprised and grateful that he'd taken the lead. I had no clue where we were going.

Cora and I tried to blend in, but we were the only non-demons walking through IT. And I had a cat on my shoulder. I tried putting him down again, but when I shifted, his claws dug in. A warning growl mingled with his purrs.

One does not anger a cat in Hell. I resumed petting him.

Passing demons glanced at us with furrowed brows, hostile but unwilling to interrupt their urgent errands to stop us. That wouldn't last. Someone would eventually stop the two out-of-place spirits wandering Hell's halls.

Well, one spirit. Like the cat on my shoulder, Cora's physical presence was obvious to anybody remotely paying attention. We needed a reason to be here. We needed the appearance of authority.

Fortunately, appearances are fickle things in Hell.

I concentrated my willpower to change my face, to add red eyes and small horns poking through my black hair.

Darkness edged my vision, and the world abruptly turned wobbly. Nothing changed. I stumbled and strained, pushing my willpower to make even the smallest change to my appearance. A pinprick of red in my eyes.

The darkness closed in, narrowing my vision almost to black. Bone-deep weariness crawled into my brain, bringing with it an urge to lay down right there in the busy aisle and stare vacantly up at the drop ceiling. I'd pushed too hard in the last several hours.

I released my willpower with a gasp and focused on walking a straight line beside Cora. I would have dropped the cat, but he had a death grip on my shoulder. For now, I was stuck in my current form as the doppelganger of Cora's ex-husband. I glanced at her, but she was too focused on keeping up with Conrad to notice me.

"Conrad," Cora hissed. "Slow down!" He did not slow

down. He turned right into another aisle and was lost from view among the cross-traffic.

We turned to follow him, but he didn't reappear. Cora broke into a brief sprint, her jewelry clattering as she ran. "Conrad?" There were demons aplenty, but no little blue dragon. She slowed to a stop. I joined her within a few steps and the flow of demons parted around us like an infernal river around rocks. Cora swore. "Now what?"

I looked around, craning my neck. The cat shifted and settled, purrs turning sleepy. Sleep sounded nice. I kept my voice low, trying to focus my thoughts. "I ... don't know. But once we find the elevators, we can't operate them without that bloody dragon."

"Why?"

"It's a security thing. Only designated spirits can traverse Hell's levels at will. Spirits like Conrad. Without him, we're stuck. We don't have time—" I cut off as the solution to our problem stepped into the aisle from a server-stack elevator to our right.

The voluptuous Kurai stormed into the aisle, her bat wings and spiky hair practically quivering with rage. I glanced at the server. Okinawa, Japan.

Odd that *Grace* had sent her there when it parsed her

soul. Not that it mattered. She was going to help us, whether she wanted to or not.

I once reaped a British spy's soul in Moscow back in the 1960s. He'd failed to infiltrate the Kremlin, thus prompting Death's presence to witness the attempt. The spy had been disappointed to meet me, but he had died with style. Which gave me an idea. An idea that I never would have tried were I not past the brink of exhaustion.

Secret Agent Grim, reporting for duty.

"Cora," I whispered. "Take the cat." I tried passing the tom to her, but his claws again dug into me. His growl this time was chest-deep and pointed.

Physical cats are much more powerful than spirits, a lesson I'd learned when Frank's cat Diana attacked the Auditor last year and dragged him back to Hell. I wasn't budging that tomcat unless he wanted to budge.

With my free hand, I reached under my jacket—and the cat—and drew *Faith*, Sam's blessed letter opener. I lengthened my stride.

Kurai turned away from us, but I caught her within a few steps. I wrapped a companionable arm around her narrow waist and slipped the dagger under her wings. The gray silk of her kimono-like suit jacket felt smooth as I pressed the blade against her back.

She froze. Her gaze snapped to mine. She smelled of blood, magic, and rage.

"Keep walking," I whispered, wiggling *Faith*. "That's a blessed blade you feel."

Kurai's red eyes widened when she recognized my soul. Her hands twitched toward the daggers at her belt, but Kurai wasn't a fool. She resumed her stride without grabbing them. "What do you want, Grim?" The words were faint and breathy.

"You're going to escort us to Level Four."

An angry retort formed on her lips. I applied more pressure with *Faith*, and the retort died unspoken. The muscles in Kurai's jaw worked before the fight drained out of her. We walked in lockstep for several strides before she nodded to her right. "This way."

We turned down yet another cross aisle that looked exactly like every other one, though with even denser traffic. Cora trailed behind us, boots loud on the flagstone floor. Her jewelry clattered until she tucked her bracelets under her sleeves. We walked in relative silence for several minutes. It was awkward; I'd never walked with my arm around someone, let alone with a knife at their back and with a cat on my shoulder, but I fell into the rhythm of Kurai's swaying hips and seething anger.

"So," I said, keeping my voice low but cheerful, "*Grace* parsed your soul and sent it to Japan. Why?"

Kurai eyed me sideways without quite turning her head. "I was once a minor Japanese goddess of war and fertility before their first emperor clawed his way to power."

My eyebrows rose. That *was* a long time ago. "An unusual combination of godly skills." I wracked my brain but couldn't remember having heard of such a goddess. Which was odd, as I thought I'd known them all. Perhaps the tiredness was affecting my memory. It pays to keep track of the spirits that humans worship. Otherwise, our post-death conversations can get ... awkward.

She shrugged. "It worked for me." A deeper scowl clouded her expression. "But the tribe I ruled was wiped out. I've been forgotten, my temple razed millennia ago. It's now an outdoor shopping mall." Kurai snorted. "Imagine the humans' surprise when I appeared in my full glory behind a rack of cheap scarves."

"You seem to have found your way back."

"No thanks to your scythe. I couldn't just return. Apparently, once *Grace* parses a soul, it remains parsed. Every time I tried to descend into Hell, I popped right back to that damned scarf rack!"

I chuckled.

"It's not funny! I was attacked by a ghost with a cursed scimitar!"

"Really?" I cocked an eyebrow. "Was his name Garrick?"

Kurai's glare turned murderous. "Friend of yours?"

"Our paths have crossed." So, Garrick was in Asia now. Interesting. I really did need to wrangle his soul into Purgatory. Eventually.

"That redneck Viking made my life hell until I escaped through a local branch of Bridewell Incorporated."

"Good for him," I said.

"And now this…" Kurai's anger resolved into a pout. She wasn't having a good day, but I didn't have it in me to feel sorry for her. If the tables were turned, she would gleefully have sent Cora and me back to the Pit.

"So," I said, eyeing Kurai sideways, "you were once a goddess. When did you become a demon?"

"I joined Hell's forces after the Shinto spirits cast me out. Lucifer accepted me, reveling in my faults instead of judging, so I swore myself to him." She jutted her jaw toward a rough-hewn stone wall that appeared through the crowd up ahead. "We're here."

The IT department opened up into a moderately sized cavern that ended in a bank of a dozen elevators. Doors chimed cheerfully open and closed as demons went wherever demons went in a hurry.

I scanned the crowd. Where the *hell* had Conrad disappeared to?

We joined the shortest queue. Kurai tensed. Her eyes flicked over the surrounding throng.

"Don't even think about it," I whispered in her ear, channeling my inner Secret Agent. It felt oddly intimate holding her so close, but I wiggled *Faith* against her back as a reminder. Kurai's jaw muscles went into clenching overdrive, but she remained silent. The queue ended and the three of us stepped into an elevator, Cora moving to my left into the corner.

Something slammed into my back. Claws dug into my spine and Conrad's cheerful voice sounded in my ear. "Heya, Bones!"

I pitched forward with a surprised yell. Kurai spun from my grasp and the tomcat and I bounced off the rear of the elevator.

The tomcat scrambled over my shoulder with a shrieking battle cry. He launched himself at Conrad, who looked briefly surprised before they both slammed into the bank of buttons beside the elevator door.

The door chimed shut. Musak greeted us, and chaos ensued.

HOLY WATER IN HELL

No plan survives first contact with a dragon. I'd felt rather proud of my impromptu secret agent plan of forcing Kurai to take us to the Pit. It was clever and daring and simple.

What I hadn't counted on was Conrad's cheerfully horrible timing. As I regained my balance, he and the tomcat rolled on the floor in a snapping snarling ball of fur and scales.

Never trap yourself in an elevator with a dragon, a cat, and a demon. Blood *will* be spilled.

They bounced off the wall to my left and knocked Cora

to one knee. On my right, Kurai drew her daggers.

A blade flashed toward my face.

I lunged back. Kurai's dagger hit the wall with a *thunk* where my head had just been. I stumbled into Cora, stepped on somebody's tail, and got bitten in the ankle. Off balance, I collapsed below the elevator's bank of buttons amid the draconic and feline roil of claws and teeth.

Cora drew her cursed dagger and lunged at Kurai. The demon blocked Cora's blade and countered with her second dagger, striking like a viper. The blade missed Cora's throat more from luck than skill as she tripped over my ankles and fell against the back wall. Her leather jacket flared open, and after a moment of panicked fumbling, Cora drew her Holy Water Squirt Gun (patent pending).

The demon twitched aside as Cora pulled the plastic trigger.

A thin stream of water struck the elevator's back wall. White smoke billowed and the wall bubbled like acid. Kurai swore and threw herself at the elevator door. She slammed into it and froze, wide eyes laser-focused on Cora's pistol, which had tracked her across the tiny room. The back wall bubbled and melted.

"Holy water," Cora said to Kurai between rapid breaths.

"Drop your daggers."

They clattered to the floor. Kurai gasped and said, "What kind of fool brings *holy water* into Hell?"

"The desperate kind." The water's acid burn against the infernal elevator spread along the wall, eating it away to reveal ... nothing. Empty blackness. We weren't in a shaft. We weren't anywhere. Hell's elevators were merely constructs of willpower allowing the mind to grasp the oddity of travel within spiritual realms.

What would happen if we fell through that expanding hole?

I blinked up from where I'd fallen to the floor. Despite her explosion of violence, I could tell that Cora wasn't trained in the martial arts like her daughter. The water pistol trembled in her hand. Her eyes were dilated, and her breathing rapid. Holy water dripped from the muzzle as her finger tensed over the trigger, sizzling where it hit the floor beside me.

No, Cora wasn't as skilled as Abigail, but she had the same fire. One did not mess with the ladies of the Knowles family.

Ripping snarls pulled all our gazes to Conrad and the cat, who'd rolled into the back corner that Kurai had just vacated. Conrad was on top for the moment, jaws snapping at the tomcat's throat. "Conrad! Enough!" Cora yelled.

The dragon paused. The tomcat scrambled out from under him and hid behind Kurai's ankles. When Conrad didn't attack again, the cat stalked around in front of the demon and sat, his tail curled around his paws. He looked inordinately pleased with himself; as if Cora's reprimand was proof that Conrad had lost the fight. Conrad hissed at the cat, then leapt onto Cora's shoulder.

Musak filled the tense silence. This time a different tune that I recognized. "Secret Agent Man." That spy I'd reaped in the 1960s had been humming it when he died. He'd called it the theme music for his life. And his death, apparently.

I snorted and pushed to my feet. Unlike that agent, I *would* live to see tomorrow.

Kurai ignored me. Her gaze swept over Cora, examining her like a scientist might examine a particularly dangerous insect. "You know that you're never leaving Hell, right? This is a one-way trip."

Cora's jaw clenched. "I'll find my way back. Once I've rescued my Abigail."

Kurai glanced at me. "*That's* why we're headed to the Pit? You want to steal souls owned by Hell? It won't work. No soul has *ever* escaped Hell's clutches."

"There's a first time for everything," I said. A lesson I'd learned the hard way when Frank cheated Death and briefly became the Grim Reaper. "Besides, escape is not our priority," I said with an apologetic glance at Cora. "Rescuing Lucifer is."

Kurai's well-sculpted eyebrows pinched downward. "But Nigel killed the Devil."

It was the same conversation we'd had with Brutus. We had to be nearing our destination, so I short-circuited the conversation. "Nigel lied. Lucifer lives. The 'Devil' Nigel murdered was Beelzebub in disguise. I'm sure the Lord of the Flies willingly joined Nigel's rebels, but somehow, I doubt he'd signed up for the last part where he lost his head."

Kurai straightened, her confused expression lightening into something resembling hope, though banked rage still burned behind her red eyes. "Lucifer lives? Where is he? And why doesn't anybody else know?"

I sighed. So much for short-circuiting the explanation. I addressed the most pertinent question and ignored the others. "We don't know exactly where he is, just that he's in one of Hell's lower levels. Despite Nigel's showy execution, he didn't dare actually kill the Devil because Lucifer's will is what holds Hell together."

Kurai snorted. "And, somehow, you're the only one who made that connection?"

I shrugged. "Everyone's too wrapped up in surviving the coup and jockeying for position in Nigel's New Order."

Cora added, "It's the same everywhere with new management. No matter how much chaos accompanies the takeover, nobody questions the new boss. That's career suicide, a statement that could be literal under Nigel's New Order."

Kurai's calculating gaze flicked between Cora and I. Tension seeped into her shoulders, and I worried that she was about to do something rash. I was grateful that Cora still had her Holy Water Squirt Gun (patent pending) trained on the demon.

"So, what now?" Kurai asked.

"Once we reach the Pit," I said, "you're free to scurry back to Nigel with news of my diabolical plot to free his father. Or you can run and hide until all this is over. I don't care. But until then, I'm done explaining."

Kurai's head cocked back. "You'll ... release me?" Her wings shifted uneasily.

I sighed. "I'm not like you. Yes, if you try something violent, Cora will melt you where you stand, or I'll banish you with *Faith*"—I brandished the blessed letter opener I still held—"but only if necessary. My job—the Grim Reaper's job—has always been about balance. Hell is out of balance, and I'm trying to fix it!"

Kurai's narrowed gaze flicked between Cora and me. Then her face went so expressionless that, were she human, I might have wondered if she'd had a stroke. I could see the thoughts flashing behind her red eyes, calculations and anger and hope, but I had no idea what direction her mind was turning. Resolve? Disbelief? Resignation?

No matter. Once we reached the Pit, I'd send her on her way. A hostage would be a burden and a distraction that we couldn't afford. I drew a deep breath and let the Musak's dulcet tones flow over me.

The elevator stopped. Behind Kurai, the door chimed open to reveal a twisting red stone hallway blocked by a massive centaur.

He was one of the guards from the Pit, bare-chested with a bow and quiver slung across his back. His eyes widened at our standoff. He stumbled back, yelled in alarm, and scrambled to unlimber his bow.

That's when Kurai attacked me.

ENEMIES AND ALLIES

KURAI LUNGED FORWARD, DROPPING to her knees beneath Cora's Holy Water Squirt Gun (patent pending). Cora fired, but the water passed harmlessly over Kurai's head. It made a bubbling line in the red stone outside the elevator. Kurai twisted toward me, one of her daggers appearing in her hand, and sliced my wrist.

I screamed but wasn't banished. Cursed and blessed blades do not affect Death, but *damn* that hurt! *Faith* dropped from my fingers. Kurai caught *Faith* in her empty hand, spun on her knees, and threw it at the centaur.

It connected with a meaty *thunk.* He looked down at

the blessed blade protruding from his chest, his bow only half-drawn. "Ah, shi—"

With a *pop*, he disappeared. *Faith* clattered to the stone floor.

Silence reigned once again, overlain by Musak. "Secret Agent Man" had been replaced by that same damned tune I'd been hearing since first arriving in Hell. Rick rolled right over me. I tried to ignore the Musak and glanced at Cora. Her wide eyes were firmly fixed on the now-empty hallway. Conrad had scrambled down her back and clung to her as if he were a living rucksack. Only his eyes poked over her shoulder.

Kurai rose to her feet and sheathed the cursed dagger she still held in her left hand. There was a flicker of motion, and her other dagger reappeared in the opposite sheath, instantly moved by her will. She massaged her palm, which was raw and red. I could see the outline of *Faith's* hilt on her skin, even though she'd only held the blessed blade for a moment.

I massaged my wrist where Kurai had cut me. It hurt, and I willed the wrist to heal. Healing spiritual wounds requires willpower just like changing forms, though significantly less as it's merely a return to what was instead of becoming something new. Yet even that skill is beyond some spirits. Xandu's missing forearm and scarred face were a testament to his weak willpower. After the strains I'd placed on myself today, stars flashed before my vision as my wrist healed. Heavens I was tired!

Within moments, Kurai was flexing her hand, all signs of injury gone.

"Why?" I asked her. "Why attack one of your own?"

A calculating look crossed the demon's expression before she tugged at her kimono-like suit jacket to straighten it beneath the belt. "Lucifer is the Lord of Darkness, the Dragon who Reigns, and my liege. If Lucifer lives, I will tear Hell apart to rescue him. He"—she pointed to where the centaur had been—"would not have listened to reason. Centaurs are idiots."

I nodded, understanding the implications of her loyalty. My impartiality between Heaven and Hell was well-known. I served both but was beholden to neither. If anything, my loyalty belonged to the souls I shepherded. It was a difficult path I trod, but one I'd chosen willingly, just as Kurai had willingly chosen to be Lucifer's servant. I'd have to keep an eye on her. The second our goals diverged, she would turn on us.

I stepped from the elevator and retrieved *Faith*. A blackened impression of the dagger remained in the stone where it had lain. I'm not a praying spirit, the Almighty has always seemed rather aloof and unhelpful to me, but I sent up a silent prayer of thanks that Cora had chosen to help me. Her weapons were significantly more powerful than I'd realized.

The others joined me, and I glanced around. "Where'd the cat go?"

Conrad answered, having resumed his parrot's perch on Cora's shoulder now that the danger had passed. "The little chicken bolted the second the door opened." He blew a tiny puff of fire on his claws then buffed them on his chest. "Couldn't handle another round with me."

And yet that 'little chicken' had easily held his own against Conrad. But I didn't see any value in pointing that out.

The elevator started to close, but Cora stopped it with a foot. She glanced around and grabbed a loose bit of red stone. The door reopened and she jammed the stone into the door's bottom corner. At my quizzical expression, she said, "In case we need a quick escape."

Smart. I turned and stalked down the winding red stone

hallway, *Faith* held low and ready. There was a moment of silence before Cora and Kurai followed, their soft footfalls accompanied by the occasional jangle of Cora's jewelry.

The narrow hallway was lit intermittently with small lanterns inset into roughly hewn alcoves. Flickering light cast long shadows. The small pools of light didn't quite connect, and I slowed every time I reached a corner or another patch of darkness.

Behind me, Cora whispered to Kurai, "So ... why was there a centaur down here? I didn't expect a demon to look like something from Greek mythology."

Kurai didn't bother keeping her voice down. "He wasn't originally a demon any more than I was. Merely a spirit from another realm who swore allegiance to Lucifer."

"So, if he's not a demon, how'd the blessed letter opener banish him?"

Kurai sounded annoyed but explained. "There are spiritual laws even older than the Rules which govern these realms. One's sworn allegiance binds their soul to their chosen realm with all its Rules and restrictions. Why do you think human souls never escape either Heaven or Hell? They are bound by the allegiance they swore in life."

Cora snorted. "I've never sworn allegiance to a spiritual

realm."

I glanced back and caught Kurai giving Cora an amused half-smile. "You think not? Interesting…"

Cora scowled, and I returned to stalking down the narrow hallway. This wasn't the same entry we'd used when the twin torment coaches had delivered us to Level Four. That elevator had dumped us right onto the plateau that surrounded the pit. This must be a side entrance. I slowed again as we neared another corner. I peered around. Nobody coming.

"What are you doing?" Kurai asked, verbal eye roll obvious.

"Being cautious?" I said, not intending the question mark.

She shoved past me and strode down the empty hallway. "*I* am your disguise," she said. "If we see anyone, just look like my prisoners."

I straightened, annoyed. But she did have a point. I sheathed *Faith* and jogged to keep up.

Within three turns, the hallway ended at the plateau lining the Pit.

Xandu's yells echoed from the distant ceiling. Kurai stopped us at our hallway's edge, and we peered out from the shadows.

"What do you mean, 'They're *gone*'?" Xandu roared. He was perhaps fifty yards away. Behind him was the main elevator we'd used previously. The centaurs knelt before him at the edge of the Pit, bows on the ground, foreheads touching the red stone. Their captain, who I recognized from the gold circlet on his brow, raised his head. His deep voice was terrified.

"They just … disappeared. One minute, they was rolling the stones by that wall"—he pointed—"the next they was gone."

"*All* of them?"

"Well, no. Just the fleshy ones. Maybe a couple others. That rainbow-haired girl for one."

Abigail! I exchanged glances with Cora.

Xandu grabbed the centaur's flowing black mane and yanked him up to eye level. It was an awkward position for the tall centaur, and he stumbled, hooves clicking on the stone.

"And how long ago was this?" Xandu growled.

"Um, three hours? Give or take. Not that time means nothin' down here," the centaur babbled. "I mean, ain't that the point? Eternal torments and all? It's not like I got a sundial or a pocket wat—"

"Fool!" Xandu roared, spittle flying. He flung the centaur back down. The captain didn't bother to catch himself but splayed subserviently at the demon's feet. Xandu leaned down, his voice lowered dangerously. "And you didn't think to tell anyone?"

"I ... well..."

I pulled Cora and Kurai back, sliding deep into the hallway's shadows. We rounded the first curve and stopped in a pool of flickering lantern light. The muted sound of Xandu venting his rage was a grisly reminder of the need to avoid getting caught. Like we needed one. There was a wailing scream that cut off abruptly, the cry of someone entering the Pit by faceplant.

Cora shook with rage. "Oh, my dear Abigail. She was in there?"

"For a time, yes," I said. "But not anymore, apparently."

Cora drew a deep breath, and her shoulders relaxed. Calm washed over her.

No, not calm. Calm implied peace and tranquility. This was something different. Fear and rage distilled into purpose. Cora's fist clenched, her rings scraping together, and her gaze met mine. "When we find Lucifer, I'm going to make him wish he'd never stolen my daughter."

Kurai sneered. "And how will you do that, *mortal*?"

Cora's fist flexed again. With exaggerated calm, she said, "I'll start with a right cross to the jaw. We'll see where things go from there, hmmm?"

Tense silence fell, filled only with the distant sounds of Xandu punting centaurs into the Pit.

"How'd she escape?" Cora asked.

I shook my head. Kurai's red eyes looked troubled, an unusual expression for her. "They must have had help. A human soul can't travel Hell alone."

"But who would help them?" I scratched my head and then pushed my shoulder-length hair back as it insisted once again on falling in front of my face. "Brutus maybe?"

Conrad's head snapped up, his silver eyes sparkling. "No, not a demon. Demons wouldn't dare help the damned." His wings fluttered excitedly. "But you know who would?"

"Nightmares," Kurai answered, her face pale.

Conrad grinned. "Yup! My kith and kin. I don't know *how* Abi and the others escaped, but I know where they went." He glanced excitedly between us, practically dancing on Cora's shoulder.

"Of course," I said, comprehension dawning. "They went to the one place in Hell where even demons fear to tread."

Kurai swore. Quietly, but in several languages and with impressive detail. Cora eyed her as the tirade continued, eyebrows climbing her forehead. I suspected she was taking notes for her own vocabulary. When Kurai finally wound down without explaining, Cora glanced at me. There was a sharp bite in her voice.

"So, where *did* my daughter go that even demons fear to tread? And how do I find her?"

I placed a comforting hand on Cora's arm. "She's in the Basement, where the nightmares live."

"...and?" she said, patience gone. "It can't be that bad. I've only met one nightmare, and Conrad's not scary at all. He's actually kind of cute."

The dragon perked up at that and flashed a dashing if toothy smile. "You think I'm cute? You ain't so bad lookin' yourself, Gorgeous."

Kurai raised both hands and backed away. "I'm not going to the Basement."

I cocked my head at her. "Then where do you recommend we go? Do you know where Lucifer is being held?"

"No, but…" A touch of panic widened her eyes. Real panic. "The Basement? *Really*?"

"We need allies and information," I said. "We'll find both in the Basement. You don't have to come, but if you want to rescue Lucifer, this is the way." I turned back to Cora.

"There's a reason that demons fear the Basement. Most nightmares are fine when off duty. Not terrifying at all, like Conrad here. But there are … others. Nightmares who never learned to separate their personalities from their day jobs. Nightmares torn from humanity's darkest, most depraved souls."

I guided Cora back toward the elevator, leaving the demon to her choice. After a moment of silence followed by a violent expletive, Kurai followed. Her tread was heavy upon the rough stone.

Cora said, "Mankind's darkest nightmares? Like what, boogeymen and vampires?"

I blew out a long breath, a touch of dread gracing even my soul. "Have you ever heard of Cthulhu?"

Behind us, Kurai resumed swearing.

Chapter 24

HELL'S BASEMENT

OUR DESCENT INTO THE Basement was quiet and tense, without even Musak—a blessing I wasn't going to over-look. Kurai leaned against the elevator's left-hand wall, arms crossed, gaze fixed on the reflective metal door. Cora and I leaned against the opposite wall, mirroring her posture, though Cora anxiously fiddled with her vest's pockets, checking her mystical supplies. Conrad was also in constant motion, bobbing on Cora's shoulder as if to a tune in his own head, his tail flicking with anticipation.

Nobody mentioned the massive hole in the elevator's

back wall. Cora's wayward shot of holy water had continued its magic in our absence, spreading like fungus, consuming everything and leaving literally nothing in its wake. The damage was worse toward the ceiling. The speaker in the corner was gone—thus no Musak—and I swear I could hear the holy water gurgling as it digested the infernal elevator. At this rate, the elevator itself would cease to exist in a few hours.

I shivered. The dark emptiness beyond that hole reminded me of Abaddon. It didn't help that there were also small holes in the floor where Cora's pistol had dripped. Small holes that were growing at only a slightly slower rate. I made a point to stand as far from those holes as I could, trying not to think about the leaky pistol sitting in my own holster. It was a powerful weapon, but I didn't dare let my wet left hip touch the wall lest I open another hole into nothingness.

I glanced at Conrad, my mind once again returning to the problem of his potential duplicity with Abigail. With his Lucifer-level access to Hell, why hadn't he taken her straight out? Was he restricted for some reason, or had he intentionally made her path more difficult? If so, to what purpose?

My gaze flicked to Kurai, and my lips pursed. Unfortunately, I couldn't ask Conrad in front of the demon. Though we served a common purpose for now, I didn't trust her. At all. And, though I had questions, I actually did trust Conrad. My questions could wait.

Finally, the door chimed open revealing a dank and dismal basement worthy of nightmares.

"Welcome to Level Six," Conrad crowed. "Hell's Basement."

The short hallway was bare cement with flickering fluorescent lights. Water dripped in the distance. Cora stepped forward but froze on the threshold when a scream pierced the silence. The scream echoed before fading into a whimper.

Kurai huddled in on herself, bat wings curled protectively around her shoulders, daggers already drawn.

I'd never visited Hell's Basement before and hadn't known what to expect. An overwhelming sense of dread pushed on me like a physical thing and I, the Grim Reaper, terror of men's souls, hesitated.

A tiny, slow whirlwind appeared before us, smoke and sand swirling and expanding upward from the cement floor. A vaguely humanoid outline climbed into view as though pulling itself from a grave. Spinning flashes of red flickered through the empty canvas of swirling sand where the apparition's face should have been.

A djinn. Or rather, the nightmare of one.

Cora gasped and stepped back, hands flying to her weapons. The sand swirled faster as the figure rose, coalescing into the crouched form of a thin man with arms that were too long, tipped by dagger-sharp fingers. He was shrouded in tattered robes and a loosely wound turban of whirlwind sand. The red flashes in the djinn's face spun faster and faster, synchronizing into a flickering red cut of a mouth. A terrifying mouth that snarled at our interruption of his eternal nap.

He had no eyes.

A shiver crawled down my spine, compounding the dread hammering upon my soul. I took an involuntary step back. My foot hit the wall.

My back didn't.

Right. Even greater terrors lay behind me, the emptiness beyond the missing elevator wall that led to oblivion.

Kurai snarled, the demon's breath coming fast as she tensed to attack. Cora's Holy Water Squirt Gun (patent pending) slipped from its holster. I drew *Faith*.

Conrad led the charge.

He launched himself from Cora's shoulder and swept into the hallway. "Heya, Bob! How's it goin'?"

Bob?

The creature snapped upright. "Conrad?" Bob's voice was raspy with a strong Persian accent, precise and clipped. "What are you doing here?"

"I'm here to see you, buddy!" Conrad snapped his wings out spread-eagle and collided bodily with Bob as though trying to land a violent hug.

He passed right through the smoky, sandy apparition, leaving a Conrad-shaped hole in Bob's chest. The djinn's shoulders slumped. "You know I hate when you do that. Right?" The swirling sand slowly filled the hole.

Conrad wheeled back, banking sharply in the narrow hallway. "You missed me, admit it, Bobby boy!"

Bob sighed a distinctly not-missing-Conrad sigh. "It's *Babil*, you miserable excuse for a lizard. Not Bob. Not Bobby. Not Bobalicious. Babil!"

Conrad grinned his infectious grin and wheeled a gliding arc between us and the djinn nightmare while singing brightly and tunelessly, "Bobbity Bob Bob Bob..."

Babil sighed again. One flashing red lip curled into a

snarl as his eyeless gaze followed the gliding dragon.

"What … do … you … want, Conrad? If you're delivering fresh meat to Cthulhu, get on with it." Babil's turned that blank, sandy stare toward us. A fresh shiver danced down my spine when Babil's flashing red lips smiled cruelly. "He's been hungry recently. Gnawing at the back of my mind. But Cthulhu always settles down after consuming a few demons."

I was not a demon. I was Death. I sheathed *Faith*, drew myself upright, and pushed back against the dread that threatened to overwhelm me.

It took everything I had. It's like Cthulhu's dread had seeped into my very bones. I'd recovered a little of my strength as we'd descended into the Basement, but this was almost too much.

Almost.

I exerted my will and shed my flesh. It wisped away like burning embers. They shriveled into nothingness, leaving me as a skeleton, naked and proud. I didn't shed everything from my human form though. Because I carried two physical objects—*Faith* and my holstered Holy Water Squirt Gun (patent pending)—I retained a belt that clung to my bony hips.

I drew from Hell's darkest recesses, from the empty nothingness beyond the elevator's missing wall, and my cowled cloak formed around me, swirling like Babil's sandy figure. My cloak settled on my shoulders, the deep cowl upon my skull. My eye sockets flashed with blue flame.

And then the world tried to tilt sideways as my willpower drained. I didn't let it. Now was not the time to show weakness. I was *Death!*

The gnawing dread within me diminished. A little.

"I am nobody's *fresh meat!*" I intoned, striding from the elevator, letting my anger overwhelm my exhaustion. "Do you know who I am, Babil?"

"Ah, Grim. There you are," Babil said, his precise tone sounding both relieved and annoyed. "I've been expecting you."

I paused. "Oh. Really?"

"You are late for the Nightmare Council." Babil raised a lanky arm to point at Cora and Kurai. Sand and smoke swirled and fell away from the arm like a trailing cloak sleeve. "But what of these two? Shall I feed them to Cthulhu?"

"No," I said firmly. "They are with me."

Babil's eyeless gaze revealed nothing before he turned to lumber down the hall. Every step left sandy footprints that faded away in the unfelt wind of his fractured soul. I beckoned the others, and we followed.

Conrad landed to trot alongside Babil. "Bobby," he said, glancing up at the djinn, "you wouldn't *believe* the day I've had. It's been freaking awesome! First, I was hanging with my friend Abi—you'd like her, she's a total badass—and we got completely lost in the Labyrinth..."

Conrad's patter washed over me as we trudged down the hall; a hall which seemed to extend into eternity without doors or crossings. The flickering florescent lights played with the shadows, hinting at terrors half-seen. As we walked, bare gray cement turned green and sickly, coated in slime that glistened and squelched with every step. It was everywhere, climbing the walls and dripping from the ceiling in thin tendrils.

I glanced at Cora, but aside from a firm grip on the hilt of her sheathed dagger, she showed no signs of fear. Her attention was laser-focused on Conrad's story. Her breath hitched every time the dragon mentioned Abigail.

Kurai was another story. Her angry, confident swagger was gone, subsumed by growing terror. Her red eyes flicked from shadow to shadow, and she twitched every time another scream echoed down the hall.

We finally reached the end of the hallway which opened into a vast cavern whose geometry felt ... wrong. Like Escher had conspired with Lovecraft to produce something beyond human understanding. The sickly green glow was stronger here. It suffused everything, directionless and pervasive.

We stood on a stone shelf in the center of a wall. Stairs angled sharply down to our right. Ramps and columns twisted before us as though cut stone had grown from dripping stalactites before giving up and melding into the walls again. Extruded shelves held wooden prison doors with small, barred windows. Claws, tentacles, and sundry appendages pressed through those openings, straining for release. And outside those doors?

Cats.

But not the cute, furry gods of Hell we'd been tripping over all day. The Basement's cats had a feral look to them. Thin, mangy, and battle-scarred. They paced anxiously. Yowls and growls mixed with cries of anguish from the cavern's imprisoned nightmares into a cacophony that grated the ear and did nothing to ease our dread.

The cavern's far end was dominated by a cell door of baffling proportions, angled like a cellar door with great iron pull rings. The entire thing was so large that it couldn't possibly fit in this cavern, distance and dimensions playing tricks with the eye that made my mind go wobbly.

If dread were directional, it was coming from behind that door.

Cthulhu.

H.P. Lovecraft's nightmare of an Elder God. His mental tentacles prodded at the edges of my mind, insidious and greasy. In my weakened state, his corrupt thoughts latched on tight and squeezed my will. He didn't speak in words but with intent and desire and a will that dwarfed my own.

How? How could *any* nightmare be so powerful?

Give up, that non-voice didn't intone. *Bow at my feet and know the joy of oblivion.*

A sob escaped Kurai. She shook her head. Her wings wrapped around her like a cloak, nothing more than a paper shield against an Elder God's madness.

I had to remind myself that he was just a nightmare.

Cora's breath came fast, dilated eyes fixed on Cthulhu's prison. But then her gaze shifted to me. Her shoulders relaxed, and she drew a bracing breath. Then she patted my bony shoulder as though comforting *me*.

My fear diminished even more. How could I not draw comfort from Cora's stalwart presence?

Babil led us to the right, down the stone steps cut into the wall. At the bottom of the steps, he stopped at the third cell we reached and pulled it open. Rusty hinges screamed their protests and revealed a wall of darkness that hung like a physical veil. Babil waved us forward.

"No," Kurai said. "I ... I can't. I won't!" She backed away.

Babil struck faster than lightning. A swirling fist gripped the pinions of Kurai's wings where they crossed before her chest, and he pulled. *Hard.* Kurai dropped to her knees. Her face froze an inch below Babil's.

"You rightfully know fear, demon," he said, clipped voice low and earnest. "Too long have nightmares suffered under Hell's rule. I should feed you to Cthulhu, but today you are fated for something far more destructive."

"What..." Kurai gulped. "What could possibly be worse than *that!*" She tried to point toward Cthulhu's cell, but her arms were trapped under her wings which Babil held pinned together.

Babil smiled a chilling smile. "The truth."

He spun and flung Kurai through the open doorway. She screamed and tumbled, flapping her wings for balance before she disappeared through the veil of darkness. Her screams cut off leaving only an echo in my mind.

Cora and I stared after her. At Babil's feet, Conrad shook his head. "Seriously, Bobby. You are such a drama queen."

"I hate demons."

Conrad rolled his eyes and then glanced up at us, his silver gaze piercing. "Come on," he said before prancing forward to slip through the veil.

Babil cocked his head at us in a contemplative manner that I didn't like. I raised both skeletal hands.

"We can walk, thank you."

That flashing, swirling smile turned wry. The djinn waved us forward.

What terrors awaited in that darkness, in the Basement's unseen depths? Yes, there was a reason Hell feared the nightmares they'd created by carving off pieces of the damned. Though demons were ever inventive in their torments, they didn't hold a candle to the depravity of the human soul.

No, that wasn't quite right. That makes it sound as

though *all* human souls are depraved. Most humans are just normal people trying to live their lives, find a semblance of happiness, and avoid screwing things up too badly along the way. Whether they succeed or not is between them and their Judgment when they reach the afterlife. Judgments are not my department.

But when a human soul *does* become depraved, when they abandon all that is good and embrace evil like a long-lost lover, *that* is when the greatest terrors are born. Imagine the nightmares of a genocidal megalomaniac. Of a serial killer. Or of that psycho who invented Musak. Imagine the power that such a nightmare might possess. A nightmare created to instill fear in souls who *reveled* in fear.

Cthulhu was one such nightmare. His insidious presence in the back of my mind made me want to run screaming in terror after only a few minutes in his eldritch proximity. His siren call of oblivion pulled at me.

If Cthulhu waited in the Basement's antechamber, what horrors lay beyond that cell's impenetrable darkness?

Cora took my elbow with her left hand. "My daughter's in there," she whispered. "I'm sure of it. What are we waiting for?"

What, indeed?

We strode arm-in-arm into the cell. Perfect darkness enveloped us. Silence fell like a curtain. Then we passed through the veil and landed in another world.

Chapter 25

HELL'S LOST LEVELS

CORA AND I STEPPED from the darkness onto a grassy hillside dotted with trees. We stopped dead. The twilit landscape dropped into a river valley dominated by a medieval city. The trees around us rustled in a warm breeze that flowed gently past, tugging at Cora's hair and my cloak like a wistful lover. The shadows of the leaves were sharp overlapping half-moons that defied logic as they danced upon the ground. I glanced up.

An eclipsed sun hung motionless in the clear blue sky. Well, mostly eclipsed. A burning crescent shone around the moon, a flaming ring that was not quite complete. I knew, somehow, that the eclipse never changed, never moved. It just sat there in transition. The perfect sun for a world that seemed to exist ... in between. This twilight world was the perfect blending of night and day that didn't belong, yet felt right.

Below us rested a city of stone and wood and shadows, nestled in the valley and straddling the broad, slow river. Light foot and cart traffic rumbled across three stone bridges spanning the river, residents about their daily lives. Something with a long black spine crested the river, a sea creature that looked far too large for the waters it swam. A broad, red-stone castle sat on the hillside directly across from us, just below the ridge. Welcoming lights flickered in stained glass windows. Laughter echoed up to us from the streets below.

This was definitely not Hell. At least, not any version of Hell I'd ever seen. This was a home for those who lived in between. For those who didn't belong to any realm.

Like me.

I caught a whiff of wild saffron and cool mint. Warm breezes and comforting shade. Tranquility washed over me like a physical sensation, and my tension faded into the background. I didn't forget it, couldn't forget the gravity of our mission, yet I found myself simply standing. Being. Absorbing my new surroundings with a sense of wonder. Cthulhu's dread which had suffused my bones was gone.

What was this place?

I glanced back. The cell door behind us was now a free-standing stone arch. From this side, the veil was not a wall of darkness, but rather a looking glass that swirled like smoke. Beyond the veil, I watched Babil swing the cell door silently closed. No squeal of neglected hinges came, just the peaceful rustle of the wind and the happy rumble of the nearby city.

Conrad's sharp whistle drew my attention. He perched on a low wall beside a well-maintained dirt path that wound down the hillside toward the city. Kurai stood ridged beside him, shocked gaze wandering the scene as though trying to make sense of it all.

Cora and I walked over, and Conrad grinned at us. "Welcome to Morpheo."

"Morpheo?" I echoed.

"Home of the nightmares," Conrad said, "embedded in Hell's subbasement." He launched into the air, flew a tight barrel roll, then angled toward the path.

Cora and I followed, her arm still hooked in my elbow. When we passed Kurai, she joined us, a silent shadow who knew that she didn't belong.

"Hell doesn't have a subbasement," I called to Conrad, despite the evidence surrounding me.

"It looks like Heidelberg," Cora said, "but from a time before the castle was destroyed. I visited with my oldest when he was assigned to Germany with the Army."

Conrad wheeled back toward us and landed on my shoulder with his customary heavy *thump*. "Bones, how many levels does Hell have?"

"Seven," I answered promptly. "Reception, Torments, the Throne Room, the Pit, the Lake of Fire, the Basement, and Abaddon."

Conrad clucked his tongue as we neared the bottom of the hill and the first buildings. "Wrong answer, Bones." He glanced back. "Kurai, you want to give it a shot? How many levels does Hell have?" He sounded like a teacher asking his class a trick question.

She gave the same answer I did, counting the levels carefully on her well-manicured claws. As she answered, our path leveled out and we entered the city. Packed dirt became a narrow cobblestone alley. We passed between white-plastered walls before stepping onto a main street. The foot traffic gave us a wide berth, nightmares clearly uneasy with our presence. There were trolls and aliens and beasts with slathering jaws. The nightmares came in every possible description, even some who looked human. We carried on across the street, our alley widening into a proper road that led directly to the nearest bridge.

What was Conrad talking about? Hell had seven levels, six for the management of souls, and the seventh reserved for Lucifer after Armageddon. It had been that way ever since...

"Nine," Cora said as we stepped onto the stone bridge.

"Bingo!" Conrad crooned. "And the prize goes to the pretty one!"

I was getting annoyed by the little dragon's smugness.

Cora said, "Dante described walking through Hell's nine circles. They wound down through increasingly horrible torments until he reached the Devil trapped in ice on Level Nine."

"Oh, right," I said. I could have kicked myself for a fool. "Hell's reorganization into a bureaucratic model only required seven levels after they streamlined soul management. Before that, yes, Hell had nine levels. I'd always assumed that the reorganization was total."

But that assumption didn't take into account the evidence I'd seen in the last few hours. The bits of backstage we'd seen, and the sections of Hell lost and forgotten in the reorganization.

We'd reached the apex of the bridge. To our right, the sea creature crested again, this time rolling to reveal entirely too many teeth in a crocodile-like jaw. I swear it waved a flipper at me.

Conrad's voice dropped, becoming low and earnest in my ear. "You ... assumed? Bones, you of all spirits should know never to assume *anything* where Lucifer is concerned."

It was a good reminder.

"But how did the nightmares do all this?" I waved my hands at the reimagined Heidelberg that was neither part of Hell's original plans nor its reorganization. We passed under a towered archway and entered the city proper. Winding cobblestone roads led inexorably up toward the castle.

Conrad cocked his head at me. I expected something flippant, but his expression turned contemplative. His gaze swung toward the castle. "Even nightmares have dreams," he said.

That was not actually an answer. But it was all I was going to get.

Conrad resumed flying and directed us up winding streets toward the castle. We passed through a broad plaza where nightmares were hawking wares in canvas stalls. It felt surreal, almost like being back on Earth. Of course, no market on Earth sold things like 'moonlit memories' and 'bottled intrigue,' and the citizens of this bizarre world ran the full gamut from familiar to mind-bending. The ones that disturbed me, however, were the nightmares without form. The coalesced mists. The shadows that moved without bodies.

Our path through the plaza narrowed between vendor stalls. I stepped carefully over the tail of something that looked like an upright crocodile wearing armor who was intently perusing a display of moonlit memories. Delicate bottles no larger than my finger bones filled narrow shelves and had labels that ranged from First Kiss to Burning Witch. Nobody said that moonlit memories were always nice.

I was so focused on the display that I didn't see the storm cloud until I walked through it.

The world went dark as sudden tornado winds whipped at me. Electricity crackled, surging upward from my feet until it coalesced on my chest and exploded into a lightning bolt. The world went blue then white. I crashed into something and collapsed to the cobblestones. Silence reigned in my persistently white world. No, not silence. A powerful ringing filled my skull. This wasn't the bells of Notre Dame. It was worse. One high note strong enough to drown the world.

I shook my head, clearing my senses. Hearing came first, shouts and accusations. Cora and Conrad and a voice I didn't know.

"...at's the Grim Reaper, Sparky!" That was Conrad.

"Don't care who he is! It's rude to walk through a body." The unknown voice was deep and rumbly and full of power. Like a thunderstorm about to break. "And the name's Jesse, not Sparky, you insolent little wyrm." I struggled to rise, but my legs only twitched. I still couldn't see anything.

"Grim, are you okay?" That was Cora, her hand warm on my shoulder. I shook my head again, and my vision cleared enough to see her concerned face. Behind her, Conrad was swooping tight circles around Jesse, the nightmare storm cloud I'd apparently walked through.

"Look, Water Droplets," Conrad's voice dripped condescension, flame leaking from his maw as he flew, "unless you wanna be evaporated right now—"

"Conrad," I said, "let him be." I clutched Cora's arm and let her pull me upright. The world tilted dangerously, then steadied. Leaning on Cora more than I let show, I focused on Jesse. He was, quite literally, a storm cloud, eight feet in diameter, black and gray and swirling with flashes of lightning that reached like sharp fingers toward the circling Conrad. The market's crowd of nightmares had cleared back. They watched with interest, but didn't interfere. Conrad stopped taunting the storm cloud but continued his tight spiral above him, trailing smoke and fire.

"Jesse," I said to the rumbling storm cloud, "my sincerest apologies. I should have paid more attention where I was walking." Jesse swirled and boiled without direction, lit inside by increasingly powerful flashes, but I felt his attention shift to me. I straightened, my strength returning. "That was an impressive display of power."

The cloud roiled, and I got the impression of a shrug. "That was nothing. But unless the wyrm backs off, you'll see real power."

I raised a hand. "No need. We were just passing through. Conrad," I said, looking up, "if you could lead the way?"

Conrad snorted at Jesse but angled down the nearest alley leading up the hill. Cora and I followed, careful to give Jesse wide berth. The nightmare storm swirled, giving the distinct impression of watching as we passed.

It wasn't until Kurai slid in behind us that I realized she'd avoided the entire confrontation. She'd hidden, blending unnaturally well into the shadows between vendor stalls. She'd made no effort to help or to diffuse the situation. Finally confident in my stride, I released Cora's arm as we walked, reminding myself of Kurai's singular loyalty to Lucifer.

The higher we climbed through the city, the more my strength returned. Morpheo's pervading sense of peace settled over me. I was surprised to find myself rejuvenated, like a residual bit of Jesse's electricity had recharged my soul. We climbed a steep ramp that clung to the hillside and ended at the castle's portcullis. I expected a guard to stop us, but the gates stood wide open. Conrad settled on my shoulder once again, and we passed through a long tunnel that opened onto a courtyard which continued to angle up the hill. Trees dotted its edges, nightmares lounging in the jumbled half-moon shadows cast by the unreal sky.

Conrad pointed up and right toward a section of the courtyard that had been raised at one end to create the only level space here. A line of tall stained-glass windows was broken by a heavy, arched oaken door. "The Council will be in there."

In front of that door we were finally stopped by guards. Wendigo. Two tall creatures who were bone-thin with long arms, claw-tipped fingers, and antlers that were battered and cracked from too many battles. Razor-sharp teeth filled their narrow jaws. Their black, soulless eyes swiveled on Cora, the only human among us. Their jaws split hungrily, tongues flicking as though tasting the air.

Menace radiated from them so strongly that Cora stopped dead when their gazes swiveled to her. After my encounter with Jesse, I understood her caution. Conrad, however, wasn't as restrained. He never was.

From my shoulder, he said, "Move it, Antlers," and hooked a thumb to one side.

They ignored him, having eyes only for Cora. The creatures spoke in unison, their necks arching forward as their clawed fingers reached longingly toward her. "Ssso fresssh.

We've not tasssted hot blood in ssso long."

Nightmares on duty were truly a terror to behold, activating primal fears in the human mind. Yet, despite the fear in her eyes, Cora's hand remained steady as she drew her cursed dagger. She brandished the blade. "Try me," Cora growled, "and you'll be tasting cursed steel and then cobblestones."

The wendigos licked their lips and moaned with blood lust.

"Hey!" I snapped my fingers at the guards, drawing their attention. "I am the Grim Reaper, and we are here on Council business. So, drop the act and let us in." I hoped it was an act. Fighting our way in wouldn't end well for anyone.

The wendigos abruptly straightened, unified motion splitting into individuals who looked slightly abashed. They fiddled with their long claws, and the one on the right said with a light drawl it hadn't possessed earlier, "Sorry about that. Just doing our job, you know."

The wendigo on the left added, "There's not much call for us to go full nightmare these days, what with Hell's torments being bureaucratic and all. Might have gotten a bit carried away."

The right one finished, "We didn't mean nothing by it, though"—it sniffed appreciatively toward Cora—"you do have lovely smelling blood."

Cora's throat worked for a second before she said, "Thank you, I think." She sheathed her dagger.

Both wendigos stepped aside, bowing so deeply that their antlers crossed. Then they straightened, and the oaken door swung open of its own accord. Their long arms gestured us inside.

We entered a formal ballroom with a circular table at its center. High crystal chandeliers flickered with candles, giving the room a secretive air. Ten nightmares sat around the table. Some I recognized, others I didn't. Frankenstein's Monster sat on the far side between a chupacabra and Teri the minotaur, whom we'd met in the Labyrinth. She grinned broadly when she saw me and blew me a kiss.

Adze the vampire sat to Teri's left, not to be confused with Dracula who sat to *his* left. Adze was half-human/half-firefly, shirtless, and emaciated; an African vampire who drank life aura instead of blood. Dracula was smoothly polished with slick black hair, a high-collared silk cloak, and manicured nails.

Sitting with their backs to me were a yeti, two werewolves, and a machete-wielding man missing half his face. On my left, directly across from Dracula, sat a white goose. There was nothing odd about her, beyond the fact that she sat among mankind's most terrifying nightmares.

In the center of the circular table stood Frank the Taxman, hands and voice raised like a zealous monk preaching to the masses. His cowl pooled at his shoulders.

"It's time to end the madness!" he shouted, finger pointed skyward and fervor pouring from him. "Time for the nightmares to rise up and take back what's theirs!"

Growling affirmations rumbled from his audience. Machete Man clanked his hilt on the table and cheered. Frank turned slowly, catching every gaze.

"Too long have the nightmares slaved in the shadows. Always scorned, always treated as 'less' simply because you are slices of human souls. You deserve more. Yet, you have accepted your lot, kept your heads down, and done your jobs. Hell's dirty work. Tormenting where torment was required, yet comforting when Hell wasn't looking. Life under Lucifer's rule wasn't perfect, but you made it work. And after Hell's reorganization, when you were shoved aside, you created Morpheo." Frank spun, raised arms encompassing the entirety of Hell's subbasement. "A haven amidst the chaos. A secret place for nightmares to finally call home. And every time Hell ripped another nightmare from a soul, no matter how heinous, you welcomed them like family."

Frank stopped and planted his fists on the table right before the goose. His voice lowered, "But the Year of the Dragon has ended. Lucifer has fallen and Nigel's New Order is ripping Hell's Bureaucracy to shreds to return to the bad old days. To rebuild Hell as it once was. Your home is threatened. Your world is about to be destroyed." Frank slammed a fist to the table. "Will you give up without a fight?"

"By Aunt Mary's rotten tooth, no!" the goose honked, echoed by her peers.

Who was Aunt Mary?

"It's time," Frank straightened, fist pumping the air, "for a revolution!"

Cheers resounded around the table.

I realized that my jaw was hanging open like a Venus fly trap, and I snapped it shut. What the *hell* was going on here?

Amidst the cheering, a voice called out from our right.

"Mom?"

I spun. Abigail flew from a line of chairs along the wall and flung herself at Cora. Cora caught her daughter with a half-choked sob. The two clung to each other. Questions, assurances, and tears tumbled and jumbled between them until they both laughed and simply embraced.

Beyond them sat the Davidsons. Inez held a sleeping Beatrix while Sam held a crutch. They looked worlds better than the last time I'd seen them. Sam's broken ankle was splinted, and they all looked ... fuller. Less stretched. They both glanced my way, and I gazed into Inez's soul. Still no date of death. She, at least, would survive. I still doubted that she knew of her pending immortality. Sam gave me a wan, lopsided smile and threw me a two-fingered salute.

"Grim," Teri's cheerful voice pulled my attention back to the table. "We're glad you could join us."

Adze the Vampire didn't share Teri's enthusiasm. He pointed behind me. "Who are they?"

"Allies," I said, striding forward. "Cora came for her daughter, Kurai has pledged to free Lucifer, and Conrad—"

"We know Conrad," Adze said, rising. His tattered dragonfly wings buzzed angrily. "Lucifer's nightmare is no ally."

"Why?" Conrad yelled, launching himself from my shoulder to the table. He glided between the yeti and a werewolf before landing with a scritch of claws on wood. "What have I *ever* done to warrant your suspicion and hatred?"

"You are Lucifer's spy!"

"If I was the Devil's spy," Conrad's voice turned saucy, "then he would have invaded Morpheo ages ago! You think Lucifer would let the nightmares build an entire world under his nose? To live happily ever after in his realm of eternal torments?" Conrad glared at the Council then threw up his paws. "No! He would have marched in here with the full power of Hell and destroyed this place. The Lord of Darkness craves power above all else. The very idea that misfit nightmares—whom he considers less than the souls you were sliced from—could find peace and joy in *his* basement would drive him mad." Conrad crossed his forelegs and glowered. "I have betrayed *nothing*!"

Silence filled the room. It was an uneasy silence, the kind that arises when someone doesn't want to admit that they were wrong.

Finally, the goose, who seemed to be in charge as much as anybody was, honked from the left side of the table. Her voice was aged and timorous but filled with resolve. "By Aunt Mary's crutch, Adze, sit down. Conrad is not our concern! That egg-sucker Nigel is. We are at a crossroads," she said. "Nightmares have lived in Hell's shadows for millennia. We have suffered and slaved and survived. In recent centuries, I don't think any would argue that we have *thrived* down here in our land of dreams, hidden from Lucifer's prying eyes." Nods around the room, though a few suspicious gazes flicked to Conrad.

"But old dragon-breath isn't in charge anymore, is he?" the goose said. "Nigel has demanded the nightmares dispersed so he can retrofit the Basement into his vision for Hell. For torments reborn and revisited on the very souls we were torn from. Do we comply, as we have always done, or do we rebel as the Taxman so eloquently argued?"

Frankenstein's Monster thrust himself to his feet, clearly a vote to rebel, but the goose raised her wing in warning. "Know this: if we lose, Nigel will destroy us. Rebellion is *not* a choice to be taken lightly." Frankenstein's Monster slowly sat back down.

Council members exchanged glances. Some looked to Frank—how the *hell* was he caught up in all this?—before the goose finally turned toward me.

"What say you, Reaper?" she asked. "You have long been a friend of nightmares. I'd hoped Teri would find you earlier to join in our deliberations, but she only found your apprentice and the mortals." So that's how they'd escaped the Pit. The goose eyed me as fiercely as only a goose can do. "Your apprentice supports rebellion. Will you?"

I stepped up between the werewolves and returned the Nightmare Council's regard. Some were worried, others determined. My own emotions were a mix, but I tamped them down and leaned on the round table.

"There is another way," I intoned.

Chapter 26

ANOTHER WAY

"I AM GOING TO rescue Lucifer," I said, "and restore him to his throne."

I expected surprise from the Nightmare Council but received only grunts of acknowledgment. Frank raised his hand sheepishly from the center of the table.

"I told them everything," he said.

Everything? While I appreciated Frank's enthusiasm, he needed lessons in discretion. Death does not divulge its secrets freely.

But, in this case, my apprentice's verbose nature *would* save some explanations. I scanned the room, pulling in everybody's gaze.

"Lucifer alone can set Hell to rights," I said, "and he need never know about Morpheo. Help me rescue Lucifer, and you stay in the shadows. Rebel against Nigel, and you face exposure." I glanced at the goose. "If Nigel invades Morpheo, do you have an escape? Perhaps a connection to the land of the living?"

She shook her head. "Not yet, but we're close. By their nature, dreams and nightmares remain apart from reality. Yet reality is shaped by the dreams of the living, so we're sure there's a connection." She bobbed her head from side to side. "We'll get there eventually, but for now there's only one way in and out of Morpheo."

I shook my head. "Then you are doomed if you fight. You may hold Nigel off at Morpheo's Gate, but Hell's forces are considerable. He *will* overwhelm you. But that's only your second greatest danger."

"What is the first?" Dracula asked, speaking for the first time. His voice was smooth and cultured with a deep Romanian accent.

"Have you considered that Nigel doesn't need to kill *you* to destroy you?"

From their worried looks, yes, they had considered that.

Even the chandeliers above us flickered as though my words instilled fear into the very room.

"Nigel has *Mercy*," I said, "the only blade that can grant a true death. A few surgical strokes with that black sword against the souls you were torn from—souls who can't fight back—and *poof*... this entire Council ceases to exist. That is not a risk I am willing to take."

I tapped a bony finger on the table. "I do not support rebellion. I support balance. I support the *Rules*, which have been in place since the parley at Megiddo for a reason. They established peace between the realms and ensured that human free will reigned supreme."

Cora's voice rose behind me, cracking with emotion. "But the Rules are broken. The fact that Abigail's here without Judgment proves it." I turned to my friends. Cora's arm was around Abigail's shoulder, holding the daughter she'd literally fought through Hell to rescue.

"Yes," I said, "the Rules are broken." I didn't point out that Abigail was stolen through some loophole before Nigel destroyed his copy of the Rules. It seemed pedantic and beside the point. "The Rules aren't perfect. Yet the system's checks and balances should have prevented this, something I intend to bring up with Lucifer when I see him. Which is my point: we must reestablish the Rules. Reset the status quo before Nigel ends *everything*. If Nigel continues his path unchecked, he will destroy *all* human free will. Heaven will retaliate and we'll have Armageddon early."

Inez rose abruptly. She had passed the sleeping Beatrix to Sam and turned furrowed brows toward me. "I'm all for preventing Armageddon," she said, "but there must be a better way than just setting Lucifer back on the throne. You make it sound good, this return of Hell to the way it was, but souls will still suffer an eternity of torments. Where's the justice in that?"

"Judgments are not my department," I said sharply.

Fire flashed in Inez's mismatched blue and green eyes, the immortal's frustration and fury coming to the fore. "Why was Hell built in the first place?"

"To punish the evil as Heaven was built to reward the righteous," I said.

She shook her head. "No, that makes the Almighty sound petty. Vindictive. Sure, He's mysterious and un-knowable, but I can't believe that God himself would be so simple in his motivations."

"You're right," I said. "I skimmed over the nuances.

Righteousness and evil are extremes on the continuum of right and wrong. If everyone were judged on whether they were 'good' or 'bad' then *everybody* would go to Hell. Nobody is perfect. If you think you are, then that arrogance is enough to condemn you. But I think Kurai said it the best."

I turned to the demon who'd been successfully hiding in the shadows of the doorway. She jumped. All eyes swiveled toward her. She crossed her arms and glowered back defiantly.

"It's all about choice," I said, holding the demon's gaze. "Call it faith or whatever you will, but salvation and damnation are Judged based on the alignment of your soul with either Heaven or Hell. An alignment that every mortal chooses whether they know it or not."

"Yes," Inez agreed, "choice is what matters here. But you're forgetting something important, Grim. The Almighty also forgives." Cora nodded in agreement with Inez, her expression turning thoughtful.

Forgiveness for my original sin? For introducing mankind to *murder*? Wouldn't that be something?

I shook my head. "The Almighty's nature is not in question here. The question is whether or not the nightmares should rebel."

"No," Inez said, "the question is whether or not we should rescue Lucifer and return to the status quo. He is evil. That's never been in doubt."

I threw my hands up in exasperation. "Yes, you're right. But this is truly a situation where the Devil we know *is* better than the one wily enough to have taken his place. It's Lucifer's *job* to mete out torments upon those who were rightly Judged and condemned. What other option is there except to rescue the rightful Lord of Darkness?"

"Overthrow Nigel as he overthrew his father," Inez said.

"And who would take charge if not Lucifer?"

Inez strode forward, every eye riveted on her. She pointed defiantly at the Council. "They do. Let the damned souls and their nightmares rule themselves for once."

"What?" I asked, taken aback. Why would Inez argue for that? There was more going on here than her dislike of Lucifer. "What do you stand to gain that is worth risking the existence of an entire realm?" I pointed toward Beatrix who snored softly in Sam's arms. "What could possibly be worth risking your daughter's very soul in the middle of a warzone in Hell?"

The fire in Inez's eyes pinched with pain. She swallowed,

and her voice turned rough. "My son. He ... chose evil. But he died too soon. Never had a chance to change. To repent." Inez's voice drifted off.

"And you would spare him his torments," I said quietly, nodding in understanding before my thoughts caught up with the facts. I froze. "What son? I remember every soul I reap, and I never took a son of yours. You have one child, and she's right there." I pointed at Beatrix again.

Inez half-turned, considering her daughter. "It took a long time to find the courage for another child." Her gaze swiveled back to mine, and she raised her right hand, turning it so that the woven gold band on her ring finger glittered in the chandelier light. "You took my son, Ferox Lepidus, almost fifteen hundred years ago," she said softly, "after he died helping Nero set Rome to the torch."

Ferox Lepidus. I thought back. Ah, yes, he'd been a centurion. A cruel and ambitious young man who'd volunteered to help burn the 'undesirables' out of Rome. He'd suffered a poetic fate; caught inside a building he'd set aflame. But that was long before Inez was born.

Inez slipped the ring from her finger. Change flowed over her like a curtain pulled back to reveal a new dawn. Her skin darkened, and her red hair became purest white.

The lines of a life long-lived fell deep upon her face. Her blue and green eyes met mine.

Shock rippled through me. I'd been wrong. So very wrong. Inez was not a new immortal unaware of her uniqueness. No, she had avoided my scythe for a very *very* long time.

I gazed into her soul and read her true name. Agnes, daughter of Jairus, born two thousand and three years ago, died twelve years later and resurrected by none other than the Son of God in the same year he resurrected Lazarus. *That* was why she had no known date of death.

She'd already died once.

Why hadn't I been called? I was brought in for Lazarus. I even reaped his soul before the Son of God called him back to the mortal realm three days later. I nearly faced an audit for that resurrection!

Yet, I knew nothing of Inez's death. Divine intervention? It had to be. The Almighty must have wanted to make a point to His followers, and Inez became immortal as a result.

"How?" I gasped at Inez.

She understood my meaning and held up her ring, pinched between thumb and forefinger. "A little gift from

Uncle Lazarus. A bit of magic that masks the souls of the immortals who walk the Earth."

"*Uncle* Lazarus?" I said, trying to wrap my head around what she'd just said. "As in, *that* Lazarus?"

Inez shrugged ever so slightly, her eyes still riveted on her ring. "He's not really my uncle. That's just what the immortals call him."

The immortals. How many were there? Inez was the only one I'd ever met. I thought back, trying to remember if I'd ever reaped Lazarus a second time.

No memory surfaced.

I wrangled my thoughts and reached for the ring. Inez clenched her fist around it, and my hand stopped.

"Your ring," I said. "Such magic should be impossible. I've been reaping souls since the beginning of time, and I've never heard of such a thing."

"And because you never heard of it means it can't exist? The world is so much more wonderful and terrible than you can possibly imagine, Grim. Lazarus has been researching the human soul for two thousand years. You might even say he's been obsessing over it. In that time, he's figured out a thing or two." Inez's clenched fist dropped to her side. Her gaze dared me to challenge her again.

Which hurt. Inez was my friend. A truly delightful woman who didn't deserve the torments visited upon her and her family. But try as I might, I couldn't agree with her plan. I couldn't support rebellion. We had to restore balance!

I shook my head. "I'm sorry, Inez, I truly am, but your son had the same choices as everyone else. He chose, aligned his soul with evil, and was Judged. You cannot change his eternal fate."

"But I can give him another chance," she said before turning to the Council.

"What of your daughter?" I asked. "A war is no place for a child."

Inez paused. She didn't face me, but half-turned to whisper over her shoulder. "I've seen more wars than I can count. Wept over the bodies of friends, of children, of those who never sought the violence visited upon them." Her gaze lifted to mine, her voice quiet and intense. "But war always came. I can't wrap Beatrix in cotton and protect her. She's *already* in Hell. War is *already* coming whether the Nightmare Council recognizes that or not. All I can do is show my daughter how to fight back. To do what's right no matter what. *That* is what I'm doing."

Inez stepped away from me. Frank had left the circular table's center, and she took his place, slipping through a narrow opening between Dracula and the yeti. Her gaze swept around the table.

"You have three choices. Help Grim rescue Lucifer, do nothing and accept Nigel's rule, or rebel. All three choices have the risk of discovery, of death and destruction. But only rebellion gives you a chance for something new. Something *better* than cowering under Hell's boot, waiting for them to crush you. You've built a better world for yourselves down here, why not extend that to the souls you were torn from?" Inez's eyes and voice hardened. "War is coming, whether today or tomorrow or ten years from now. Better to face it on your own terms. The choice is yours."

The Council exchanged glances. They looked worried, as well they should be. Yet, slowly, one by one, they rose to their feet and cast their votes to rebel. I cursed them for fools.

The nightmares were going to war with Hell.

TRUTH AND DRAGONS

As the Nightmare Council dove into war preparations, Kurai sidled silently up to me. Her red eyes were haunted, and her wings once again wrapped her shoulders like a cloak.

Behind us, Cora and Abigail were deep in conversation, their heads nearly touching as they caught up on the past few years since Abigail had died. Both their faces were streaked with tears. Half-listening to their conversation, I heard the details of the escape from the Pit.

Teri the minotaur had arrived via a backstage passageway looking for me on the Council's behalf. Hell's security wasn't nearly as tight as Lucifer imagined. When she didn't find me, Teri rescued the others and brought them here. I was mildly surprised that Abigail hadn't somehow saved them all, but despite her strength, she was still a human soul and subject to the limitations that implied.

Kurai finally broke the silence between us. "I understand now," she said, her gaze fixed on the Council.

"Understand what?" I asked.

"What Babil the djinn said about destructive truth."

The Council was debating how best to strike at Nigel's fledgling empire. Frank and Inez were deep in the conversation, adding advice the nightmares seemed to value.

Kurai said, "We always thought that nightmares were something less. Only slivers of souls, barely deserving Hell's contempt, let alone our notice." I nodded. It was a common condescension among demons. "But they are so much more. The power I felt from Cthulhu..." She shivered. "And this place. Morpheo's not just a lost level of Hell. This is a whole new realm. Like Mudang or Valhalla, but unique and with its own rules." She snorted, but it was a sound of wonderment, not derision.

"Yes," I said, "but those are merely observations. What *truth* have you learned?"

"Nightmares are our equals. Perhaps even our betters in some things." She drew a shuddering breath. "Which has terrifying implications about the humans they were torn from."

I nodded in agreement. "Underestimating the potential power of nightmares has always been one of Lucifer's blind spots." I eyed the Council. "A failure that is about to tear Hell apart."

Sam joined Inez and Frank at the table, hobbling on his crutch. Beatrix walked beside him holding one finger of his free hand. Her tangled brown hair half-covered her face. The girl watched the nightmares with wonder and a little fear, which was understandable. They were terrifying to behold. But then her gaze swiveled toward me, the walking, talking skeleton wrapped in a black cloak and cowl. In the Pit, I too had scared her. Was she still afraid of me?

Beatrix chewed on a fingernail, watching me through her shield of hair before releasing her father's hand and walking over. She huddled in on herself as she approached but seemed oddly determined. She stopped in front of me and just stared up into my flaming eye sockets, shoulders hunched. Her fingernail chewing accelerated the longer the silence stretched. Realizing that Beatrix wasn't going to speak first, I knelt and met her gaze at eye level.

"I'm glad Teri rescued you," I said.

"Who?" Beatrix asked, the word mangled by the finger between her teeth.

"The minotaur. Tall nightmare, bull horns, ring in her nose. Really bad breath."

Beatrix giggled. "Stinky breath!" she said, loudly enough that Inez glanced over. Her mother eyed us thoughtfully before giving me a small nod and returning to the war planning. Despite our differences, Inez trusted me—trusted Death—with her daughter.

Beatrix gnawed on her nail some more, and silence fell between us again. I wasn't good with children. Yes, Death sees entirely too many children, but I don't exactly have long conversations with them. Finally, I asked, "Is there something you need?"

"Tell me a story?"

"Here? Now?" I rocked back on my heels, surprised at her audacity. The nightmares were planning a rebellion, and I should be out rescuing Lucifer. I'd already wasted enough time spinning my wheels in Morpheo.

Yet, none of that mattered to Beatrix. Her world view was as small as she was. She'd just survived months in the

Pit and was now surrounded by literal nightmares. She was scared and reaching out for the only comfort she knew. A way to make sense of the world through the lens of stories. Yes, her parents were here, a comfortable constant in this world of horrors. Perhaps it was their presence that gave her the courage to approach me. To ask Death for a story.

Such courage should be rewarded.

I nodded gravely to Beatrix the Brave. "Very well. A short story."

Beatrix beamed at me, radiant joy hitting me like sunshine after a storm. She crawled onto my bony knee and nearly knocked me over. I dropped my other knee to the ground and steadied myself awkwardly, wrapping one arm around the girl's waist so she didn't fall. At no point had she stopped chewing her fingernail.

"So," I asked at a loss, "what kind of story would you like?"

Beatrix's finger—the one not in her mouth—shot toward Conrad. He was sitting with unusual quiet on the back of Dracula's chair, not part of the discussions, but paying keen attention. "A dragon story!" Beatrix yelled. Conrad's head snapped toward us. His eyes narrowed.

I chuckled. After today, I had quite a few dragon stories.

"Did you know that Conrad can change shapes?"

Beatrix's eyes widened.

"It's a remarkable skill for a nightmare, but even so, he's not very good at it."

Conrad stuck his tongue out at me, but I could see a hidden smirk when his gaze flicked toward Beatrix. She giggled.

"Most nightmares are trapped in their original terrifying form." Beatrix inhaled sharply, and I quickly added, "But you needn't fear them. Not in Morpheo. Here they are free to be whoever they wish. Some are gruff and cranky like Adze, and others kind and gentle. But their appearance will never change. Take the yeti there..." I nodded at the yeti with his back to us, soft white fur overflowing his chair. The fur rippled whenever he moved. "He is and always will be a yeti, large and terrifying and a surprisingly accurate representation of what a real yeti looks like."

Beatrix's eyes bulged. "Real?"

I nodded. "They're incredibly rare, practically extinct. I've seen them in the course of my duties as Death because explorers and mountaineers often confuse 'intrepid' with 'idiotic.' But this story isn't about yeti. It's about The Amazing Conrad the Dragon who couldn't quite become a puppy."

From the back of Dracula's chair, Conrad sniffed dramatically at me and turned his attention to a monologue from Frankenstein's Monster. Yet I could tell that Conrad was still listening to me.

I lowered my voice and leaned toward Beatrix. "Earlier today, Conrad and I were up in the mortal realm. People aren't used to seeing little blue dragons, so he disguised himself."

"As a puppy!" Beatrix clapped her hands, finally pulling that finger from between her teeth.

"Almost..." I let the word linger in the air. "He had the whiskers, hair and tail, but ... have you ever seen a blue puppy?"

She shook her head.

"Or one with wings?"

Beatrix giggled.

"Exactly," I said, then paused, thinking. Conrad wasn't limited like other nightmares. Though we hadn't discussed it, I was increasingly convinced that he had Lucifer-level access throughout Hell.

Did he also have Lucifer's knowledge?

My gaze fixed on the little dragon. Conrad must have

felt Death's flaming stare because his head swiveled back toward me. It cocked to the side as though he were asking, 'Wassup, Bones?'

Beatrix tugged on my cowl, pulling my gaze down. "What'd Conrad do?"

"Well, there we were," I said, returning to my story, "riding in a cab to Cora's house when—"

The ballroom door slammed open, interrupting me. It bounced off the wall with a crash and Babil flew in with a whirlwind of sand and shadows. Beatrix leapt from my lap and scrambled back to hide behind her father's leg. Sam tucked a protective arm around her. I rose as all eyes followed Babil. The djinn formed beside the goose's chair and spoke with breathless intensity.

"They're here. Hell's Legions are breaking into the Basement."

Chapter 28

BATTLE DUCKS

SILENCE FELL. SILENCE SO grave and deep that the creaking shift of Sam's crutch felt loud and disruptive.

The goose narrowed her eyes. "Well ... lay a golden egg and call it Mary." She leapt onto the table and hissed an unintelligible string of sibilants. There was a flash of light and the space inside the circular table became a window similar to the one we'd seen in Hell's Reception, though horizontal. I was too far away to see much on the flat surface, but the Basement's sickly green glow was unmistakable. It reflected onto the Council as they rose to gaze downward.

One of the werewolves growled with a furry contralto. "They've bypassed the elevators. That's one of the old ramps into the Basement." Ramps from Dante's day that had once connected Hell's levels. She glanced at Frankenstein's Monster. "Will the barricades hold?"

"Don't count on it," he said.

The goose turned to Inez. "You were right. The war has come to us." To the rest of the Council she said, "Assemble at the Gate! Go!"

Her words were like fire beneath the nightmares. They leapt into action, scrambling for the open door behind me.

Inez and Sam followed more slowly. Beatrix trailed, again clutching Sam's hand.

I stepped into their path, my arms spread. "Wait, please. This is not our war. We must rescue Lucifer. Anything else is a distraction."

Inez shook her head. "Sorry, Grim. You're doing what you think is right. So am I." She pushed past me. Not in an unkind way, but with determination, and she slipped the gold band back on her finger. Change flowed over her as she passed, her wrinkles fading as her white hair turned fiery red.

Sam threw me an apologetic smile. "I'm with her. Always will be."

"You knew, didn't you? About her immortality."

He nodded. "I told you before, I *really* won the jackpot with Inez. If she's going to war, so am I."

I waved toward his crutch. "The first demon you meet will tear you to pieces."

Sam snorted. "There's more to fighting than swinging a sword. You forget, I'm a logistician. I plan. I organize. There'll be plenty to do behind the lines."

"But ... what about Beatrix? You can't take a child to war!" Beatrix's blue eyes gazed up at me from behind Sam's leg.

The yeti, who'd waited behind the other council members, came up behind Beatrix and swept the little girl into his arms. She shrieked in terror, wriggled like a bug on its back, then went very still, wide eyes fixed on the white-furred nightmare cradling her like a baby.

"We will safeguard the child," he rumbled, eyes fixed on Beatrix. He gave her a gentle smile, one without teeth. "In fact, she can help."

"Really?" Beatrix said, her voice small. Her fingers twitched like she didn't know what to do with her hands. She finally settled on grabbing a handful of silky fur near the yeti's jaw and running it through her fingers.

"Mmm..." he said. "That feels nice. Tell me, do you like stories?"

Beatrix nodded.

"Good," he said. "Because Morpheo is a dream realm. Down here, with a little help, your dreams can come alive. We've dreamed up some fearsome defenses, but I suspect that you"—he tapped her nose with a claw—"have a *great* imagination."

Beatrix drew in a wondering breath. "I could make a unicorn?"

"Is it a fearsome unicorn?"

"Uh huh!" Beatrix said, hands suddenly waving with excitement. "And I can make dragons and goblins and ... and *ducks!*"

"Ducks?" I said, glancing at Sam.

He chuckled. "We took her to a duck pond a couple of years ago. They swarmed her for the bread, and, well, a two-year-old isn't much bigger than a duck. She didn't stand a chance." He looked away sheepishly. "Yup, we made memories that day."

The yeti nodded. "Giant battle ducks. I like it."

Sam's head snapped up like he'd suddenly realized

something. He narrowed his eyes at the yeti. "I'm all about using giant battle ducks against Hell—in fact, I really want to see that—but I know how nightmares are made. You're not tearing *anything* from my daughter's soul."

The yeti shook his shaggy head. "In Morpheo, dreams come alive through imagination and need, not violence. Come, and I'll show you." He turned toward the door which Inez was holding open, waiting for her family. The yeti strode out on silent paws, asking Beatrix what her battle ducks would look like. Sam hobbled to follow, but I stopped him with a hand on his shoulder.

"Sam, wait."

His face hardened. "You're not changing my mind."

"No, it's not that," I said, reaching into my cloak. "I just thought that a little *Faith* might help in your coming battle with the forces of Hell." I presented Sam's blessed letter opener. "Good luck."

A wry smile lit his eyes as he took the blade. "With *Faith*, who needs luck?" He slipped it into his belt and threw me a two-fingered salute. "Thanks."

Sam hobbled from the ballroom. Inez spared me a sad smile before she pulled the door shut with a resounding *boom.*

***

The nightmares were gone, leaving me in the Council chambers with Frank, Cora, Abigail, and Kurai. Oh, and Conrad. At some point he'd rejoined Abigail, once again perched on her left shoulder like a blue-scaled parrot.

Frank stood separate from the women, throwing Cora nervous looks while fiddling with the sleeve of his cloak. Clearly, the silence was too much for him. He cleared his throat and said, "Uh, hey Cora."

Cora crossed the short distance between them and slapped his face with a ring-laden hand. Hard.

"Ow!" Frank rocked back. "What was that for?"

"You planned your own death, using ingredients *I* provided to swap souls with Grim, and didn't even tell me?"

Frank rubbed his jaw. "I, uh, meant to. Really. But it was dangerous. Didn't know if I'd survive. I knew you'd cry and—"

"Coward."

Frank's shoulders hunched. He wasn't winning this argument, so he turned to me, still rubbing his jaw. "So, where to, Boss?"

"You argued so enthusiastically for war, I'm surprised you didn't rush out with the Council."

He shrugged, regaining some of his confidence. "I've always had a soft spot for the underdogs, and I hope they win. But the real battle is rescuing Lucifer. I'm a Reaper. My place is with you."

I couldn't have agreed more. "But we still don't know where Lucifer is," I said.

Conrad raised a sheepish paw. "I do."

All eyes turned toward the nightmare. Toward *Lucifer's* nightmare ... who could point unerringly toward the spirit he'd been torn from. He pointed downward. "Morpheo's inside Level Eight. There's still one more missing level of Hell. What Dante called Hell's Ninth Circle."

The Ninth Circle was Lucifer's court before the reorganization. Not that Hell had shown Lucifer's court to Dante when he'd toured the place. Dante had only seen Lucifer trapped in ice for eternity. And now Hell's Ninth Circle truly was a prison for the Lord of Lies. How ironic.

Cora hitched her leather jacket and nodded sharply. "Okay. How do we get there?"

I turned to her, surprised. "We? Now that you've found Abigail, I thought you would be looking for a way to

Purgatory and then home."

Cora and Abigail threw me matching looks. One of those looks that said I'd completely missed the point. Abigail asked, "You never read Dante's *Inferno*, did you?"

"I don't get a lot of reading time as Death. You try keeping up with mankind's mortality rate. But I reaped Dante's soul, and he gave me the basics. Authors always babble on about their books."

Abigail shook her head. "Dante didn't leave through Hell's front door. His exit was *below* Lucifer's prison on Hell's Ninth Circle. The only way out is through. We're with you all the way." Her rainbow hair slipped off her ear, half-covering her face, and she pushed it back and looked at Conrad. "So, where's the entrance to Hell's Ninth Circle?"

Conrad grinned and turned to Kurai. "You remember that giant cellar door in the Basement?"

Dread realization spread across demon's face. "Oh, hell no!"

"Yup!" Conrad crowed. "To reach Lucifer, we have to go through Cthulhu."

Kurai swore. Loudly and in several languages.

***

By the time we reached Morpheo's Gate, the hillside was blanketed with nightmares preparing for war. The twilight air was thick with sweat, fear, and determination. Many were preparing layered fortifications. The stone walls we'd passed on the trail were now impressive redoubts coated in brambles and spikes. Even as I watched, the spikes grew and twisted. They were so sharp, even their shadows glinted in the eclipsed sunlight.

This was a dream realm. Imagination was their only limit.

I glanced at my team as we ran, surprised to be thinking of them as 'my team.' Death is a lonely business. I'd been on my own for so long that I'd had forgotten what it was like to trust another soul. To enjoy their company, even as we headed into the awaiting terrors of Lucifer's prison.

Up the hill, an army of nightmares pressed together at Morpheo's Gate, pushing and straining to pour through the small doorway into the Basement. Trolls and minotaurs, vampires and shadows, geese, wolves, squid, and more. Lots of tentacles and too many teeth. And claws. Everything had claws.

We'd passed the Davidsons and the yeti at the edge of the city, down at the bottom of the hill. Sam and Inez were assisting a collection of little blue men with red beards and kilts as they pulled bombardment munitions from a warehouse. Trolls positioned trebuchets and catapults nearby. The little blue men seemed more inclined to action than logistics, but as we'd passed, Sam had chivied them into an assembly line, stacking munitions that weren't iron. They looked like giant marbles, multicolored and swirling with their own internal light. Nightmare magic waiting to wreak havoc among any who would dare enter their realm.

Beatrix and the yeti had been with them, deep in conversation.

We were halfway up the hill when an abrupt and very loud, "Quack!" from behind made me jump. We stopped and turned. A duck the size of an elephant thundered up the trail, waddling wildly as it chased a sparkly pink unicorn. The oversized mallard was mostly brown with a green head, yellow bill, and terrifying eyes.

No, not eyes. Eye. The right side of its face was scarred as though it had lost a fight with a cat whose size I didn't want to contemplate. Beatrix's battle duck was fierce indeed.

The unicorn ran past, not even slowing. It was a bizarre

mix of adorable and menacing with a spiraled steel horn and matching sabertoothed fangs. Pink glitter trailed behind it. The queued nightmares cheered as the unicorn joined them.

The battle duck rocked to a stop in front of us. Its right eye was milky and blind, but the left considered us sharply, as though wondering if we were the enemy. Or food.

"Quack!"

My companions and I all took a step back.

I glanced down the hill. Another battle duck was taking form between Beatrix and the yeti, a swirl of feathers and magic and dreams. I swear I heard Beatrix's giggles echoing up the hillside.

A deep growl snapped my attention back to the path. A goat-headed monster stood between us and Morpheo's newest creation. Krampus. He had gangly arms, long and twisted horns, and was layered in matted black hair. Krampus growled something at the battle duck.

The mallard rolled its fearsome yellow eye but stepped around us.

Krampus gave me a respectful nod before turning to growl at a many-tentacled ... *thing* nearby that was creating a slime pit between two wall sections.

We joined the queue at the Gate and pushed forward. We had to reach the Basement before Hell's forces broke through. Before the war began. Hopefully, we could slip past unnoticed as the nightmares prepared.

We jostled for position, Conrad rejoining us to land on Abigail's shoulder. We finally passed through the gate right behind Beatrix's unicorn and returned to the Basement.

The sounds of war struck me first.

A fist struck me second.

THE NIGHTMARE WAR

I STUMBLED BACK, CLUTCHING my jaw. Kurai caught my shoulders and shoved me aside. She drew her daggers. The demon who'd struck me was a muscled brute: twice as tall as me, red-skinned, and shirtless. Oversized mountain goat horns curled past his jaws. He roared with battle fury.

Kurai launched herself at the demon, screaming her rage as she plunged both daggers into his chest. The demon stumbled back in surprise. A meaty fist wrenched Kurai free. He tried to smash her against the sickly green stone wall, but she twisted in his grip, dropped briefly to the ground, then sprang back toward him. Her wings wrapped his head, cocooning the two of them together.

I didn't wait to see what happened next, but it didn't sound pleasant. More nightmares pushed through the Gate behind us. Jesse the storm cloud roiled and boiled to our left, larger than before. His lightning snapped out with staccato booms, and demons went flying. One unlucky demon struck him—or, rather, *at* him as a storm cloud had nothing solid to strike—and chains of electricity wrapped the demon in jagged, jumping lightning. The demon convulsed until Jesse released him to collapse in a smoking heap.

I dodged right, pulling Cora and Abigail with me. Frank followed tight on our heels. Cora drew her water pistol and held it low and ready. Her wide-eyed gaze darted from side to side.

Abigail was weaponless, but not for long. She flexed her will, and a bladed staff materialized in her hands. It looked vaguely Japanese with a long black shaft capped by a curved short sword. The weapon looked natural in her hands.

Battle raged around us. Demons poured out of a ragged hole in the cavern's far wall, a screeching horde that sent a shiver down my spine. Many still wore their rumpled suits, but the wave of violence gave lie to Hell's veneer of civility. It was like a prelude to Armageddon.

In the distance, I saw Nigel and his cronies watching from just inside that hole. I recognized the Auditor's distinctive lanky form as he leaned on *Grace.* My scythe. Its curved blade reflected the Basement's green glow.

Demons and nightmares fought everywhere on the Basement's twisted walkways. There was no front line and gravity seemed optional in this Escheresque madness. Combatants fought sideways or even upside down. Screams of anger and agony flowed over me. The true horror was they couldn't kill each other. Victory would come to the side that inflicted the most suffering.

We ran, keeping to the right side of the cavern, dodging and hiding and trying our best to remain on ground level. Now that we were back in the Basement, Cthulhu's dread once again seeped into my bones. Behind my fear and adrenaline surged an overwhelming numbness.

Join me in oblivion, it whispered without words. *True death awaits.*

I gritted my teeth and ignored Cthulhu's siren call. It wasn't easy. I felt stronger, refreshed even from my time in

Morpheo, but the power of Cthulhu's will was not easily brushed aside.

"There!" Conrad said, launching himself from Abigail's shoulder to swoop low toward Cthulhu's cell. Not that he needed to direct us. It was hard to miss those massive doors sitting angled like a cellar entrance. Frank put on a burst of speed and ran up the path to catch up with Conrad.

Dave and Dale, the twin torment coaches we'd met in Customer Annoyance, leapt at Frank from behind a pillar. The Taxman shrieked and flailed his fists with absolutely zero effect.

We *really* needed to talk about his battle responses.

The demons dodged his blows easily and—moving as with a single mind—planted twin punches into his gut. Frank wheezed and collapsed. He rolled over; pushed to his hands and knees. The twins drew matching knives. Evil grins spread as they raised their blades to stab him in the back.

Abigail sprinted up the path. Her bladed staff whirled, deftly removing a demon's hand before completing its spin to crack him in the side of the head. He collapsed like a ragdoll. His severed hand, still clutching the knife, arced upward before wisping away in black smoke.

"Dave!" the other twin gasped, shocked gaze following the severed hand. He should have looked behind him.

Barely a step behind Abigail, Cora shot Dirk in the back of the head with her Holy Water Squirt Gun (patent pending). His head disintegrated. The rest of him followed, disappearing with a *pop*, banished to the Lake of Fire on Level Five. Abigail prodded his unconscious twin with her foot while Cora scanned for more threats. Frank remained on his hands and knees, struggling for breath.

Something made me look up. Whether it was claws on stone or that sixth sense when you know someone's watching you with homicidal menace, I couldn't say, but a squad of demons armed with wicked-looking blades stalked toward us down a vertical path. I drew my Holy Water Squirt Gun (patent pending) and aimed upward. Though this was the first time I'd drawn it, the leaky pistol was half empty, the rest of my ammunition soaking the cloak at my left hip. Dribbles of holy water rolled down the barrel and over my fingers as I aimed up at the demons.

Those in the front eyed the spot where Dirk had been and exchanged nervous glances. Little splashes of holy water still sizzled on the ground. As one, their gazes swiveled to my neon green pistol.

I cocked my head to one side, channeling confidence I didn't feel. They slowed.

Kevin's face appeared from the back of the squad, peering around demons larger than him. Abigail's former boss from Torments bore a whip and a cruel snarl. The whip snapped and he yelled, "For Nigel! Attack!"

The demons must have feared Kevin more than they feared banishment. Their expressions firmed and with a yell, they charged.

I pulled the trigger.

Holy water shot upward but fell far short of my attackers. Half of it splashed back on me while the other half was caught by the Basement's variable gravity and made a sizzling line on the vertical path.

Damn. I'd never fired a squirt gun before, and I'd expected a bit more range. Apparently, these were close combat weapons. I braced myself, pistol aimed, and waited for the charging squad to reach me.

That's when I noticed the black tomcat. He sauntered onto the vertical path between us from behind a bend in the surrounding stone. It was the same tomcat who'd found me in IT. Most of the Basement's feral cats had disappeared, choosing discretion as the better part of valor as this was not their war, but not him. The battle-scarred tom strolled onto the path without a care in the world. He sat as though fully expecting the charging squad to go around him.

He wasn't alone.

Diana flowed after him, tail high, looking like a queen on parade. As though she considered the Basement's eldritch horrors commonplace. She sidled up to the black tom and rubbed against him in a sultry manner that had no place on a battlefield. However, I suppose cats have their own priorities. The tom arched into her, licking Diana's neck.

Annoyance flickered through me. Really? Diana couldn't be bothered to bring me to Hell, but when it came time to flirt, she was raring to go! My annoyance, however, was short-lived.

The lead demons saw the cats and yelped in terror. They leapt aside, splitting the squad like a river around a rock, but those behind them didn't see the obstruction. Clawed feet slammed into the intertwined cats.

Diana and the tom flew in a yowling, snarling ball. They landed on their feet only yards from me. They turned on their attackers, fur standing on end, and the tomcat's yowl chilled the marrow in my bones. It was deep with promises of violence and vengeance. Then the cats did something impossible.

They changed their physical forms.

The tomcat twisted and grew, mutating into a beast twice the size of a tiger. Muscles bulged. A ridge of black spikes erupted along his spine, and his fangs lengthened like a sabertooth's. The path crumbled under his enormous claws.

He roared.

Diana's change was less dramatic but no less terrifying. She grew into a monster-sized version of herself, slightly smaller than the tom, with the same fluffy white hair and squished face she always had. But that face was no longer cute and demure. The anger of an offended goddess filled Diana's eyes. Her roar matched the tom's, deep and angry.

As one, the two cats leapt. The demons tried to run, to escape the enraged mutant monsters, but they didn't stand a chance. They were mere spirits. These were cats of flesh and blood with stronger willpower than all of them combined.

Willpower. That was the only explanation for the impossibility I'd just witnessed. Diana and the tom had combined Hell's mutable spiritual nature with their iron willpower to change their physical forms. That was Lucifer-level willpower. Did every cat have this strength of will?

Probably.

Between them, the cats tore the demon squad to shreds. Literally. Within moments only bits of demon remained, which then wisped away into the ether just as Beelzebub had when he died. Kevin and his squad were no more.

I slowly lowered my weapon as the echoing screams faded. I'd thought only *Mercy* could grant a true death. To end an immortal soul. This explained Hell's fear of its feline residents.

One does *not* anger a cat in Hell.

Vengeance satiated, both cats shrank back to their original forms. They wound about each other, giving licks and entwining tails before they flopped unceremoniously in a tangled puddle of fur on the vertical path. Their tails and ears twitched happily as though all was now right with the world even as war raged around us.

My promise to make Diana a goddess among cats was pointless. She already was. A goddess both terrifying and wonderful. The squad's decimation had taken only seconds. I would never again underestimate a cat.

Both cats' gazes swiveled toward me. I nodded my thanks.

Beside me, Cora and Abigail stared wide-eyed at the cats. From their shocked expressions, I suspected that they too were reevaluating their world views of cats.

Abigail shook herself and helped Frank to his feet, stepping over the still-unconscious Dave the now one-handed demon. "You good?" she asked Frank.

Frank nodded, sucked in a few breaths, and squared his shoulders. "Yeah."

"Then let's move!" Cora said, pushing past him to take the lead.

We were a hundred yards from Cthulhu's cell when the doors began to push upward. With a groan that shook the walls, those doors that were too big to be real, yet too real to be ignored, creaked open. Great claws as big as the Basemen's green pillars curled around the edges of the doors.

We were fifty yards away when Cthulhu's head pushed through the gap, octopus tentacles writhing with an entrancing rhythmic sway. I couldn't look away. The green and black monstrosity rose from the depths, towering like a titan.

We were nearly there when the doors crashed open, knocking down pillars and pathways like kindling, crushing demons and nightmares alike. I stopped running, as did my companions, though our destination lay scant yards ahead. We simply stood and stared at the magnificent terror towering above us. It bore an octopus-like head atop a rubbery, vaguely humanoid body. The Basement's ceiling twisted and moved, expanding upward to make room for the eldritch terror. Seawater and slime dripped from Cthulhu. It landed with splashes like a waterfall around us.

Powerful dread numbed me. The call of oblivion sang to my soul and overwhelmed my willpower. I wanted nothing more in that moment than to answer the call of Cthulhu. To sink into nothingness.

<u>**Chapter 30**</u>

ELDRITCH HORROR

THE NIGHTMARE WAR FROZE as all eyes turned to the eldritch horror dominating the basement. The Elder God who demanded submission. Silence spread, cloying and thick and steeped in fear. Weapons clattered to the stone. Abigail's bladed staff disappeared, untethered from her will. Demons dropped to their knees, weeping. I craned my neck to gaze up, up, up into Cthulhu's glorious visage. The world smelled of seawater and slime and death. Oblivion beckoned. I yearned to answer that call, to sink into nothingness. Forever.

Conrad slammed into me, a wall of blue scales that blocked my vision. His wings wrapped my head as Kurai's had wrapped that brutish demon scant minutes before. I scrabbled at him, clutched his body, and strained to pull him loose so that I might gaze upon the wonder of—

Conrad punched me. Twice. Quick left-right jabs that rocked my skull. "Snap out of it, Bones!" he hissed.

I fell back. Crashed to the slime-slicked stone.

Conrad grabbed my skull in both paws and gazed deep into my soul with his slitted eyes that shone like the moon. "You are the Grim Reaper," he said. "You are *Death*, the terror of men's souls. That"—he pointed a wing at Cthulhu without shifting his gaze from mine—"is but a caricature of *your* power. The power of Death."

I yanked at him, straining to throw him off me, but Conrad wrapped his tail around my neck, pulling us closer until our foreheads touched.

"We have to rescue Lucifer!" he said, shaking my skull with his intensity. "Only Lucifer can stop Nigel's madness and forestall Armageddon. I need you, Bones. Not Abi. Not Cora. Certainly not that buffoon, Tubby. You. So, snap out of it!"

His paw pulled back to punch me again, but it paused

when my eye sockets flared bright.

"One does not smack Death like a piñata," I intoned. "But ... thank you."

Conrad's gaze flicked from flame to flame in my eye sockets as though weighing the clarity of my mind. He nodded, leapt from me, and I rose. The call of Cthulhu still pulled at my soul, but I resisted. I focused on the task at hand.

Get everyone into Cthulhu's chambers. Find Hell's Ninth Circle. Rescue Lucifer. Stop Armageddon.

Easy.

Nigel's mocking laugh rang out, echoing across the silent cavern.

"Is that all you have? An oversized squid?" he yelled. Drawn steel rang. I glanced back. Nigel, along with the Auditor and his lackeys, were the only demons still on the shelf where they'd broken through into the Basement. Hell's newest lord looked small in the distance. David to Cthulhu's Goliath.

But I knew how that story ended. Goliath had whined inconsolably after I reaped his soul.

Cthulhu stepped forward, dripping seawater and slime. He ignored us, his dread gaze fixed on Nigel. We were less than ants beneath his feet. The Basement shuddered with Cthulhu's every step. Nightmares and demons alike scattered before him. Twisting paths and towering columns shattered and collapsed as he strode through them like cobwebs in a forest.

Nigel leapt down from his shelf and charged, *Mercy* raised for the attack. This would be a battle for the ages, and I'd seen a lot of battles. All of them, in fact.

But this one, I'd have to miss.

I grabbed Abigail's face and wrenched her gaze from Cthulhu's lumbering form. Fear warred across her features before her eyes cleared, and she pulled away. "I'm fine!" she said, shaking her head. "He just ... surprised me."

"You're not the only one. Help your mother," I pointed to Cora before grabbing Frank. It took a bit more to bring my apprentice around, but fortunately, I didn't have to resort to Conrad's piñata technique.

Conrad squatted on Kurai's shoulder, whispering into her ear. A shiver wracked the demon, and her gaze snapped to mine. There was no fear upon her face. Anger and determination, yes. But not fear.

I ran for the cellar door entry into Cthulhu's chambers and gazed down. It was like peering over a cliff at midnight. Black water lapped against unseen stone far below, rippling with the tremors of Cthulhu's every step.

The others joined me. Frank peered down and whistled. "That's the way to Hell's Ninth Circle?"

Conrad nodded from Kurai's shoulder.

"Then what are we waiting for?" Frank said and jumped. "Geronimo!"

He pulled his legs up, wrapped his arms around his knees, and hit the water like a cannonball.

We *really* needed to have that talk about maintaining the Reaper's dignity.

Cora and Abigail followed. Cora simply jumped with her nose plugged while Abigail executed a swan dive.

Now that was *much* more dignified.

None of them surfaced. What lay within those murky depths?

I exchanged glances with Kurai. She gestured me forward, and I was about to jump in when something behind her caught my eye. A bit of green plastic half-hidden behind rubble from the cellar doors' cataclysmic opening. A futuristic-looking water pistol.

My hand flashed to the holster under my cloak. It was empty. I leaned past Kurai to get a better look. "Hold on.

I think I dropped my—"

Conrad launched himself from her shoulder and hit my chest like a battering ram. "Let's go!" he yelled.

We didn't even teeter on the edge. Conrad's momentum threw me backward into thin air. I scrabbled to catch hold of something. Anything.

I failed.

We tumbled into the darkness. I flailed, screaming at the idiot dragon who'd separated me from the only weapon I had left.

His wings snapped open just before we hit the water, then he used me like a diving board for a draconic version of Abigail's swan dive.

I didn't have time to congratulate him on his form. I splashed head-first into the murky salt water with zero dignity.

Chapter 31

THE DRAGON

HEAVY DARKNESS ENVELOPED ME: cold, wet, and salty. Despite the ignominy of my entry into the water, I was not unfamiliar with the briny depths. Mankind has long challenged the ruthless vagaries of the sea—the Phoenicians, the Vikings, idiots on supposedly unsinkable cruise liners. Many claim to have conquered the sea, sailing it with impunity. Thumbing their noses at Death.

Yet I, the Grim Reaper, am always there, waiting for when they fail.

Death comes for all.

And now I was coming for Lucifer. But not as a shepherd to guide his soul to eternity, but as a savior here to set him free.

The Devil. The irony of that statement was not lost on me.

I sank into the depths. Silence wrapped around me like a comforting blanket. The Basement's green glow illuminated the water above, but only darkness spread below. Liquid night. I could barely see Conrad's silhouette below me, swimming straight down.

A change in pressure announced Kurai's entry into the water. Had she retrieved my Holy Water Squirt Gun (patent pending)?

Abruptly, the water around me disappeared, and I fell into open air. I tumbled a scant few yards and crashed onto a rough, slick floor. It was a stone shelf, broad and deep, whose ceiling was the water above. I rose. Though I had plenty of room to stand, the breadth of the shelf made the ceiling feel low enough that I wanted to crouch.

It was a stairstep. Not big enough for something as gargantuan as Cthulhu, but perhaps fifty feet across and half that deep. Backed by stone on three sides, the open side revealed a cavern of ice and stone. We were near the cavern's ceiling, the giant stairwell's next step just visible beyond the ledge.

We must have passed through some sort of portal within the water. This wasn't where Cthulhu had lived. It wasn't big enough. This was, indeed, Hell's Ninth Circle.

I could tell because it was freezing cold.

Nearby, Cora and Abigail squeezed water from their clothes and hair while Frank just stood there looking like a drowned rat in his Reaper's cloak. I stepped toward them, shedding water as I walked. It formed little rivulets on the stone that streamed down to puddle between us. Once it pooled together, the water poured slowly upward, defying gravity to rejoin the water that was our ceiling. By the time I reached them, I was bone dry.

Frank watched the water flow upward, eyes wide. "How'd you do that?"

"Willpower," I said. "You keep forgetting that you aren't mortal anymore. As a spirit, you can change your appearance and even environment to whatever you wish—if your will is strong enough. And I wouldn't have accepted you as my apprentice if you *weren't* strong enough." He just had to realize it!

Frank nodded, face scrunched as he tried to exert his will. Water slowly started drifting upward from his cloak.

He didn't manage complete dryness, but at least he no longer looked like a drowned rat. Merely a damp Taxman.

Abigail stopped wringing her hair and straightened. She narrowed her eyes. The water in her hair, cloak, and clothes whisked away much faster than mine and Frank's had. It shot toward the seawater ceiling like liquid bullets.

Cora watched, her breath forming a cloud in the cold. "But I *am* mortal, so I guess I'm stuck as a drowned rat?" A shiver ran through her, and she rubbed her arms. Then she started digging into her pockets and dropping water-logged spell ingredients onto the stone.

Abigail scratched behind her earring-studded ear. "Is that salt?" she asked as Cora pulled two water-logged baggies from her cargo pockets. Cora nodded.

"For creating a circle, either to bind a spirit or keep them out." The bags made a *splooch* sound when she dropped them next to the matches and candles. "So much for that idea." When she finished emptying her pockets, all that remained was her jewelry: rings, bracelets, and necklaces that clicked and clattered as she adjusted her clothing.

Kurai dropped to the shelf beside us. Her hands slapped the stone as she caught herself in a half-kneel. The demon rose and snapped her bat wings out to their full span. Salt-water sprayed like scythes to the sides before drifting up-wards in twin clouds. Mist rose from her skin and clothes, water flashed to steam by the heat of her endless fury.

I nodded in appreciation. Willpower with a flair for the dramatic. I'm sure Frank would get there eventually. I re-minded myself that he was still young. Not even a century of life and less than a year as a spirit.

Conrad whistled to us from the edge of the step. He was peering downward, ears perked and tail twitching happily. "Come *on*!" he said. "We're nearly there!"

As we strode to the edge, I leaned close to Cora, "My pistol is gone. I saw it behind some rubble before Conrad knocked me into the water. I might have dropped it when Cthulhu's power overwhelmed me, but I *didn't* hide it behind the rubble."

She glanced sharply at me, and her hand shot inside her jacket. The black leather rustled. "Shit," she said, voice low. "Mine too. I know I holstered it."

I glanced at the excited Conrad. He looked like a puppy who'd returned home. He'd been the only one of us un-affected by Cthulhu's power. He was the only one who could have taken our weapons. But why?

The same questions must have graced Cora's mind.

Her gaze flicked to Conrad as we approached him, and her voice lowered. "I still have the cursed dagger and the rest." She caressed Saint Patrick's iron cross among her necklaces. Rings and bracelets clinked together. "Just … be careful, Grim."

"Always," I whispered back.

An enraged dragon's roar split the air. We all jumped. "Grim!" a booming voice called. "Release me!"

I knew that voice. We had found Lucifer, Lord of Lies, Prince of Darkness, the very Devil himself. I looked down upon Hell's Ninth Circle.

A cavern of black stone and blue ice spread out below us. Our massive stairwell curved downward and to the left before ending at an expansive frozen lake.

A giant blue dragon struggled in the center of the lake, encased in ice. Only his head and shoulders were free. He looked like an oversized version of Conrad, only much older and much angrier.

Eternal torches sputtered and spat in irregular sconces wherever stone poked through the encasing ice. The ice refracted the torchlight, splitting and twisting it until shadows danced within its misty blue depths.

Conrad leapt from the stair and glided down toward

the lake. Abigail jumped down to the next step down then turned to help her mother. I leapt to join her—

—and landed on the ice a dozen yards from Lucifer. I stumbled, catching myself before I fell. I glanced around. Kurai appeared beside me, not looking surprised at all. Cora, Abigail, and Frank were still back where we'd started, struggling down that first step.

I shivered. It had been a long time since Lucifer had used his willpower directly upon me. But this was why I'd come. To free the Devil from his captors and return him to power.

But where were his jailors?

Conrad glided down and landed on the glass-smooth ice before the Dragon. He bowed low and Lucifer's leathery lips pulled back into a toothy smile. His gaze lifted to mine.

"Thank you for coming, Grim." The Devil's voice echoed through the cavern, deep and melodious.

"I see no jailors," I said. "Why have you not escaped?"

"You think I haven't tried?" Lucifer roared. He tucked his head and white-hot flame poured from his maw. It obliterated the ice near his foreleg, flashing it into steam. Yet, before he could even shift his weight, the surrounding ice snapped forward with a crackle like shattering glass.

Faster than thought, it trapped him firmly again.

If only I had my holy water! I could have melted that ice as though it had never been. The Devil would then be free of his prison, once again able to bestow his will upon Hell and...

Realization slammed into me, and I stumbled back. The click of my bone heel on the ice echoed through the cavern, but I barely heard it. My thoughts raced. Connections clicked.

Lucifer had just pulled me onto the ice with his will. He was as strong as ever. Able to affect me and the very nature of Hell itself. Nigel could never have imprisoned Lucifer here unless the Devil *let* himself be imprisoned.

And he'd conveniently separated me from my allies, leaving me only with Kurai and Conrad.

I once again wished I had my holy water but for a very different reason.

My jaw clenched as I reached a single inescapable conclusion.

I hadn't come to save Lucifer. He'd brought me here, reeling me in like a fish on a hook.

But why?

Chapter 32

THE DEVIL IN THE DETAILS

"YOU DON'T NEED RESCUING, do you?" I asked Lucifer.

The Dragon eyed me with slitted silver eyes. A wry draconic smile revealed massive teeth, and he shook his head in a slow, definitive 'no.' "You always were a quick thinker, Grim. It's one of your more endearing traits. And it saves so much time. No need for tedious explanations."

He blinked and the world around us changed. We were still in an icy cavern, but it was warmer. Comfortable, as though the ice was mere decoration now. The lake disappeared, replaced by acres of polished red marble floor. A modest dais rose from the center of the floor bearing an ornate golden throne. Tree-like marble columns stretched to the ceiling in ordered rows that radiated from the throne like rays of the sun.

Lucifer lounged upon the golden throne in his angelic form. Olive skin, laughing silver-blue eyes, and shockingly white wings that matched his hair. Hair that was crew cut and spiky with the casual flair of a Hollywood star.

He'd once been called The Morning Star, back when he'd been the Almighty's right hand. Before he'd rebelled and been cast from Heaven.

Conrad swooped down to land on Lucifer's forearm, but the Devil caught him by the throat before he did. The little dragon squawked and flailed for half a second then went deathly still, his eyes wide. Lucifer's silver gaze bored into Conrad's. His lip curled.

Conrad spoke in a strangled rush. "I did everything you required, my lord. The blessed weapons are gone, Morpheo is under attack, and Grim is here."

Lucifer grunted. "Good." He released Conrad who dropped to the red marble before fluttering up to roost on the back of Lucifer's golden throne. The little dragon looked at me, guilty expression warring with pleasure at his master's paltry praise.

The Lord of Lies plucked a grape from a little fruit platter that appeared beside the throne. He popped it into his mouth and smiled at me.

"Why?" I asked. "Why work so hard to manipulate me into coming here? You are the Devil. A summons would have been easier."

"Yes," Lucifer said, "but that wouldn't have served my purpose."

"And what is your purpose?"

"The same as it's always been. To take my rightful place on Heaven's throne."

"By turning Hell over to your madman of a son? He's on the brink of starting Armageddon!"

"Oh, you know I won't let it come to that. Not yet."

"Then why let Nigel take power at all?"

"Come, Grim. You're thinking only one layer deep. Go deeper." Lucifer plucked another grape and reached up as though passing it over his shoulder to Conrad. The dragon strained his neck for it, but Lucifer popped the grape into his own mouth and chewed with a grin. Conrad slumped back.

The Devil was enjoying himself. The Battle of the Basement raged above us, Nigel threatened Armageddon, and he was munching grapes without a care in the world.

Why? Why was he not worried?

I crossed my arms. Think deeper, Grim. Play the Devil's game until you know the rules.

Then change the rules.

"Nigel couldn't have executed his coup unless Hell truly had schisms," I said. "He played to the discontented, gathering followers"—ah, that was it—"and bringing them into the open."

Lucifer nodded. "Rebellion was percolating before my son returned from Abaddon. Better to control the boil and identify the leaders than to lose my throne. I won't be cast out again."

"You want Heaven's throne, but you don't have the power to take it," I said. I expected anger at such a harsh truth, but Lucifer's eyes merely turned hard for a second before he nodded, waiting for me to continue.

Frustrated voices rose in the distance behind me. I glanced back and flinched. Kurai stood directly behind me, silent and brooding. Not that I'd forgotten her presence, but did she have to loom so close? What was her role in all this?

Frank, Abigail, and Cora were only halfway down the stairs, scrambling, hurrying. Not that they could help. I was in a debate with the Devil himself. If only I had my scythe. *Grace* could stop time and let me—

Of course.

I spun back to Lucifer. "You didn't want me. You wanted my *scythe*!"

"Don't be dense, Grim." Lucifer shook his head. "Would I have gone to this much trouble if I didn't want you? Of course, I also want your scythe *Grace*. Imagine, the power to stop time, to have all the time in the universe, and how did you use it? To take confessions." He snorted.

"But I don't have *Grace*. The Auditor's minions stole it."

"As they stole *Mercy* from your darling Evelyn. I'll admit surprise that—of all my demons—the Auditor gained possession of not one, but *two* of the three great blades. Too bad he's a true believer in Nigel's coup. He was such a capable administrator."

Grace and *Mercy*, both in Hell at the same time. Something tickled my mind, and I thought out loud. "The Almighty cast you from Heaven using Gabriel and the sword *Justice* as His instruments. Soon afterward, you created *Mercy* to even the odds. To challenge the Almighty with a blade capable of granting true death. Kill God and take his throne. But then He sent Evelyn to infiltrate Hell. She stole your trump card, the sword designed to slay the Almighty, and you couldn't get it back, though I'm sure you tried. Not long after that, everything went wrong at Megiddo and Evelyn got trapped in Abaddon with *Mercy*. That must have rankled, having *your* sword in the one place you couldn't reach."

My words trailed off as memories rolled through me. Gabriel forced me to abandon Evelyn and *Mercy* in Abaddon. Had that been part of Heaven's plan all along?

Had the Almighty himself betrayed Evelyn just to keep the blade of unmaking from Lucifer's grasp? The Almighty was righteous and holy, but I couldn't shake the thought that He might sacrifice Evelyn to further His inscrutable plan.

Lucifer's lips pursed, my spiraling thoughts thankfully unknown to him. "The keys to a successful plan are patience and flexibility." He spread his hands. "And now *Mercy* and *Grace* are within my grasp. I merely need to stretch out my hands and they will be mine."

"Not quite," I said and pointed up toward the battle that raged even now in the Basement. "You failed to account for the nightmares."

"I accounted for everything!" Lucifer snapped, sudden fire flashing in his eyes. Blue flickering flames, like mine.

The fire dimmed and then vanished. The Devil smiled up at his nightmare, which made Conrad look obscenely happy. "I never said I had only *one* rebellion brewing. Why do you think I created Conrad? Why else would I tear away a piece of my very soul? I needed eyes that could go where I could not." The nightmares had been right. Conrad was Lucifer's spy, the cunning little serpent. He'd played me like a violin, guiding me to this moment. The Devil waved a dismissive hand. "The nightmares are weak and of no concern."

That was a mistake. One I hoped would return to haunt him.

"The question remains," I said. "Why am I here? What do you want me to do?"

"For now? To watch." Lucifer rose and waved a hand. The marble between us rolled back like a scroll, revealing a thick window that looked down into the Basement ... which was above us. I shook my head at the incongruity.

Lucifer controlled Hell. As I'd told Frank when we first arrived, one could go mad applying the laws of physics to a spiritual realm.

Lucifer alighted from the dais, stepped to the edge of the window, and squatted with his forearms on his knees. His wings trailed behind him. Conrad fluttered down and tried to land on Lucifer's shoulder. The Devil shook him off irritably, and the nightmare dropped down beside him to watch the battle. A battle that, now that I'd had time to think about it, was entirely too convenient. The nightmares hadn't rebelled against Nigel yet—they'd voted, but hadn't gotten beyond words—so why attack?

"Conrad," I said, "when did you betray the nightmares? You never left my side in Morpheo."

The little dragon cocked his head and then jumped across the thick window with a single flap of his wings. He landed heavily on my shoulder and craned his neck to meet my gaze. His silver eyes looked so much like Lucifer's. "Remember when you lost me in IT?"

"Yes. I had to accost Kurai just to find the elevators, but that was before..." I trailed off, glanced back at Kurai—who smiled humorlessly at me—and said to Conrad, "That was planned, wasn't it?"

He shrugged. "She helped point you in the right direction while I was busy."

I considered that. "When you disappeared, you went to Teri the minotaur, told her I was in the Pit, and then told ... someone that we would end up in the Basement. And"—my thoughts were racing now—"that the nightmares were going to rebel, which led Nigel to attack." So many places that plan could have gone wrong.

And yet it hadn't.

Conrad nodded, and I rocked back on my heels, awed and a bit overwhelmed at the vast complexity of Lucifer's plan to bring me here. To orchestrate this moment.

"Quiet," Lucifer commanded. "You'll want to watch this part." He waved a hand again, and the glass separating us from the battle below disappeared, letting sound join sight.

I expected blood-curdling cries and the clash of steel. Instead, I heard the singular unearthly scream of Cthulhu. The discordant wail washed over me, dropping me to my knees. Cthulhu's comforting dread subsumed everything I was, his siren call to oblivion urging me to throw myself through the window.

Then the scream died. The call of Cthulhu ended, snapping like a rope under too much tension.

I fell forward onto my hands and gazed down through the window. Conrad clung to my shoulder, flapping his wings for balance as I hit the marbled edge. Below us, barely a column or ramp remained standing. Mangled demons and nightmares lay scattered among the rubble; victims of war unable to die, yet too wounded to carry on. But all that was background.

The back of Cthulhu's head filled my vision, a monstrosity of tentacles frozen in mid-motion. He knelt atop the rubble, one massive, mottled green hand pressed to the ground as though squashing a bug.

Mercy's blade pierced that hand from below, looking no larger than a toothpick. A hole formed around the blade, smoke curling outward, expanding the wound until Cthulhu's entire hand wisped into nothingness.

Nigel stood proud upon the slick green stone, *Mercy* upthrust. The demigod screamed his victory.

Cthulhu disappeared slowly at first, then more rapidly as the essence of his slice of soul died the true death. His voiceless call caressed my mind one final time. Though there were no words, I knew what he said.

Finally ... oblivion.

A cheer rose from Hell's forces as Cthulhu wisped into nothingness. They surged toward Morpheo's Gate. The nightmares had regrouped, forming a defensive line around the Gate. I saw Beatrix's sparkly pink unicorn near the front, her spiraled horn slashing like a rapier.

Nigel walked among the wounded. He paused at each nightmare. Without a word, he dispatched them, one by one, with *Mercy.* True death followed in his wake, silent as the grave.

Then Nigel reached the front line, and the true massacre began.

"No!" I screamed. I looked across at Lucifer. "Stop him!"

"Why would I do that?" he said. "The nightmares rebelled against *me.* They are nothing. Besides, it's such a delicious irony for my problems to solve each other."

I shot to my feet. I pointed a bony finger at the Devil, wanting to rage at him, but my fury was too deep for words. Couldn't he see? Life is precious! Even after death, the soul lives on. He had *no idea* how amazing nightmares were—despite having his own nightmare. They'd built an entire world, and Lucifer was going to let them be slaughtered like sheep.

And what of Conrad? Would Lucifer dispatch Conrad once the nightmare 'threat' was eliminated?

Malice twinkled in the Devil's eyes. Yes, he would.

"Damn you!" I screamed.

"There you are," Lucifer purred, rising to his feet. "Truth comes out in anger. Tell me, Grim, what do you *truly* want?"

"I want to set things right! Return the world to the way it was. The way it should be!"

He shook his head. "There's no going back, Grim. Only forward. But the status quo isn't why you're here. Truth in Death is your motto, so tell me the truth."

I ground my teeth.

The Devil thrust a finger at me and demanded, "What do you want? What is Death's heart's desire?"

"To save my friends!"

Lucifer reared back in mock surprise. "The Grim Reaper has friends? What a fascinating idea. I wasn't sure my little nudge would work."

"Nudge?" I said.

"Your brief mortality. That escapade as Frank Totmann." Lucifer chuckled. "What, you think Alvin Bureaucracy found an ancient Sumerian soul swapping spell by himself? He's good, but he's not *that* good."

I stumbled back in shock. Alvin ... betrayed me? I knew he'd given Frank the spell, but Alvin claimed he did it out of pique.

Lucifer was still talking. "And then Frank's girlfriend just *happened* to have the key ingredient, the bone dust of a Sumerian priest? Cora should take greater care with her online shopping. You never really know who you're buying from."

My mind spiraled in on itself, fighting to untangle the twists of Lucifer's plan to get me here. How long of a game was he playing? How many more would suffer until he got what he wanted? My mind flashed to Beatrix in the Pit.

"You shouldn't have taken the little girl," I said, feeling hollow and powerless. "An innocent has no place in Hell."

"But why should it matter?" Lucifer's tone was lightly mocking. He was toying with me. "She is but one of billions of souls. You've seen atrocities before. Stood aside impartially while the innocent were slaughtered."

I shuddered. Yes, I'd seen more atrocities throughout history than I could count. "Death does not interfere. I merely shepherd the souls of the fallen. Those are the Rules. But everything you've done here," I pointed toward the open window, voice rising, "is an abomination! Stealing the living? Letting Nigel *permanently* end the nightmares because they're inconvenient? Saving my friends *will* restore the balance to Hell and forestall Armageddon. *That* is my heart's desire."

Lucifer stalked around the open window, sliding toward me like a serpent preparing to strike. "And what would you give for your heart's desire?"

"Anything."

"And yet," Lucifer said sadly as he reached me, gaze flicking from my head to my toe, "you have nothing to give. No power. No scythe. No position. Nothing whatsoever of value."

I gazed deep into the Devil's eyes, and I saw the raw blistering truth. I had nothing. No trick up my sleeve. No magic sword to save the day. All I had was me.

My soul.

And that was enough.

"Me," I said. "I offer my—"

"No!" Cora's voice rang from behind me. I spun. Cora, Abigail, and Frank ran toward us across the acreage of marble. Kurai crouched between us, daggers drawn.

"Stop!" Lucifer's voice reverberated with sudden power.

He thrust out his palm and pure willpower on a scale I could only dream of flowed from him like a shockwave. It slammed into them with a flash of white light. Frank and Abigail went flying, tumbling end over end. Abigail's cloak split and snapped out like wings, righting her tumble. She banked, riding the waves of Lucifer's willpower like a kite in a storm.

But not Cora. Cora didn't even flinch when Lucifer's power hit her. She didn't even slow.

Kurai threw herself at Cora, daggers slashing at her throat. White light flashed, and the infernal blades bounced off Cora's skin as if she wore invisible armor.

Shock rippled through me. That was a holy shield. But where had Cora gotten one? The last time I'd seen a holy shield had been on Joan of Arc.

And then I remembered. Cora's jewelry. She wore dozens of 'magical' baubles and bracelets. Even Cora wasn't sure if any of them were real, but somewhere among that clatter of protection amulets and rings was an artifact of true power. An item blessed specifically to protect the faithful from the powers of Hell.

I hadn't realized that Cora was among the faithful. I don't think she did either until this very moment. But there's nothing like coming face to face with the Devil to make you choose sides.

Cora dropped a shoulder into Kurai's chest and knocked her aside. The demon fell back, landing on her ass more in surprise than pain. Lucifer threw more blasts of willpower at Cora. She barreled through them. A screaming freight train of leather and camouflage-clad justice.

Conrad squawked from my shoulder and shot into the air. The Devil's gaze flicked after his nightmare, but his supreme confidence didn't crack. He didn't see Cora's right hand pull back, her fist wrapped around the blunt iron of Saint Patrick's cross.

Somehow, in all his millennia, I doubt the Devil ever got sucker punched.

Chapter 33

A Deal with the Devil

THE PURE SURPRISE ON Lucifer's face just before Cora's fist connected was exquisite. Her punch threw him back, powered by blessed iron and a mother's righteous fury. He fell through the open window and tumbled down into the Basement.

I caught Cora before her momentum carried her right after him.

"That's for stealing my daughter!" Cora screamed as the Morning Star fell.

Yells from below were followed by pointed blades and cheers from Hell's forces. The Devil was back! Lucifer snapped his wings out, righted himself, and landed near Nigel. His gaze whipped back up to us. His growl was audible from up here.

"I think you've pissed off the Devil," I said.

"Good," Cora spat, flexing her hand around the iron cross. I couldn't tell if it was because she'd hurt her hand, or to prepare for round two. "There's truth in anger."

I glanced at her. "You could hear us?"

"You weren't exactly whispering and the acoustics in here are fantastic."

A sword appeared in Lucifer's hand as though drawn from the ether. It was double-edged with a broad hilt and wreathed in deep blue flames—a mockery of Gabriel's sword *Justice*. Clearly, Lucifer had decided it was time to put an end to his son's uprising. Nigel barely had time to brace himself before his father attacked. Lucifer's flaming sword blurred as he struck again and again, tracing arcs of fire through the air. Thunder crashed and the entire basement rumbled with the power of the Devil's fury.

Nigel didn't stand a chance.

Lucifer pressed him, practically running as Nigel struggled to keep his footing, to keep that flaming blade from his throat. The demigod's retreat stopped abruptly when his back slammed into a collapsed green column. Lucifer batted *Mercy* aside and stabbed his son through the chest. The flaming sword bit deep, pinning Nigel to the stone like a bug on display.

Nigel screamed. Lucifer pushed the blade deeper, twisting it before letting go and stripping *Mercy* from Nigel's grip. He stepped back and let his son writhe furiously against the blade impaling him.

The Devil turned, his gaze sweeping the highly attentive faces of Hell's forces. They'd paused their assault on the Gate to watch Nigel's defeat. "You are either with me," Lucifer said, "or with the rebels." He brandished *Mercy* in a clear threat. "Choose wisely."

Hell's forces roared their support and charged the Gate. "For Lucifer!"

"I think," I said to Cora, pulling her back from the window, "that we're beyond 'truth in anger.'"

"Right," she said slowly. "I say we make ourselves scarce before old snake breath comes back." She turned to go, but I placed a hand on her shoulder.

"Where would we go?" I asked.

"The exit! It's got to be around here somewhere." Her head whipped around, gaze piercing the far corners of the ice cavern.

Kurai laughed from behind us. It was not a kind laugh. "There's no exit," she said, climbing to her feet.

"But in Dante's *Inferno*—" Cora began.

"Dante's visit was nothing more than marketing." Kurai spat that last word. "We showed him what we wanted him to see, then sent him on his way. *Nobody* leaves Hell unless Lucifer lets them go. And after your little display of pique, I doubt he's feeling generous."

Cora swore, low and with impressive variety. She'd learned well from Kurai. She crossed her arms and stomped away from the window.

Abigail landed beside her mother, her reaper's cloak billowing like a parachute to cushion her fall. Far behind her, Frank was once again running across the marble. Lucifer's attack had thrown him nearly back to the stone stairs. I turned back to the window and looked down.

Lucifer was flying toward us, *Mercy* in his hands, its sheath now at his hip. He'd left Nigel pinned to the wall with a pair of nervous-looking demons as guards over the furious demigod. Beyond them, the battle of the Basement continued. The nightmares were sorely pressed, losing ground against Hell's reinvigorated forces. It would only be minutes until Morpheo's Gate was breached.

One of Beatrix's battle ducks pushed through the Gate with a loud, "Quack!" and towered over the battlefield. Its beak snapped forward and grabbed a demon. The demon flailed and fought, but in two gulps, it was gone. The nightmares rallied briefly, but even a battle duck's fury wouldn't save them.

Lucifer swept through the window and landed, gaze riveted on Cora. She backed away, knuckles white around her iron cross. She tried to push Abigail behind her, but her daughter just squared her stance. The bladed staff reappeared in Abigail's hands. Lucifer pointed *Mercy* at Cora with clear intent. "You would *dare* strike me?"

"Stop," I said, stepping between them.

Lucifer brandished *Mercy*, the blade hovering inches from my face. "You have no authority here, Grim. No power to make me do *anything*!"

"You're wrong."

His face went purple.

"I have the power of choice," I said. "Of free will." Then I did the most dangerous thing I've ever done. I turned my back on the Devil.

Cora looked nervous, her fist white-knuckled around

Saint Patrick's cross. Her eyes flicked to watch Lucifer over my shoulder. Abigail shifted beside her. From the look in her eye, she would have attacked Lucifer already if I weren't standing between them.

I wasn't immediately struck down by *Mercy*, so I spoke loudly to ensure everyone heard. "I *choose* to protect my friends." I'd never had friends among mortals before, and I wasn't about to let Lucifer have them. My gaze flicked between Cora and Abigail. "We could fight our way out of Hell, but I doubt we'd all make it. And what of the nightmares? Running like scared rabbits won't help them. They've built something amazing: a place to call home amidst the horrors of Hell." An ache filled me to have a home like Morpheo, but I pushed it down. Rest and peace were not in my future. "They deserve a chance to become something more than chattel to be slaughtered at Lucifer's whim. I choose to protect them as well, and in that protection, to reestablish balance where it has been sorely lacking."

I turned back to Lucifer. He'd lowered *Mercy*. His fury had dimmed. Conrad glided over and landed on his shoulder. For once, Lucifer didn't shake the little dragon off. Twin silvered gazes watched me, inscrutable.

"I know why I'm here," I said. "It was a trap well-laid, and I walked willingly—if unknowingly—into it. I should have known better, but regrets for the path not taken are wasted. So, I willingly offer you the one thing I have, the one thing you worked so hard to get: me. My soul and my servitude."

There were yells of disbelief behind me, but a beaming smile split Lucifer's face. He opened his mouth, but I raised my hand before he could speak.

"I do not offer myself cheaply." I closed my fist, then raised my index finger. "First, you will immediately return the living to the mortal realm. The Davidsons, who are in Morpheo, and Cora." I nodded toward her without averting my gaze.

Lucifer arched an eyebrow. "Hell does not release souls, regardless of how they arrived."

"That's a policy, not a Rule. You set the precedent when you let Dante walk free. This is not negotiable."

Lucifer's lips pursed, but he nodded. I raised another finger.

"Second, you will cease your attack on the nightmares, free them, and relinquish all claim to the realm they call Morpheo. They can choose to work for you as other spirits have done, but their days of involuntary servitude have ended. Beyond that, you and the Nightmare Council can negotiate terms, but you *will* negotiate with them as equals."

Lucifer eyed me thoughtfully while Conrad cocked his head back to eye his master. This was a gamble. Lucifer's argument against returning Cora and the Davidsons was for show. He didn't care about them, and he knew that he had to give *something* in exchange for my servitude. Yet, how he reacted to the emancipation of the nightmares would reveal how desperately he wanted me.

The Devil nodded, his face a mask. "Very well. Anything else?"

Damn. Not even a quibble. Time to go for broke.

"I'm just getting warmed up," I said and raised a third and fourth finger. "Release Abigail's soul to me and return every stolen soul to Purgatory to await proper Judgment. I'm sure the Office of Micromanagement has a full listing." Lucifer's eyebrows rose, but I barreled on, remembering the empty chambers I'd found in Purgatory. My thumb extended for my fifth condition.

"Release Minos the Judge from wherever Nigel stashed him." I raised my other index finger. "Sixth, you or yours will *never again* interfere with the impartiality of Judgment."

I paused, thinking, then raised fingers seven and eight. "Oh, and I need two scythes. One for Frank and one for Abigail." There were twin gasps from the women behind me, and I glanced over my shoulder the Abigail. "You'll make one hell of a Reaper if you wish to join me."

She straightened from her fighting crouch, bladed staff still in both hands, and eyed me thoughtfully. Behind her, Frank finally came running up, gasping after having run across the entire marbled expanse for the second time. Abigail glanced at him, then at me, and nodded. "Hell, yeah." She pushed a stray bit of rainbow hair behind one ear and grinned.

Lucifer considered my eight upraised fingers. "That's a lot to ask in exchange for your paltry—"

"I'm not done yet." The Devil's eyes bulged at being interrupted. He'd have to get used to it if he planned to keep me around. Finger nine extended. "Change your ridiculous policy about no coffee, candy, or chocolate in Hell. No need for your minions to suffer as the damned do. If you want to forestall another uprising, letting the employees have a cup of joe is a nice place to start."

My second thumb extended for a count of ten. "And you *will* reestablish your half of the Rules *as they were originally written*. I would not have Armageddon start too soon because you decided to get fancy with loopholes."

Lucifer drew a deep breath. Was he going to argue? This was only the second time I'd ever negotiated employment terms, and I hadn't expected to get this far. Ah, hell, why not drop one more nail in my coffin?

I clenched my fists and lowered them to my sides. "Finally, I get one additional demand to be granted—without question—at the time of my choosing."

I swear I saw smoke curling from Lucifer's ears. His jaw clenched so hard that I could hear his teeth grinding. But then the anger flashed away, replaced by that charming, confident smile. "So long as it's within my power to grant and does not violate the Rules, so be it. I accept your conditions."

Relief washed over me. I'd done it. My friends were safe, and balance was restored to Hell. All I'd had to sacrifice was my soul.

Chapter 34

THE DRAGON LOOPHOLE

LUCIFER SNAPPED HIS FINGERS and the world around us changed again, but this time more slowly. The expansive throne room split into three sections like a pie centered on the open window into the Basement.

The dais and throne pulled back from the window, giving room for a long parquet-inlaid table to rise from the marble. Red stone flowed off the table like gel before solidifying into floor once more. A dozen chairs rose to join the table, claw-footed and heavy. The conference room setup was arranged so Lucifer's throne sat at its head.

The section of the cavern to the throne's left where Cora, Abigail, and Frank stood shifted from a marble expanse to a smithy with rough flagstone floors. A forge and anvil rose from the stonework as the conference table had. Racks of tools soon joined them with a selection of metal stock and wooden rods of varying lengths. Lava boiled and raged in the forge with such heat that I could feel it from yards away. I could smell it too, an intense brimstone stench.

The final piece of the pie to the throne's right, where Kurai stood, became an office, the kind you'd expect in a medieval castle, but with only three wood-paneled walls like a set piece from a stage. Three bookshelves rose from the highly polished hardwood floor, filled with aged, leatherbound volumes. The Rules. They didn't appear damaged, and yet they must be. How else could Nigel have so blatantly violated them? How else could I have lied?

Before the shelves rose a heavy oak desk and a very modern and comfortable-looking swivel chair of black leather. Upon the desk sat an inkwell with a crow-feather pen.

The open window into the Basement remained where it was, the centerpiece of the ice cavern. The roar of battle echoed up to us. Lucifer gave curt orders to Conrad to call off the assault and bring the Davidsons and the Nightmare Council to the throne room. Conrad nodded and dropped from the Devil's shoulder. He fell like a stone through the window before snapping his wings open.

Lucifer snapped his fingers again and a section of marble behind his throne turned liquid. Minos the Judge rose through it like Poseidon rising from the sea. He was muscled and bare-chested with a distinguished beard and crown. And he was easily three-times my height. A snake's tail curled out from behind him, twitching angrily. He shook a fist at Lucifer.

"There you are, you snake! How *dare* you imprison me? It's a clear violation of the Rules. If you damaged your half of the Rulebook—"

Lucifer raised placating hands. "Minos, apologies." The Lord of Lies bowed his head ever so slightly. "It was not I, but my son Nigel who imprisoned you as part of a coup that I have only just put down."

The Judge's eyebrows pulled down into a sharp V. "And the Rules?"

"My Keeper of Records is even now repairing them. Isn't that right?" Lucifer turned toward the faux library.

The Keeper? When had she arrived?

I turned. Only Kurai stood before me. Her gaze met mine and she smiled.

Then she changed.

It started at the tip of her nose and flowed back toward her bat wings like she was stepping through a mirror. The buxom goddess of love and war transformed into a petite wingless Amazon. Her spiky black hair grew into a long brown braid, and her kimono-like suit became a leather jerkin crisscrossed with straps.

Only the burning anger in her eyes remained the same. I should have known. Should have seen. "You were manipulating me and Nigel the entire time, weren't you?" I asked. "Playing all the sides against each other at Lucifer's bidding to bring me here." No wonder I didn't remember her as a goddess in ancient Japan. It had all been a ruse.

And yet, I'd never read the truth in her eyes, in her soul. The Keeper was a true chameleon spirit. A Kitsune. A tricksome fox who could become whoever she wanted to be.

The Keeper flicked a small knowing smile at me but didn't answer. Instead, she sat at the broad oaken desk. She swiveled in her chair, retrieved a heavy tome, and then opened it on the desk. The binding was damaged. Several thick parchment pages slid free. The Keeper reached into a drawer and retrieved a heavy needle, leather bindings, and a single fresh sheet of parchment. She set the binding materials aside. With a delicate dip of the feathered pen into the inkwell, she began to write.

But I wasn't in the mood for mysterious non-answers. While Lucifer placated Minos, I stepped toward the Keeper's desk, hoping to rattle her confidence. Just a little. "What about Abaddon, Keeper? Was it part of Lucifer's plan to have me thrown into the realm of eternal Darkness?"

The Keeper's lips pursed. Her pen paused, and she said, "The Dragon's plans are eternally flexible. I was supposed to be in Nigel's throne room to stop him throwing you in, but then *she*"—the Keeper flicked a venomous glare at Abigail—"sent me to the mortal realm with your scythe." The Keeper's gaze returned to her parchment, and her pen resumed its scritching as she wrote. "And yet it all worked out according to Lucifer's infernal will. You escaped, I found you again, and brought you here, which is all that matters." Her voice had a smug tone I didn't like. So much for rattling her. I turned away, letting the matter drop.

Lucifer was laying the charm on thick with Minos. "Let us return you to your chambers. This elevator"—a Minos-sized door slid open in the nearest column—"will take you straight to Purgatory. Again, my sincerest apologies."

Minos harrumphed. "You're not getting off that easy. I'm initiating a full audit of Hell's records. If you stole a *single* soul without Judgment—"

Lucifer raised placating hands once again, his voice soft and penitent. "Already taken care of. The souls stolen by my son and the Auditor will be returned to Purgatory presently. The Keeper will ensure that the loophole they used is stitched shut."

Loopholes. There were entirely too many loopholes in the Rules. But that started an idea tickling in the back of my mind.

Minos worked his jaw for a moment, then said, "Good. I shall return to inspect your half of the Rules once they are repaired. Don't think you can slip new loopholes past me."

Lucifer glanced at me and then at the Keeper. The scritch of pen on parchment was ominously loud. "Wouldn't dream of it."

With another harrumph, Minos departed. Lucifer

strode into the smithy and retrieved a heavy leather apron that hung from the side of the forge.

***

The next several hours were surreal. Lucifer set about forging scythes while the throne room became a hive of activity. Demons came and went from elevators in the columns, making reports, receiving orders, and dashing off to return Hell to business as normal. Lucifer attended to them all while staying focused on his task. Metal rang, fire crackled, and steam hissed as he created nearly perfect replicas of *Grace.*

As he'd done millennia ago when he created my scythe, Lucifer demanded Abigail and Frank each turn over something formed of their own willpower. Something he could forge into the scythes to bond them to their blades. Abigail gave him her bladed staff.

Frank looked briefly dumbfounded. He didn't have Abigial's strength of will to create something he wasn't already intimately familiar with. But then the Taxman rummaged in his pockets and retrieved a wallet.

"Cash or credit?" he asked with a smirk.

Lucifer cocked an eyebrow, said, "You can't afford my rates," and took the entire wallet.

Conrad returned from his errands and flapped about Lucifer's throne room like a sparrow, humming to himself as he watched the results of his duplicity at the Devil's behest.

When he swooped nearby, I said, "Conrad, a question."

The little blue dragon banked sharply and landed on my shoulder. His breath smelled slightly sulfuric but with a hint of sweetness. He must have stolen some grapes from the platter by Lucifer's throne when the Devil wasn't looking. He tilted his head. "Wassup, Bones?"

"When we first met, you kept arguing with Abigail to leave. To escape Hell, which would have violated your primary mission to lead me here. Why?"

Conrad's chin dipped, and he looked embarrassed. His head swiveled to watch Abigail by the forge. "I like Abi. A lot. Lucifer would never let her soul go, so I wanted to give her a chance to escape."

"Then why not take her directly to Purgatory before we even met? You have full access as Lucifer's nightmare. Why play games about getting lost in the Labyrinth?"

Conrad looked pained. "There's no keeping secrets

from the Devil. When he learned of Abigil's intent to escape, he devised the plan for you and me to meet in the Labyrinth. His subtle way for our paths to cross."

"And yet, once we met, you still tried to leave with Abigail," I said. "Why go against the Devil's will?"

Conrad's draconic expression turned sharp. "Nightmares have free will, just like everybody else. You were Lucifer's priority. She became mine. But she wouldn't leave you, so our priorities merged. Problem solved."

"Yes. Free will is the key," I murmured. "She'll do well as a Reaper." I considered the dragon on my shoulder, my mind flicking back to earlier thoughts of loopholes. "What will you do now?"

He shrugged, making his wings ripple across his back. "Back to my old job, I guess. Lucifer's spy and nightmare messenger." He didn't sound excited about the prospect.

I glanced at Lucifer as he hammered a scythe blade on his anvil. The Devil had me well and fully trapped in his service. He'd thought of everything.

But try as he might, he couldn't *control* everything. Or everyone. "You know," I said, "I think she likes you too. A lot." My gaze turned ever so slightly toward Abigail. She and Cora watched Lucifer's work; heads close as they whispered to each other. Frank stood awkwardly nearby as though he wanted to join the conversation but didn't know what to say. "It's a lonely job being Death," I said.

Conrad followed my gaze to Abigail. He didn't say anything, but the tilt of his head was thoughtful.

Chapter 35

THE RULES REBOUND

THE DAVIDSONS AND THE Nightmare Council arrived together, escorted by Brutus. The prune-faced demon led the Council to the conference table before the Devil's throne. They sat and, once they realized that Lucifer wasn't immediately joining them, began whispering urgently among themselves.

Brutus and the Davidsons strode to where I waited with Cora and my apprentices. Sam, Inez, and Beatrix seemed unharmed from the battle. Brutus pointed at Cora then hooked a thumb over his shoulder, "Come on. Time to go home."

Cora turned and wrapped Abigail in a tight hug. Her daughter returned the hug just as fiercely. "I'll be fine, Mom."

Cora pulled back. "You sure? I can probably convince Brutus—"

"I'm sure. I'm going to be a Reaper." A wry smile creased her lips, and she pointed to her skull-emblazoned shirt. "How cool is that? Now, go home and have a nice glass of wine for me."

Cora snorted. "Wine? After today, I'm going straight for the whiskey."

Our heads snapped toward the Nightmare Council at the sounds of heavily dragged furniture. They were rotating the conference table away from Lucifer's throne. Once it was perpendicular to the throne, the Council pushed all the heavy chairs back in place, and everyone sat again. The goose sat at one end of the table, Adze the Vampire at the other. The only empty chair for Lucifer remained on the near side facing his own throne. If he chose to sit on his throne anyway, half the Council would have their backs to him.

I smiled. Lucifer had made a mistake underestimating the nightmares. He thought they were weak? Jesse the

Cloud felled me with ease at Morpheo's market, and Jesse wasn't the most powerful nightmare. Not like the council. They were going to wring Lucifer dry in negotiations.

I turned back to the Davidsons. Inez once again looked like a normal woman in her mid-thirties with red hair. Weariness and sorrow weighed heavily upon her features. She'd failed to change her son's fate but clutched her daughter on her hip as though determined not to lose another child to Hell.

Brutus motioned impatiently for the mortals to follow him, but I raised a forestalling hand.

"Inez," I said, "we need to talk about Lazarus and the other immortals. How many—"

"I'm not betraying them." She shook her head, eyes tight.

"Humans are not meant for immortality in the flesh."

She cocked an eyebrow at me and glanced at the Keeper at her desk. She was sewing the new page into the leather tome. "It's not against the Rules."

"No, it's ... how do you know that?"

Her lips pursed, but she didn't answer.

"What aren't you telling me?"

"Leave it alone, Grim. The immortals aren't hurting

anyone. If anything, we're helping. But right now, I just want to take my family home."

I clenched my jaw. Of course. This was not the time. Her son remained in Torments and Inez's living family did indeed need to go home. I inclined my head, conceding the point. Inez nodded sharply and turned toward the elevator. Brutus and Cora walked with her.

Sam nodded at me, said, "See ya around, Grim," and trailed after his family.

Yes. He would see me. I would give the Davidsons time to recover from their ordeal, but Inez couldn't avoid me forever. We would have that talk.

Lucifer yelled behind me, and I spun toward the forge. "What do you mean, Nigel's *gone*?" The Devil grabbed the demon messenger's horn and slammed the side of his face onto the anvil. He raised his hammer.

The demon struggled in the Devil's grasp. "My ... my lord. The Auditor and his captains snuck in. Freed him. Please don't—"

"The Auditor is missing too? With *Grace*?" Lucifer roared. The demon whimpered and went limp, eyes squeezed shut as he waited for the hammer to fall.

Damn. My scythe was gone. I didn't know what Lucifer

had planned for me, but I'd assumed it involved *Grace.*

Lucifer screamed and threw the demon from the smithy. The messenger cartwheeled madly and bounced a couple of times before coming to rest near the window that remained open into the Basement.

"Find them!" Lucifer screamed. The demon scrambled and dove through the hole. He wasn't a winged demon, but falling into the Basement must have been preferable to facing his lord's wrath.

Silence filled the throne room as Lucifer fumed, staring after the messenger. Finally, he spun and hung up his apron. "Where's Charon?" he bellowed.

"Here, my lord!" the Ferryman called cheerily from one of the elevators.

My lord? Since when did Charon work for Lucifer? He looked much more chipper than when Frank and I had seen him at the river Acheron. And what was he even doing here? I'd made a deal with him to go reap souls in my stead. Had Charon been part of the plot to bring me into Lucifer's servitude? I glared at him, but the elderly spirit just waved at me as he sauntered toward the forge, his cloak's hood thrown back around his neck.

Lucifer motioned Abigail and Frank forward. My bony

eye ridges rose when I saw that he'd forged not two but three scythes. Was one for me? I started to follow my apprentices, disappointed to receive only an imitation of *Grace* but stopped when Lucifer shook his head at me. The Devil passed the scythes out, one each to Frank, Abigail ... and Charon.

Why did he get one? Was this a reward for helping bait the trap that led me here? The Ferryman caressed his scythe and gazed at it with a mix of greed and wonder.

Lucifer gathered their attention and began without pre-amble. "Unlike *Grace,* the power of these scythes is limited. They'll lead you to the next soul in need of reaping and will send the soul to Purgatory for Judgment. That's all."

Behind the three, I nodded in understanding. Only the Almighty could grant power over time and space. No in-stantaneous traveling, and no freezing time for these new Reapers.

"Divide the Earth as you will, but between the three of you, you should be able to manage what Grim used to do by himself."

Wait. What? "You're replacing me?" I said.

Lucifer barely glanced at me. "For now," he said without further elaboration.

Frank and Abigail exchanged glances. Then Frank narrowed his eyes at Lucifer. "Just to be clear," he said, "we don't work for you."

Lucifer's gaze could have melted iron. His silky-smooth voice hardened. "Death serves both Heaven and Hell."

Frank added, "But is beholden to neither."

Would you look at that? Frank really had paid attention to my lessons!

Frank pointed toward the Keeper who was still rebinding the volume on her desk. "It's in the Rules. None shall interfere with Death's duties. Not even you."

Lucifer's lips pursed in annoyance. I thought he might lose his temper again, but instead, he just nodded toward the elevators. "You have your scythes, go reap some souls."

Charon bowed deeply and headed off. Abigail and Frank turned to me.

"You'll do just fine," I said, and I meant it. They'd make mistakes, for sure, but their hearts were in the right place. Charon, on the other hand...

He had experience, but I was worried about his connection with Lucifer. He'd require watching.

Abigail nodded and extended a fist toward me. I eyed it for a moment, unsure what it meant, then bumped my knuckles against hers. She smirked and spun for the elevator. Her cloak swirled behind her.

Frank surprised me with a bear hug that nearly crushed my bones. I stumbled back, then awkwardly returned the hug, patting him on the back.

"Don't trust him," Frank whispered. "Not for a second."

"Never," I whispered back.

"If you need anything, anything at all..."

I patted Frank's back again, and he released me. With a sideways glance at the Devil, the Taxman jogged to join Abigail and Charon at the elevator. A sudden thought struck me as they departed and, if I'd had lips I might have smiled. The special Rules and restrictions governing Death weren't burned into Frank's and Abigail's souls. Charon was bound by Death's Rules—I'd ensured that happened after he started London's Great Plague—but Frank and Abigail were wild cards in whatever game Lucifer was playing.

Conrad, who'd resumed his cheerful flight around the throne room, swooped toward the elevator after the new Reapers. He slid inside just before it closed. Another wild card. I could have cheered. The little dragon had chosen the life he wanted over the one Lucifer demanded of him. I wondered how long it would take the Devil to realize that his nightmare was gone.

Lucifer grabbed the sheathed *Mercy* from where he'd leaned it against the forge and turned to me. I didn't like the way he smiled. Too many teeth. He threw his other arm companionably around my bony shoulders and guided us to the Keeper's desk. As we crossed the threshold between smithy and office, oak-paneled walls and an arched ceiling formed around us, completing the illusion that we were in a castle instead of the bowels of Hell's Ninth Circle. There was even a large stone-framed window that looked out upon snow-laden fields.

Once we were sealed off from prying eyes, Lucifer's smile dropped. He stopped us in front of the Keeper's desk. "You're probably wondering why I went to such trouble to bring you into my service," he said.

"The thought had crossed my mind. Especially when you gave away my job."

"Don't worry," Lucifer said, leaning close and lowering his voice as though sharing a secret. "You're still the Grim Reaper. Just with more focus in your work."

"Meaning?" I crossed my arms. The Keeper tucked the

last of her binding thread away. As she did, I felt the weight of the Rules—of Death's Rules—settle over me once again, as if my bones were being squeezed. No more lying for me.

"Only that you'll be reaping the most important souls." Lucifer slid the Rulebook closer and scanned the neatly printed text. "Check it over, and ensure the Keeper captured all your demands."

I leaned on the desk and read. It was all there, a perfect transcript of everything I'd demanded in exchange for my eternal servitude to Lucifer. Two empty signature lines waited at the bottom. Updating the Rules to sell my soul to the Devil didn't directly involve the Almighty, so it didn't require ratification by Heaven. I flipped a few pages, noting which Rules had been torn out. Only Rules involving Death. Only Rules whose violation might go unnoticed by Heaven. For a time, at least.

The Keeper pushed the inkwell toward me. I hesitated.

Lucifer said, "I've kept my side of our bargain so far. A sign of good faith. But faith can be broken. For the sake of your friends, don't do anything foolish." He still held *Mercy* sheathed in one hand and shifted it ever so slightly. His threat was clear.

I signed the amended Rules. Lucifer countersigned.

Pain seared my bones. I dropped to my knees and screamed. And then, as abruptly as it had started, the pain was gone. A ghost of a memory that felt like a noose around my neck. I'd just given up a sliver of my free will. I had to do whatever Lucifer demanded. Remaining on my knees, I looked up at the Devil.

"What would you have me do?" I asked.

He arched an eyebrow, and I ground my teeth. I didn't want to say what came next. But I had no choice.

"My lord."

Lucifer smiled. It was the smile of someone who just got everything he'd ever wanted. He unsheathed *Mercy* and examined the curved blade thoughtfully. Then he flipped his grip and extended it to me.

"With this blade," he said with formality, "I name you the Devil's Assassin."

Heaven help me.

No. Heaven couldn't help me, I'd sold my soul willingly. I stared at *Mercy*'s hilt.

"Take it, Grim," he said.

I rose and took the blade. It felt wrong to be holding the sword that Evelyn had carried for so long. It was light in my hands, balanced so well that I barely felt the weight. A sudden impulse to strike Lucifer down flowed over me, but my hands didn't even twitch. My signed contract forbade such treachery.

"The Devil's Assassin," I said, horrified. "Who am I to kill?"

"The Auditor and Nigel. They no longer serve my purposes."

I nodded, not as bothered by the mission as I'd expected. The Auditor was the embodiment of evil, and Nigel never should have been conceived. Still, I asked, "What changed? You could have easily killed Nigel when you defeated him."

"True, but I stayed my hand with thoughts of binding him in the Lake of Fire as an example to any who would challenge me." The Devil shrugged. "But that was merely one option, and not worth the effort of trying to take him alive again. I have bigger plans, as you know, that require your scythe *Grace*. To retrieve it, you'll have to kill Nigel and the Auditor."

Yes, they wouldn't relinquish *Grace* easily.

Lucifer continued. "And then you will retrieve the last great blade: *Justice*."

I pulled back. "But, my lord, the Archangel Gabriel

holds *Justice.* I can't kill Gabriel!"

Lucifer's eyes flashed. "You can and you will."

Pain seared my bones again, nearly dropping me to my knees. Lucifer's command was absolute, his will overriding my own. I was the Devil's Assassin. I would kill the Archangel Gabriel.

Chapter 36

THE BUREAUCRAT

DESPITE THE PAIN OF Lucifer's will imbued into my bones, I forced myself upright. I refused to cower before the Devil any more than absolutely necessary. "Why me?" I asked. "You have demons much more inclined to assassination than me."

"Because you, Grim, have what my demons do not: open access to Heaven. Gabriel trusts you."

"Gabriel hates me."

Lucifer shrugged. "Perhaps, but he won't refuse you an audience. My demons would never get close to him." He waved a hand, and one of the library's walls split and reformed into a stone-arched doorway. "You have your mission. Do not fail."

***

My departure from Hell was much simpler than my entrance. The Keeper escorted me to an elevator while Lucifer left to join the Nightmare Council for negotiations. We rode to Purgatory serenaded once again by the Musak rendition of "Never Gonna Give You Up." It was like Hell wanted to give me one last punch in the head before kicking me out to do the Devil's bidding.

I didn't want to complete my mission, to assassinate Gabriel. But I could feel Lucifer's willpower driving me forward. I had no choice.

The Keeper glanced pointedly at *Mercy* in my hands. "You may be the Devil's Assassin, but entering Purgatory with a bared blade is a bit over the top, don't you think?"

Right. I was used to having a scythe in my hands. One does not sheath a scythe. I slid *Mercy* home into the sheath at my hip with a *shink-thunk* that was more forceful than necessary.

The Keeper waved an annoying finger at my face. "You'll

need to blend in. Do something with your face. Something more subtle than Death's grinning skull."

I wanted to argue for argument's sake, but what could I say? I leaned against the elevator wall for support and changed form for the seventh time today. A holy number, according to the Almighty, full of strength and power. Perhaps he was right because exhaustion didn't wash over me this time.

Or, more likely, I was too angry to be tired.

I expanded my skeleton into the same body I'd worn when I arrived at Cora's front door. Had that been only hours ago? It felt like a lifetime. My cloak shifted into a simple black blazer over a dark gray shirt with matching slacks.

The Keeper eyed me appreciatively. She stepped close enough that I felt the warmth of her presence and then ran her fingers through my lanky black hair. The gesture ended in a tender caress on my cheek. "Oh, I like that," she said. "So ruggedly handsome. You'd be surprised how many doors a pretty face will open."

I shuddered at her touch and pulled away.

The Keeper let her hand drop. "My turn," she said with a purr and changed her form. Again, it looked like she was stepping through a mirror, or rather that a mirror was sliding over her. The tip of her nose elongated into a wolf's snout and her body grew gray fur. Her tight Amazon warrior's armor became a pristine white robe. Lovetta the Guardian of Purgatory threw me a wolfish grin with just a hint of the Kitsune underneath.

I bit back a curse.

Lovetta the Guardian, Kurai the middle manager, and the Devil's own Keeper of Records. All were the same spirit. It was in the eyes. The Keeper's burning anger was banked, but still there now that I knew what to look for. This damned Kitsune had manipulated me from the beginning.

No, worse than a Kitsune. A bureaucrat. That was what her three forms had in common. She served in positions that let her smile while making everyone else's lives miserable.

Bureaucrats truly are of the Devil.

Lovetta threw me a wolfish wink before the elevator door slid open. The ordered chaos of Purgatory washed over us, a thrum of voices and the press of souls. We'd arrived near the Soul Processing Desk, stepping out of a wall that hadn't had an elevator when Frank and I had first arrived.

Lovetta strode out and waved cheerily. "Chiti! Did you miss me?" She sounded like an airheaded secretary. I wasn't fooled.

Chiti growled at her. "There you are! Minos came back and started yelling about Judgments. We're swamped in Form-5s!"

"Pshh," she waved her hand dismissively. "We have all the time in eternity. I've got something *much* more important. Gossip!" She reached the desk and leaned close for a stage whisper. "Nigel's coup failed, and he's on the run with the Auditor." Both Chiti's and Leandros's ears perked up, though they looked troubled. They'd been in on the coup, somehow; at least on the periphery. Did they know Lovetta's true identity?

I almost told them out of pure spite, but I held my tongue. Death does not succumb to petty revenge. My revenge would be profound. And permanent.

I caressed *Mercy*'s hilt as I stepped from the elevator and turned away from the Guardians. I slipped under the rope and milling souls shifted aside to let me pass. I walked aimlessly among them, among the souls I'd been charged to shepherd. The souls whose very fate was now in jeopardy because of decisions I'd made.

I'd made a mistake. The Devil I knew was not better than the one who'd replaced him. My meddling had only advanced Lucifer's plans to take Heaven's throne. Once he had all three great blades, he would challenge the Almighty himself, and I wasn't positive that Lucifer would lose that fight.

I snorted, remembering something Evelyn had said during that fateful dinner with the Davidsons before Xandu struck her down and stole *Mercy*.

There is good and there is evil. Shades of gray are merely light tainted with darkness.

Lucifer, the Dragon, was pure evil, more devious and cunning than I'd ever imagined. I had to escape my bondage; break the Rules as Lucifer had done before I was forced to do something the realms would never recover from.

Before I killed Gabriel and stole *Justice*.

My anger must have shown on my face because the souls awaiting Judgment pulled back as I passed. They quieted as Death strode among them, though they didn't recognize me as such. Death is supposed to be emotionless. Calm. I'd been the neutral party between Heaven and Hell for millennia, unconcerned about their war as I shepherded humanity's souls.

I was impartial no more.

Lucifer would rue the day he manipulated me into becoming the Devil's Assassin. But how? This wasn't a problem I could solve alone. I needed help. I needed someone practiced in cunning and deceit and manipulating the Rules.

I needed Conrad.

Purpose filled my stride. Conrad and I would defeat the Devil. Together we would break the chains he'd wrapped around my soul.

Death and the Dragon.

Curious about what happened during Kurai's banishment in Okinawa? Find out in "Valhalla and Cocktails," available only in *Grimsworld Tales* along with origin stories for many of the characters you've come to love.

https://books2read.com/grimsworldtales

Thank you for reading *Death and the Dragon!*

Did you know that book reviews make authors go all soft and gooey inside?

It's true. We love hearing back from readers! Long or short doesn't matter, just share your thoughts.

If you would kindly leave a review on Amazon, Goodreads, or wherever you shop for books, you will have my eternal thanks.

Join the Lost Bard's Letter at https://davidhankins.com for more (free) lighthearted stories.

ACKNOWLEDGEMENTS

Where to begin? As with any project, *Death and the Dragon* came to life through the work of some absolutely amazing people. First and foremost, special thanks to my wife Michelle for her keen insights while reading multiple drafts.

Many thanks to my daughter Beatrix for some truly delightful jokes for *Death and the Dragon*. (Speaking of jokes, I have to note that the problems in the Unhelpful Helpdesk were true stories from my life, changed only enough to fit the narrative. Sometimes truth really is stranger than fiction, and the jokes write themselves.)

My alpha readers are the best! L. Briar, Brittany Rainsdon, and Shannon Fox, I couldn't have done this without you. And if I'd tried, Grim would have been stumbling over plot holes bigger than the Pit. Thank you!

Once again, to my illustrator Sarah Morrison: You've

outdone herself. I absolutely LOVE your cover on *Death and the Dragon*! And that interior art of Cora? Perfection. I'm looking forward to seeing what you do with *Death and the Immortal*.

As always, editor Dan Hilton provided a marvelously sharp eye with his red pen. It's the little details that make all the difference.

Death and the Dragon was my second Kickstarter, and I'm absolutely thrilled by everybody's support! Special thanks to editors Scot Noel (*DreamForge Magazine*), Mike Jack Stoumbos (Wonderbird Press), and Danny Hankner (*Story Unlikely*) for donating books, magazines, and subscriptions as Kickstarter backer rewards.

And, of course, so many thanks to all the Kickstarter backers who helped bring *Death and the Dragon* to life! You rock!

Kickstarter Backers: Alysha Cheah - Alexander Nirenberg - Alexandra Engrand - Amy "Guthington" Wethington - Andrejs Zolotuhins - Andrew R - Angelique Fawns - Annarose Willhite - AslansCompass - BDan Fairchild - Ben - Brenda Hankins - Brittany Rainsdon - Candice R. Lisle - Carla Bermudez - Cat Girczyc - Cat & Cthulhu - Christina Baclawski - Cindy Lou Who - CL Fors - Contessa Timmerman - Dan Hardez - The Honorable Danny Hankner - Darren Lipman - Dave Holets - David Scoggins - Dead Fish Books - Diane St Romain - Dodie Sullivan - Dybbuk - Dylan Pucilowski - EB - Eric Stallsworth - Eric Keller - Evan Anderson - Franziska - Fred Wehling - Gary Phillips - GMarkC - H. Mark Little - J. R. Johnson - Jack Holder - Jacob Garfinkel - Jakub Narębski - James Moon - James S Caraballo - James 'The Great Old One' Burke - Jared S Campbell - Jarrod Williams - Jason Palmatier - Jeanna - Jenny Perry Carr - Jesse Cloud @cloudy_reviews - Jim - John Markley - Josh Erikson - Joshua Gerdez - Joshua Hair - Joshua Palmatier - Juliette Reneaume - K. Z. Richards - Karen M - Karen Chong - Karla Heubner - Karmi Rivera - Kathryn M. - Kelly McMahon - Leana - Laughing Briar - Laura Dion - Leslie B - Leon Glaser - Lily Raven - Luke Leveque - Marie Fisher - Mark Leslie - Mark Wyckstrom - Melissa Graham - Micha Rieser - Mighty V - Mike Dubost - Michael the Horologist - Duke and Laura Holley - Manny Kincaid - Myke Tea - Molly J Stanton - Natalie Boon - oli-obk - Paul Janke - Peter Michael Gray - Rachel - Rachiel R. - Ricardo Monascal - Rikard - Rob Steinberger - Ruth Ann Orlansky - Sarolta - Sam Paisley - Samantha Newberry - Sandra Skalski - Scot Noel -

Scott Casey - Scott M. Sands - Shannon Fox - Shanon M. Brown - Spencer Sekulin - Stephen W. Buchanan - Stephen Michael Kellat - Steve & Beckey Sanchez - Steven Clark - Tech Support 1 & 2 - Timothy Hankins - TJ Knight - Tracy Hughes - Tracy Popey - Victoria P - WaterNai - Wingnut - Wouter de Wit

Last, but certainly not least, thank you to YOU, the reader who actually read all the way through these acknowledgements. I hope you enjoyed *Death and the Dragon*.

Until next time,

David

About the Author

Award-winning author David Hankins writes from the thriving cornfields of Iowa where he lives with his wife, daughter, and two dragons disguised as cats. His writing began in the oral tradition of convincing his daughter to Go To Sleep with inventive stories. That usually backfired. After years of Just One More Story, David began transcribing his midnight ramblings in an attempt to keep his storylines straight. Children are ruthless about mistakes in their fairy tales. David writes lighthearted speculative fiction because that's what he loves to read and—this is the important bit—there's not nearly enough humor in the world. He aims to change that, one story at a time. You can find him at https://davidhankins.com